When had touching Summer, holding her, begun to feel so right?

Scowling at the thought, Gavin tried to convince himself he was imagining things. Their marriage was a business arrangement, nothing more or less, and even if it hadn't been, he wasn't looking for a relationship.

But knowing that and remaining indifferent to Summer were two different things.

Continuing to scowl, he vowed to keep his hands to himself from that moment on, and just that easily, he set himself an impossible task. Because now that he'd decided not to touch her, she only had to shift slightly in her seat beside him for him to want her.

It was, he decided grimly, going to be a long year.

MONTANA MAVERICKS: WED IN WHITEHORN

Brand-new stories beneath the Big Sky!

MONTANA MAVERICKS

LINDA TURNER

With grandparents who were in the circus and a family tree dotted with horse traders, freedom fighters and a card shark or two, it was only natural that Linda Turner gravitated toward writing—she is the descendant of a long line of characters. Adventure is in the blood, the road less traveled just waiting to be explored. Consequently, it was her sense of adventure that led her to Washington, D.C., to work at a Boy Scout camp for a summer. And that doesn't even begin to touch a cross-country bicycle trip, tracking a thief in New Orleans and dealing with ghosts in her parents' home in San Antonio. Single and unattached, she has her bags always packed, and she's just waiting for a chance to get on the road again. Scouting out locales for her books is a perfect excuse to travel—not that she needs one. Life is too short to sit home all the time. When she's not traveling in between books, she's at home in San Antonio, writing and reading and spending time with her family and friends.

MONTANA MAVERICKS

LINDA TURNER

NIGHTHAWK'S CHILD

Silhouette Books

Published by Silhouette Books

America's Publisher of Contemporary Romance

Special thanks and acknowledgment are given to
Linda Turner for her contribution to the
MONTANA MAVERICKS:
WED IN WHITEHORN series.

SILHOUETTE BOOKS

ISBN 0-373-65057-4

NIGHTHAWK'S CHILD

Visit Silhouette at www.eHarlequin.com

Printed in U.S.A.

MONTANA MAVERICKS

Wed in Whitehorn

*Welcome to Whitehorn, Montana—
a place of passion and adventure.
Seems this charming little town has some
Big Sky secrets. And everybody's talking about...*

Gavin Nighthawk: The respected surgeon with
a chip on his shoulder seemed the sole suspect in
Christina Montgomery's vicious murder. But Gavin
hadn't done the deed, though the fact that he'd fathered
her child in secret seemed to suggest otherwise. Yet he
wasn't alone in proclaiming his innocence....

Summer Kincaid: A friend from reservation days,
Summer knew the brooding dad couldn't kill anyone. So
she proposed a shocking arrangement: they would wed
to afford Gavin all the power and propriety of the
Kincaid name...and to ensure Gavin gained custody of
his baby girl. The deal was to last a year, but Summer
found herself wanting it to last a lifetime.

Audra Westwood: When ex-lover Micky Culver comes
forward as a surprise witness, Nighthawk's guilt and
Audra's days as Lexine's puppet seem at an end....

Alyssa Nighthawk: Gavin's precious baby has finally
come home, but will her newfound family be able to hold
her close forever?

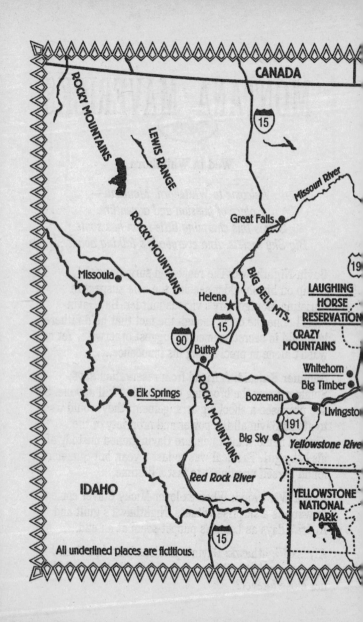

CANADA

ROCKY MOUNTAINS

LEWIS RANGE

ROCKY MOUNTAINS

Missoula

Great Falls

Missouri River

Helena ★

BIG BELT MTS.

LAUGHING
HORSE
RESERVATION

CRAZY
MOUNTAINS

Butte

Whitehorn

Big Timber

Elk Springs

Bozeman

Livingston

ROCKY MOUNTAINS

Big Sky

Yellowstone River

Red Rock River

IDAHO

YELLOWSTONE
NATIONAL
PARK

All underlined places are fictitious.

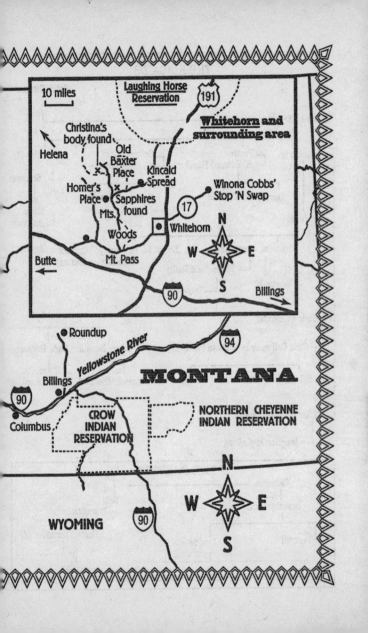

MONTANA MAVERICKS: WED IN WHITEHORN
THE KINCAIDS

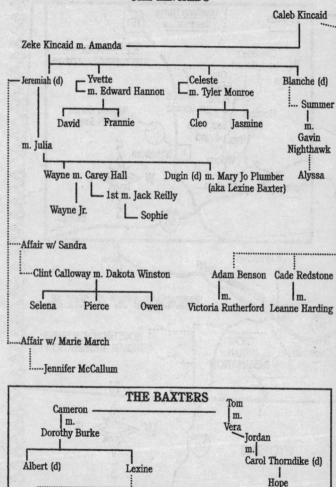

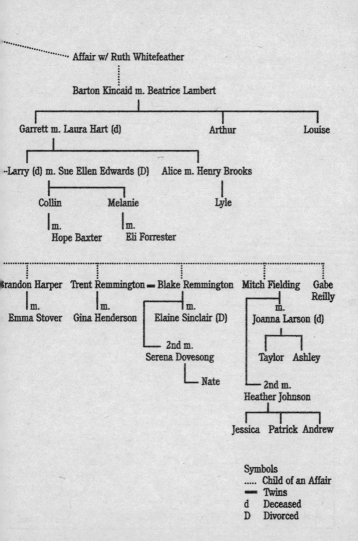

Affair w/ Ruth Whitefeather

Barton Kincaid m. Beatrice Lambert

Garrett m. Laura Hart (d)   Arthur   Louise

Larry (d) m. Sue Ellen Edwards (D)   Alice m. Henry Brooks

Collin   Melanie   Lyle

m.   m.
Hope Baxter   Eli Forrester

Brandon Harper   Trent Remmington — Blake Remmington   Mitch Fielding   Gabe
                                                                          Reilly
m.   m.   m.   m.
Emma Stover   Gina Henderson   Elaine Sinclair (D)   Joanna Larson (d)

                                    2nd m.   Taylor   Ashley
                                    Serena Dovesong

                                         Nate   2nd m.
                                                        Heather Johnson

                                                 Jessica   Patrick   Andrew

Symbols
..... Child of an Affair
— Twins
d   Deceased
D   Divorced

Prologue

The previous August

Gavin stared down at the message that he was wanted in his boss's office as soon as possible and swore under his breath. He didn't have to know what this was about to know that it wasn't good. Whatever else Michael Preston was—and as Chief of Surgery at Whitehorn Memorial Hospital, he'd been called more than a few choice names over the years—he wasn't insensitive to the pressure of the work his surgeons performed. He wanted them calm, cool, and collected when they walked into the operating room, so he made sure any discussions he had with his residents was restricted until after surgery. Or at least, he always had before.

But then again, he'd never had one of his surgeons accused of murder before, either.

His square-cut face set in harsh lines, Gavin was tempted to ignore Michael's missive and to meet with him later, after surgery. Whatever beef Preston had could wait. Gavin's patients came first with him. Since his arrest, work was the only thing that kept him sane. With the rest of his life in turmoil, he couldn't take a chance on screwing up his residency. Scowling, he strode down the hall to Michael's office.

Seated at his desk, the older man was waiting for him,

his expression grim. Gavin greeted him with a curt nod. The nerves in his stomach clenched in a fist, but he had no intention of letting Preston or anyone else see him sweat. He'd learned the hard way to protect his thoughts. His own face impassive, he shut the door behind him and stood stiffly in front of Preston's desk. "You wanted to see me?"

To his credit, Michael didn't try to lighten the moment with frivolous chitchat, but instead got right to the point. "Sit down, Gavin. A situation has arisen that I think you need to be made aware of."

He preferred to stand, but this wasn't the time to draw lines in the sand. Dropping into the chair positioned across from Michael's desk, he stretched his long legs out in front of him and mentally braced for whatever was about to come. "You might as well give it to me straight. This has something to do with the trial, doesn't it?"

He didn't bother to deny it. "You know the hospital's policy regarding the charges against you. You're innocent until proven guilty."

"If you called me in here to tell me the hospital knows it's only a matter of time before that happens, you wasted your time," he said flatly, irritation flashing in his dark eyes. "I know the evidence looks damning, but I didn't kill Christina Montgomery. And somehow I'm going to prove it."

"I hope you do," the other man said honestly. "You're a damn fine surgeon. We need you around here. The problem, though, isn't the administration. It's your co-workers. More than a few of them have doubts about your innocence."

He wasn't telling Gavin anything he didn't already know. He was aware of how a majority of the staff felt about him. As had most of the people in town, they'd rushed to judgment the second they'd heard he'd been charged with

Christina's murder. Trying and convicting him, they hadn't stopped to consider the fact that all the evidence against him was circumstantial or that he wasn't a violent man. He was a doctor, for God's sake, and in the business of saving lives, not taking them.

And if he was going to kill someone, it certainly wouldn't be the mother of his baby girl. He'd never loved Christina—their relationship had been little more than a one-night stand—but he certainly hadn't hated her or wanted her dead. If anything, he'd felt sorry for her and had only tried to help her once he'd found out she was pregnant. And because of that, people now thought he was a murderer.

"I can't control what people think," he said curtly. "If they want to believe I'm a murderer, that's their problem."

Leaning back in his chair, Michael sighed heavily. "I wish it was that simple, Gavin, but it's not. They're refusing to work with you."

Surprised, his dark brows snapped together in a scowl. "Who is?"

The older man gave him a speaking look. "I won't name names, but suffice it to say, it's enough people to create a problem with scheduling. That's why I wanted to speak to you before you went into surgery. You can't operate this morning. I couldn't put together a surgical team that was willing to work with you."

Gavin couldn't have been more stunned if Michael had reached across the desk and backhanded him. *No one wanted to work with him?* How could such a thing have happened? He was a good surgeon. A damn good one! He'd worked hard to get where he was, and he was proud of that. Unlike his white colleagues, he'd come from the wrong side of the tracks—the reservation—and had to fight every step of the way to make something of himself. It hadn't been easy. Not that he was looking for accolades, damn it, he assured himself with a scowl. He wasn't. He just wanted some respect from his peers. And now Michael was telling him that no one wanted to work with him. So much for respect.

It was over, he thought numbly. The career he'd spent years building, all the hard work, the life he'd mapped out for himself as a leading surgeon...it was all over. Unless he could find a way to clear his name, the dreams that had gotten him through college and medical school were dead.

Disheartened, disillusioned, so frustrated he wanted to rage at the world, he could think of nothing to do but accept the inevitable. As long as he had a murder charge hanging over his head, he couldn't work.

"I won't quit," he told his boss coldly. "I know there are some people in this hospital who would like to see the last of me, but I'm not quitting. I'll take a leave of absence instead and return to work the day after I'm acquitted."

If Michael thought there wasn't a chance in hell of that happening, he wisely kept that to himself. Instead he nodded in agreement and rose to hold out his hand. "That's fair enough. I wish you luck, Gavin."

It went without saying that they both knew he was going to need it.

One

Two months later

The Hip Hop Café was *the* place to be when gossip was running high, so Summer Kincaid wasn't surprised to find the place packed to the rafters when she stopped in for lunch. Ever since Gavin Nighthawk's arrest that was all anyone was talking about. The second Summer stepped inside, the gossip, rife with speculation, hit her right in the face.

"I always knew there was something not quite right about that boy. He always seemed so full of anger. It's because he's *Indian*, you know. He wants to be white. Everyone says so."

"And he's so big. I bet he killed that poor girl without even breaking a sweat."

Across the diner, Judge Kate Randall Walker sniffed in irritation and said loudly, "That's what's wrong with this country. People rush to judgment without waiting to hear the facts of a case, and I think it stinks."

Not surprisingly, that didn't sit well with a majority of the diners, especially Lily Mae Wheeler, the queen of the town gossips and a general busybody who was, as usual, holding court from the first booth inside the door, which she considered "hers." She'd been known to make up news on a slow day just to have something to talk about, but that wasn't necessary today. There was nothing she enjoyed more than putting a negative spin on things and destroying someone's reputation.

Arching a plucked brow at the judge, she narrowed beady little eyes at her. "Are you saying he's *not* guilty?"

"I wouldn't know," Kate replied coolly. "That's for a jury to decide. In the meantime, the man has a right to live in peace."

Tossing her head to draw attention to her permed curls, which she'd died the outrageous color of cotton-candy pink to match what she claimed was her sweet personality, Lily Mae waved her hand and just that easily dismissed the old-fashioned notion that a man was actually innocent until proven guilty. "Well, of course *you* would think that. Everyone knows you're a liberal. Personally, I don't think *Doctor* Gavin Nighthawk should be allowed to walk around free, let alone with a scalpel in his hand. *I* certainly wouldn't let him operate on *me* or someone I loved!"

Taking a seat at the counter, Summer could only privately shake her head at the asinine remark. Lily Mae had a well-known reputation for saying whatever came into her head. The more educated people in town didn't take her seriously, but there were, unfortunately, others just like her who believed that Gavin was a dangerous man who needed to be locked away from decent society.

And that frustrated Summer no end. As a child of mixed heritage, she had, thanks to the insistence of her white aunts, spent her summers on the Laughing Horse Reservation getting to know the Native American side of her family, and there she'd had a chance to watch Gavin from afar. They'd never been close enough to even be called friends, but there'd always been something about the tall, gangly boy that she'd admired. He'd had a kindness to him that some of the other rougher boys hadn't had, an inherent gentleness that came out whenever he came in contact with those who were weaker or slower or older and in need of help.

He had, however, never made any secret of the fact that he couldn't wait to leave the reservation and its poverty behind. He'd had dreams, and he hadn't let anyone or anything stand in his way. Through hard work and determination, he'd earned a full scholarship to college and left the day after he graduated from high school.

Summer had lost touch with him then and had no idea that he'd gone on to medical school, just as she had, until he'd returned to Whitehorn for his residency at the same hospital where she worked. Thrilled, she'd thought at first that fate had had a hand in bringing them back together, but it didn't take her long to discover that there was little resemblance between the kind, gangly boy she had known on the Laughing Horse Reservation and the bitter, brooding man he had become. She didn't know this new Gavin, and honesty forced her to admit that she wasn't sure she wanted to. While she was comfortable with who she was and her Native American heritage, he had turned his back on his people to make a name for himself in the white man's world, and that angered her. Still, she only had to remember the boy he had been to know that he would have never been able to take a life.

Anyone who doubted that only had to look at his work. If ever a man was born to be a surgeon, it was Gavin Nighthawk. As an immunology resident at Whitehorn Memorial Hospital, she'd observed him in the operating room numerous times and had nothing but admiration for his skill. Unlike other gifted doctors she knew, however, he wasn't one of those arrogant, holier-than-thou surgeons who forgot about his patients once he worked his magic on them on the operating table. He truly cared about his patients and was a gifted healer.

No one seemed to remember that, however, when it came to Christina Montgomery's murder. Before she'd died, everyone had known that she was sad and lonely and pregnant, in spite of her best efforts to hide her condition. The whole town had speculated on who the father of her baby was, but she'd taken that information with her to her grave. It wasn't until months after her body was discovered in the woods that law enforcement officials discovered that the man who impregnated her was also the same one who'd delivered her baby and was the last one to see her alive— Gavin Nighthawk.

For months he'd kept his silence about the whereabouts of the baby and his own involvement, and that was enough to condemn him in most people's eyes. The fact that everyone knew that he'd never cared about Christina but had turned to her on the rebound after his affair with Patricia Winthrop went sour had only made things worse.

"He's going to prison, anyway. He might as well resign now."

"Do you think the state will revoke his license? Do they let murderers practice medicine after they get out of jail?"

"Who said he'll get out? He killed the mother of his baby. No jury in their right mind is going to let him off with anything less than life for that."

All around her, people speculated on Gavin's fate as if he was just some character on a soap opera and not a real man at all. And Summer hated it. She longed to stand up and shout at his detractors, to make them see him as he really was, but she was a quiet, unobtrusive woman, and that wasn't her way. It wouldn't do any good, anyway. She couldn't control what people thought, couldn't make them see him for the boy he had once been. To them, he was a hard, angry Indian with a chip on his shoulder who didn't make friends easily, and they had little sympathy for his fate.

And that, more than anything, was what scared her. She'd done everything she could to help him by convincing her uncle Garrett to hire Elizabeth Gardener, one of the best lawyers in the state, to defend him, but now Summer wasn't sure that even Elizabeth could save him. The tide of public opinion had definitely turned against him, and unless something drastic happened, he appeared to be a doomed man.

The bell on the door rang merrily then, signaling a new arrival, and everyone instinctively turned to check out the newcomer. When Gavin Nighthawk himself stepped into the café, silence fell like a rock.

"Speak of the devil."

In the crowd that packed the restaurant, Summer couldn't have said who made the comment, but whoever it was obviously meant for Gavin to hear it. Standing tall and proud at the entrance, his expression stony, he surveyed the throng of diners through cold, black eyes. Holding her breath, Summer wouldn't have blamed him if he'd turned and walked out, but he was made of sterner stuff than that. Silently daring anyone to stop him, he strode down the long length of the café to the only empty table in the place.

The silence engulfing the place like a shroud broke the second he turned his back on the rest of the room and pulled out a chair. Hushed whispers flew about the café like angry bees. There was no doubt that he was the main topic of conversation, but he didn't acknowledge the gossip by so much as a twitch of an eyebrow.

Still, Summer couldn't help but feel sorry for him. Everywhere he went, people no doubt treated him the same, as if he was some sort of social outcast with a horrible disease, and that had to hurt. Her heart breaking for him, she glanced over at him, noted the rigid set of his shoulders, and thought she had never seen such a lonely man in her life.

A wise woman would have left him alone, but Summer had never been particularly smart when it came to Gavin. There was just something about him that always drew her to him, and she couldn't fight it now any more than she could at the hospital, where she wandered into the operating room observation area so she could watch him work. Without a thought to the consequences, she impulsively grabbed her iced tea and flatware and joined him at his table.

She couldn't have shocked him—or herself—more if she'd appeared in front of him naked. Glancing up from the menu Janie Austin, the manager of the café, had handed him, he scowled at her as if she'd just lost her mind. "What the hell do you think you're doing?"

At his low, angry growl, Summer asked herself the same thing. He obviously wanted to stew in his aloneness, and she'd invaded his space without bothering to ask his permission. He had every right to be irritated, but she didn't intend to let him scare her off. "Joining you for lunch," she said quietly. "You look like you could use a friend."

If she expected gratitude, she didn't get it. "I'm not the kind of man you want as a friend," he said flatly, returning his attention to the menu. "If you don't want to be tarred and feathered for associating with a murderer, I suggest you get your cute little butt up from this table and get away from me."

Shocked—no man had ever mentioned her butt, cute or otherwise—she felt a blush climb into her cheeks and seriously considered leaving him in peace, just as he'd suggested. But when she looked around and saw the hostile looks *she* was receiving from the other diners just because she'd dared to befriend him, she knew she was doing the right thing.

Stubbornly staying right where she was, she settled back in her chair and watched him try to ignore her. "So," she asked quietly, "how is Alyssa doing?"

That brought his head up, just as she'd known it would. The citizens of Whitehorn might not think much of Gavin as a man, but none of them could dispute the fact that he was crazy about his little girl. At the mere mention of her name, his face lit up with a love that couldn't be denied.

"Rachel and Jack are taking good care of her," he said gruffly. "I owe them for that."

Rachel Montgomery Henderson, Alyssa's aunt, was, in fact, devoted to the baby. After Rachel had launched an exhaustive search for Christina's baby last winter, Gavin had removed the child from the home of Cheyenne elder Lettie Brownbear and left her anonymously on Rachel's doorstep with a note to take care of Alyssa until he could come for her. When he was charged with Christina's murder and the truth came out that he was Alyssa's father, he'd arranged for the baby to continue to stay with Rachel and her husband, Jack. The decision had been a wise one. They loved her as if she was their own and saw that she had a loving, stable home.

Still, Summer knew that it had to be difficult for Gavin, knowing that someone else was raising his child. "Do you get to see her very often?"

"As much as my schedule allows," he began. His mouth twisted into a grimace of a smile. "Of course, that was before the hospital staff decided they couldn't work with an accused murderer."

"You didn't murder Christina," she replied with quiet confidence. "Even if you didn't love her, she was the mother of your little girl. You would have never hurt her, let alone killed her.''

No, he wouldn't have, but he was surprised that she realized that about him. No one else seemed to. ''Tell that to a jury of my peers,'' he said bitterly. ''If they're anything like the clowns in here, I'm fried.''

He tried not to think about it because it tore him in two, but the closer the trial drew, the harder it was to ignore the fact that the evidence piling up against him was damning. Thanks to the generosity of Summer's uncle, Garrett Kincaid, he had a good attorney in Elizabeth Gardener, but he had a grim feeling that not even Elizabeth was going to be able to pull his feet out of the fire on this one. Too many people wanted to see him burn.

''I can take whatever they dish out,'' Gavin continued, his face carved in harsh lines, ''but Alyssa's the one I'm worried about. If I'm convicted, I'll either spend the rest of my life in prison or face the death penalty. Either way, Alyssa's going to grow up without a father, and that's not fair to her, damn it! She's just a baby—she didn't ask for any of this. But she's the one paying the price for whoever killed Christina, and there's not a damn thing I can do about it.''

He looked sick at heart, and Summer couldn't say she blamed him. His daughter's fate hung in the balance as much as his did, and that was the real tragedy here. Summer knew from firsthand experience what it was like to grow up without a father, and she wouldn't wish that on anyone. Her own father, Raven, had disappeared before she was born, leaving a hole in her life that had never been filled. To this day, whenever she looked in a mirror, she searched for him in her own features. Had his eyes been almond-shaped like hers? Had his hair been the same shiny black?

Was he the one she had to thank for her wide, expressive mouth and quiet personality?

Because her mother, Blanche Kincaid, had died a week after she was born and no one knew Raven the way she had, Summer had been left with a legacy of questions about her father that she would never have the answers to. Her mother's sisters, Yvette and Celeste, had raised her in a loving home and while they had never said a bad word against Raven, they had never been able to tell her why her father had left town when he'd known her mother was pregnant with her. Had he really been paid off by her uncle Jeremiah? Was Raven Hunter the type of man who would do such a thing to the woman he claimed to love and the baby they had created together?

Her aunts didn't think so, and Summer wanted to believe them, but deep down inside, doubts lingered that she couldn't banish. And her heart twisted at the idea of Alyssa growing up with those same kinds of doubts. She was an innocent child. She had a right to grow up knowing that her father was an honorable man who loved her—and the right to really know him. That wasn't going to happen if he was convicted.

Her heart breaking for both Gavin and the baby, Summer wanted to tell him to have faith that the real killer would be caught soon, but he wouldn't thank her for what would be little more than trite words to him. In the eyes of the police and D.A.'s office, they were satisfied that they had charged the right man with the crime. If the reaction of the other diners in the café was anything to go by, just about everyone else felt the same way. Which meant Gavin's fate was doomed.

Seated three tables over from Gavin and Summer, Audra Westwood picked at the salad she'd ordered, pretending to eat, her green eyes sparkling with glee as she avidly listened to the heated comments flying around the café. All around her, people shot Gavin Nighthawk dirty looks and grumbled about the man's audacity. He was nothing but a cold-blooded killer, and he had no business forcing himself on decent, law-abiding citizens. If he had any kind of conscience at all, he would confess to killing the Montgomery girl and save the county the expense of an extended trial.

Hardly able to contain the smile that kept tugging at her collagen-enhanced lips, it was all Audra could do to just sit still. Everything was working out just as Lexine had predicted. In the eyes of the majority of the townspeople, Gavin was guilty as sin. Now all she had to do was keep her mouth shut and wait for the trial to start. With all the circumstantial evidence against him, not to mention public opinion, Gavin wouldn't stand a chance. He'd be convicted and lucky if he didn't get the death sentence.

Poor baby, she thought wickedly. That was the breaks. He'd appeal, of course, but that didn't concern her. Once he was found guilty in a court of law, the case would be closed as far as the local police were concerned. Gavin would be shipped off to prison, gossip would die down, and with time, the murder of Christina Montgomery would be forgotten. And no one would know that the real killer still walked the streets.

Holding that knowledge deep inside like a treasure, she fairly purred with satisfaction as she leaned across the table to Micky Culver, her live-in boyfriend. "Did you hear what that man behind you just said?" she whispered. Her smile sultry, she mimicked softly, "'I'm not paying six-fifty to eat with a murdering Indian.' Can you believe it, Mick? Everything's going to work out just the way we want it to!"

His brown eyes hard and his mouth compressed into a

flat, angry line, Micky arched a scraggly brow at her. "What do you mean 'we'?"

Far from offended, she only laughed. "C'mon, baby, you know you don't mean that. You don't want anything to happen to me. You love me."

Grudgingly, he had to admit that was true. When Audra had come to him in despair, penniless after she'd been swindled out of her inheritance by her mother's lover, he'd thought he'd died and gone to heaven. Finally, he had a chance to prove his love for her! He'd taken her in, given her a home, and thought they would spend the rest of their lives together.

But lately he'd begun to have doubts. He'd known she was no angel—neither was he—but she was enjoying Gavin Nighthawk's predicament more than she ought to. The man had a little girl, for God's sake, and she needed him. But Audra didn't seem to care about that. All she was interested in was getting her own butt out of a sling, and if that meant an innocent man would go to prison for a crime she'd committed, she didn't seem to have a problem with that. But he did. In fact, it bothered him more and more each day.

Micky wanted to blame Audra's cold-blooded attitude on Lexine. Ever since Audra had gotten involved with her birth mother and started visiting her in prison, she hadn't been the same. She'd become harder and self-centered. But as much as he hated Lexine Baxter's influence, he knew she couldn't make Audra do anything she didn't want to do. Audra was a grown woman, responsible for her own actions. Because of her, Gavin Nighthawk was in a tight spot, and she was delighted.

"Who are you?" he asked, truly puzzled. "I don't know you anymore. I'm beginning to wonder if I ever did."

"Don't be silly." Audra laughed, not taking him seriously. "Of course you know me, honey. I'm just like you. That's why we get along so well."

There'd been a time when he would have agreed with her. Neither of them had much use for the law when it got in the way of what they wanted. He'd done some time in jail and didn't fool himself into thinking that before it was all said and done, he wouldn't repeat the experience. But unlike Audra, he wasn't proud of what he'd done. He was just weak sometimes, and when life closed in on him and he didn't know where the rent money was coming from or how he was going to eat, he did stupid things. But he'd never physically hurt or killed anyone. He'd robbed from folks who could afford the loss and had insurance to replace what he'd taken. Still, he wasn't pleased with himself.

But nothing seemed to bother Audra at all. Was she really that cold? That mean? He didn't want to think so, but he couldn't be sure. And that was what worried him.

"Are you really going to do this?" he rasped in a low whisper that didn't carry beyond her ears. "Are you just going to sit there and let that man go to prison for something you know he didn't do? Would you really do that?"

Surprised that he even had to ask, she all but laughed in his face. "Are you kidding? You're damn straight, I would! It's a tough world out there, baby, and a girl's got to do what a girl's got to do. Anyway," she said with a toss of her short, bleached-blond hair, "he's only getting what he deserves. She was the mother of his baby—he should have married her and taken care of her instead of leaving her out in the woods by herself to get in trouble."

"So it's *his* fault that you came along and killed her?" he whispered incredulously. "Is that what you're saying?"

Pushed into a corner, she shrugged. "Well…yeah. If she'd been where she was supposed to be, none of this would have happened."

Unable to believe she could justify murder so easily, Micky actually felt nauseated. Pushing away the steak sandwich he'd barely touched, he threw down his napkin and abruptly rose to his feet. "Something in here's making me sick to my stomach," he said coldly. "I need some fresh air."

And for the first time in their relationship, he walked out on her, leaving Audra staring after him in stunned surprise.

Laughing Horse Reservation was north of town and home to the Northern Cheyenne tribe. It was here that Summer had spent the summers of her childhood, getting to know her father's people and their traditions. And it was here that she had first been introduced to medicine when she was taught the ways of tribal medicine. She'd loved it, loved caring for her people, and when she'd returned to Whitehorn after college and medical school for her residency in immunology at Whitehorn Memorial Hospital, one of the first things she'd done was open a clinic on the reservation.

It was hard, working two jobs, but she was doing the right thing and had no regrets. Life on the reservation had improved some since she was a child, but poverty was still rampant and medical care practically nonexistent. It was the very young and the very old who suffered the most, and she did what she could to help them. She even took her services on the road, making rounds on the reservation once a week, driving from one home to the next long into the evening, visiting with patients, examining them, caring.

Usually she loved making house calls because they gave her a chance to reconnect with her heritage and memories of long-ago summers. But as she left the Hip Hop Café behind and headed for Janet Crow's house on the far east side of the reservation, all she could think about was Gavin

Nighthawk. There had to be something she could do to help him.

Troubled, she thought she hid it well. Taking Janet's blood pressure as the older woman chattered about her new granddaughter, Summer smiled and nodded and made the appropriate responses. But Janet was shrewder than she'd given her credit for. The older woman waited until Summer had listened to her heart and pulled the stethoscope from her ears before she arched a brow at her and said, "All right, missy, what's wrong?"

"Well, your blood pressure's higher than I'd like, but—"

"No, not with me," she cut in with an impatient wave of her hand. "I'm an old woman—it's my time in life to fall apart. I'm talking about you, girl. What's wrong with you? What are you brooding about?"

"I'm not brooding," Summer began, only to swallow the rest of her words when Janet gave her a hard look with brown eyes that were as sharp as a hawk's. She might be seventy-five and not as healthy as she could be, but she had earned her place as a tribal elder. She didn't miss much.

"All right," Summer sighed, knowing when she was beaten. "It's the trial, okay?"

Janet didn't have to ask which one. "His days of freedom are numbered," she said flatly. "I hope he's wise enough to enjoy them while he can."

"So you think he'll be convicted?"

Janet's shrug was uncaring. "It makes no difference to me."

"But he was born and raised here on the reservation!" Summer protested, stunned by her attitude. "He's Cheyenne. Don't you think the tribe owes him some kind of loyalty?"

"Why? Where was his loyalty when he moved into the

white man's world?'' she countered swiftly, resentment glittering in her eyes. "He grew up on the land of his ancestors, spent his boyhood running free among his people. But we were never good enough for him. Even as a boy, he made it clear that he wanted nothing to do with his Native American heritage."

Summer winced. "It was the poverty he hated, Janet. The lack of hope."

She disagreed. "It was the white man's way he admired, the white man's world of money and success and fair skin that he wanted, and as soon as he was old enough, that's what he went after. He doesn't care about us. Why should we care about him?"

She had a point, one that Summer couldn't, regrettably, argue with. It was common knowledge that Gavin's parents had raised him to want a life different from the one found on the reservation. And while there was nothing wrong with encouraging him to be ambitious, they'd gone too far. He'd never been content with who and what he was, and the end result was that he was a man who fit neither in the white man's world he sought nor the Native American heritage to which he was born.

And Summer found that incredibly sad. She walked with ease in both worlds and was accepted everywhere she went. She couldn't imagine what life must be like for Gavin, and her heart ached for him. He'd rejected his own people and didn't have a clue what he'd given up.

"He made some mistakes," she acknowledged. "Some big ones. But I can't say that I wouldn't have made the same ones if I'd been raised the way he was."

"You would have never turned your back on us the way he has," Janet said indignantly, her dark eyes flashing. "You're not that way."

"I might have been if Aunt Celeste and Aunt Yvette had

only cared about money. So don't judge Gavin too harshly," she cautioned. "None of us know how we would have turned out given the same circumstances. And think about this. If we turn our back on him when he's in the worst trouble of his life, what does that say about us?"

Put that way, there was little the old woman could say. "You are wise beyond your years," she replied with a grimace of a smile. "I will try to remember the disservice his parents did him and not judge him too harshly, but I doubt that the rest of our people will do the same. It galls many of them that he hasn't even offered to help you at your clinic. The work you do there is just as important as what he does at the hospital, and you could use his help."

"He's got enough on his plate right now without worrying about whether I could use an extra pair of hands at the clinic," she said dryly. "Anyway, I'm handling things just fine. Opening the clinic was one of the best things I ever did."

"You're working too hard."

Summer grinned. "It's not work when you love what you're doing."

"It is when that's all you do," she argued sagely. "There's more to life than taking care of sick people. You're a pretty young woman. When was the last time you went out to dinner with a nice, good-looking man? Every girl needs some romance to make her heart sing."

Summer couldn't help but smile fondly. Janet was just like all the other tribal elders—they all felt, because they cared about her, that they had a right to dabble in her love life. Or her lack of one, she ruefully added. Not that she was looking for a man. Her work was all that she needed, the only thing she wanted, but no one could seem to understand that.

"I appreciate the concern, Janet, but I don't have time for romance."

"You would if you didn't work so much. Or take on other people's problems—like Gavin Nighthawk's. You *are* going to help him, aren't you?"

Put on the spot, she couldn't deny it. "If the opportunity presents itself. My conscience won't let me do anything else."

Not surprised, Janet sighed heavily as Summer began to repack her medical bag. "I knew you would. You always did worry about other people more than you worried about yourself. Your mother would be proud of you."

The unexpected words of praise brought the sudden sharp sting of tears to Summer's eyes. "Thank you," she said huskily. "I like to think she would be."

"Just watch yourself, okay? You're such a tenderhearted soul and I don't want to see you get hurt."

"By Gavin?" she said, surprised. "For heaven's sake, Janet, we're barely friends. The only reason I'm going to help him is because I can't stand by and let an innocent man go to prison for a crime he didn't commit."

"Just remember that that 'innocent' man likes blond white women. Don't let him break your heart."

Summer promised her she had no intention of letting him or any other man do any such thing, but on the way back to her clinic, she almost laughed at the very idea of Gavin looking at her as anything but another doctor. Granted, there was a connection between them that she couldn't explain, but there wasn't anything the least bit romantic about it. They just came from the same background.

That was all it was, she assured herself. He looked at her and saw the girl from a past he wanted to forget, a girl who'd eagerly absorbed all the ancient knowledge the reservation had to offer. And every time her eyes fell on his chiseled features, she was reminded of the silent, brooding boy who'd walked alone across land that she loved.

Decades later, he was still walking alone, and it was that, more than anything, that tore at her heart. Everyone needed someone to talk to, to forget their troubles with, to vent to, and Gavin seemed to have no one, not even family. Long ago, he'd walked away from the people who could have at least offered him emotional support now, and there was no way to turn back the clock. He was in the worst trouble of his life, and he had no one.

Except her.

That caught her by surprise, and she immediately tried to reject the idea. She hadn't been kidding when she'd told Janet that they were barely friends. He hadn't asked for her help and didn't want it. She would do well to remember that.

But all the way back to the clinic, all she could think of was Gavin and the look on his face at the Hip Hop when he'd heard the things being said about him. With every snide remark, his expression had grown colder and more remote, and all Summer could think of was that he must have suffered the same verbal abuse everywhere he went from the day he was charged with Christina's murder.

Dear God, how had he stood it?

Haunted by the image of his loneliness, she slept little that night. He was innocent. Deep down in her heart, she knew that as surely as she knew that he wouldn't thank her for interfering in his life. Still, she couldn't worry about that. She didn't care if he ended up hating her guts, she had to find a way to help him. The question was...how?

The answer came to her with the rising of the morning sun. Already hard at work at the hospital, her eyes sandy from lack of sleep, she was examining a newborn in Pedi ICU when an idea popped full-blown into her head.

Stunned by the very outrageousness of it, she stopped in her tracks and told herself it would never work. He would think she'd lost her mind, and she couldn't say she'd blame him. So would everybody else.

Sure she was suffering from sleep deprivation, she tried to dismiss the idea and concentrate on her work instead, but she was fighting a losing battle. The idea stuck like a burr to her imagination, and with no effort whatsoever, she could see it working. She could help him. All she had to do was explain the idea to him and persuade him to give her a chance.

Yeah, right, she thought derisively. When pigs could fly. Don't even think about going there, she warned herself. Even if he didn't laugh in her face, he would never go for it. If she wanted to save them both some grief, she'd forget the whole thing.

She should have. It would have been the wisest course of action. But she didn't, unfortunately, always do the wise thing. Instead she followed her heart and dared to take a chance. The decision made with no conscious effort on her part, she found herself heading for his house at the end of her shift and knew she had no other choice.

His house wasn't in one of the more affluent subdivisions of Whitehorn—as a resident at the hospital, he could afford little more than a tract house at this point in his career. But it was still obvious to Summer as she pulled up before the brick and glass contemporary structure that he'd left his past—and the reservation—far behind. Wincing at the coldness of the place, Summer almost turned around right then and there to head for her clinic. This was never going to work.

But she couldn't bring herself to drive away, not when this might be her only chance to save him from a life in prison. Her heart in her throat, she stepped from her car and slowly started up the walkway to his front door. With every step, the knots in her stomach tightened with trepidation. There wasn't a doubt in her mind that she was doing the right thing, but that didn't make her task any easier. Because she knew that if Gavin accepted her offer, her life would never be the same and neither would his.

Two

He wasn't thrilled to see her. In fact, he was downright rude. Scowling at the sight of Summer Kincaid on his doorstep, Gavin made no move to invite her inside but stood blocking the threshold as if he was going to slam the door in her face at any second. "What do you want?" he growled.

That wasn't the greeting she'd hoped for, but Summer supposed she couldn't blame him for being less than hospitable.

"I need to talk to you," she said quietly. "May I come in?"

He didn't budge an inch. "No. I'm not in the mood for company."

That much, at least, was obvious. His chiseled jaw as hard as granite and his brown eyes nearly black with hostility, he was primed for a fight and ready to take on the world. If she'd been smart, Summer would have apologized for disturbing him and waited until another time to approach him with her proposal. But she'd had to psyche herself up just to get this far, and if she didn't speak her mind now, she was afraid she never would.

So she stubbornly held her ground and looked him right in the eye, silently daring him to throw her off his property. "I'm sorry about that, but I'm not leaving until I've had a chance to talk to you. We can do it right here on the doorstep in front of God and everyone or you can invite me inside. The choice is yours."

Irritated, Gavin arched a dark brow at her. He'd talked to her more in the past two days than he had in the past two years, and he had to admit he was surprised by her obstinacy. She was a quiet little thing and usually didn't say much. But something had lit a fire under her, and if the glint in her eye was anything to go by, she'd shout whatever she had to say to him to the rooftops if he didn't give her a chance to speak to him in private.

He shouldn't have cared. The whole world already knew just about everything there was to know about him—she couldn't possibly have anything to say that couldn't be posted across the front page of the Whitehorn *Journal*. Or at least, he didn't think she did.

Frowning down at her, he hesitated, then with a muttered curse, he jerked the door open wider. "All right," he said harshly. "Come in and say what you have to say. But make it quick."

Then get out.

He didn't say the words, but Summer heard them nonetheless. Another woman might have been offended, but she refused to take his hostility personally. She'd wanted an opportunity to speak to him and he was giving it to her. Nothing else mattered.

Slipping past him through the door, she stepped into the living room, only to stop short. She supposed she had to give him credit. With inexpensive glass and chrome tables and what appeared to be a few good pieces of secondhand modern furniture, he'd created a surprising sophistication without spending a lot of money. If there were no plants, no warm colors, none of the softness needed to turn a house into a home, she doubted that he cared. After all, he wanted acceptance in the white man's world, not warmth.

Following her into the room, Gavin said roughly, "Well? What is it you barged in here to say? Spit it out and let's get it over with."

Jerked back to her reason for being there, she hesitated, not sure how to begin. Too late, she realized she probably should have given more thought to her proposal, but at the time she'd come up with it, it had seemed like the perfect plan to exonerate him. Now she wasn't so sure.

Heat singeing her cheeks, she tried not to squirm as he pinned her with a gaze that was as hard as nails. "I've been thinking about the trial—"

"You and everyone else in town," he drawled. "What about it?"

"I think I can help you."

His eyes narrowed sharply. "How? Have you heard something? What do you know about Christina's murder?"

"Nothing!"

"Then how the hell do you think you're going to help me?" he demanded impatiently. "By being my *friend* and standing up with me in court the way you did at the Hip Hop?" He made "friend" sound like a dirty word. "Thanks for the offer, but I don't think the jury's going to give a damn about how many so-called friends I have when the prosecution has evidence placing me at the murder scene. So if that's all you came for—"

He turned away, dismissing her without even hearing what she'd come there to say, and something in Summer just snapped. She'd meant to lay the groundwork for her offer before she actually made it so she wouldn't completely shock him, but he'd taken that opportunity away from her.

Left with no choice, she blurted, "The jury might not care about your friends but I bet they'd be impressed by a wife who believed you and stood by you through all this.

"Especially," she continued when he jerked back around to face her with a scowl, "if that wife was from one of Whitehorn's leading families and was a well-respected member of the medical community."

"I don't have a wife," he said flatly.

"No, you don't," she said simply. "But you could. Think about what that would say to a jury. After you were accused of a horrible murder, a woman with an impeccable reputation pronounced her love for you and married you. No woman in her right mind would do that unless she thought you were truly innocent."

If he was impressed with her reasoning, he didn't show it. His brown eyes suspicious, he said, "Just what exactly are you suggesting?"

"That we get married."

The words just seemed to pop out of their own accord and hang in the air between them like a blinking neon sign. And too late, Summer realized just how forward they sounded. Horrified, she hurriedly said, "Don't misunderstand—I'm not saying that I'm in love with you! How could I be? We hardly know each other. Any marriage between us would be one strictly of convenience."

"Of course. I never expected anything else."

At his dry tone, she blushed to the roots of her hair. "This isn't about sex," she said stiffly. "It's about helping you."

"Which you seemed determined to do, and I can't for the life of me understand why." Frowning, he studied her with puzzled eyes. "What's in this for you?"

Not surprised that he'd so quickly reduced things to the bottom line, she didn't insult his intelligence by pretending she was a saint sacrificing herself just for the sake of helping him. "Your help in my clinic on the reservation for one year," she said bluntly.

"In exchange for marriage?"

She nodded. "Also for one year. You know I'm not the type to flaunt my family connections, but you have to admit that marriage to a Kincaid can't do anything but bolster your standing in the community. And that just might help clear your name. Once the trial's over and you're vindicated, my family connections will help when you go back to court to regain custody of Alyssa."

She made it all sound so simple. All he had to do was marry a Kincaid, and his life would magically return to normal. His name would be cleared, people would look at him in a different light, and he could go on with his life as if Christina's death and the subsequent murder charges leveled against him had never happened. And the price of a ticket to this fairy tale was only a one-year marriage of convenience to a woman who didn't love him any more than he loved her. And his help at her clinic, he reminded himself. After all, it was only fair that she get something out of the arrangement, too.

Stunned, he should have laughed in her face. That was what any sane man would have done. He was already in enough trouble—he didn't need to take on more by agreeing to a marriage that by its very nature was doomed to failure. And what would it really accomplish, anyway? True, the Kincaids were a powerful family in Whitehorn, but it wasn't the family that was on trial. It was him, and few people seemed inclined to cut "that Indian boy from the wrong side of the tracks" any slack. He didn't think marriage to a Kincaid would change that.

But can you be sure of that? a voice in his head wondered. *Summer Kincaid is well liked and respected. If she pretended to be in love with you and married you, people just might start to wonder what she saw in you and if they might have misjudged you. Granted, it's a long shot, but at this point, it's the only chance you've got. You'd be a fool to turn your back on the only person who's helped you from the very beginning. Thanks to her intervention, her uncle hired Elizabeth Gardener to represent you, and now she wants to help you again. Why are you hesitating?*

That was a good question. Aside from himself, he also had to think of Alyssa and how this might benefit her. If, through some miracle, he was able to actually clear his name, he still might have to fight to get his daughter back. He'd have a much better chance of winning that fight if he had a wife the likes of Summer Kincaid by his side to act as Alyssa's mother. And he wasn't losing his daughter, damn it!

Considering all that, he should have jumped at her offer like a drowning man being thrown a lifeline. But if the events of the past year had taught him anything, it was to look a gift horse in the mouth. Not everyone who appeared to have his best interests at heart did.

"I'll think about it," he said stiffly, "and get back to you."

She nodded. "Just don't take too long. For this to work, we've got to convince people that we're really in love, and we can't do that overnight. With your trial only a few weeks away, we don't have a lot of time."

No one was more aware of that than he. Ever since the trial date had been announced, he'd felt as though there was a guillotine over his head, waiting to fall. And it scared the hell out of him. "I should have an answer by morning."

That was the best he could do, and she had no choice but to accept it. "Then I guess I'll talk to you tomorrow," she said stiffly. "You can reach me at the hospital until two, then I'll be at my clinic."

She walked out without another word, leaving Gavin staring after her with a frown. He'd thought he'd known who and what Summer Kincaid was, but now he wasn't so sure. Why was she going out of her way to help him? What did she really want from him? Would she really go to such lengths to get help at her clinic or was that just an excuse to get involved in his life? Until he had some answers, he wasn't making a decision about anything.

Self-doubt didn't hit Summer until later that night when she was getting ready for bed and had nothing to distract her from her own thoughts. She'd actually asked Gavin to marry her. Dear God, what had possessed her? He must think she was desperate, or out of her mind, or both, when nothing could have been further from the truth. When she'd made the suggestion, she hadn't thought of anything beyond helping him out of the awful bind he was in. But now she had to wonder what she was going to do if he actually agreed to marry her. She'd made it clear that there would be no sex, but they would still have to live together, still have to act the happily married couple. She'd never been an actress, never had much use for pretense. How in the world was she going to pull this off if he said yes?

He wouldn't, she assured herself quickly. His back was already to the wall—if he'd thought marrying her would help him, he would have said yes in a heartbeat. Probably he was trying to find a way to let her down easy and spare her feelings. He'd call in a few days, thank her for the offer, and politely tell her he didn't think it would work. And that would be the end of that.

She'd done everything she could to help him, she told herself as she pulled on her pajamas and turned back the covers to her bed. If he insisted on going through this all alone, there was nothing she could do.

Resigned to the fact that she would, in all likelihood, watch him be escorted off to prison, she was about to crawl into bed when her doorbell rang. At nine-thirty at night she seldom had visitors. Unless it was someone who didn't have a phone coming from the reservation with a medical emergency.

Concerned, she hurriedly pulled on a robe and rushed to the front of her small, two-bedroom house, flipping on lights as she went. She hoped it wasn't Hannah Eagle. Six months' pregnant, she'd had three other pregnancies that had ended in miscarriages. It would kill Hannah if this one did, too.

But when Summer quickly unlocked her front door and pulled it open, it wasn't Hannah's husband John standing on her porch. Instead, she found herself face-to-face with the last man she expected to seek her out at that hour of the night. Gavin Nighthawk.

"Gavin! What are you doing here?"

"I need to talk to you," he said huskily. "I apologize for showing up without calling, but I was driving around and somehow just ended up here." His eyes dropped to the thin material of her gown and robe. "I didn't wake you, did I?"

She was respectably covered—there was no reason for her to be embarrassed—but in the harsh glare of the porch light, she could feel a painful blush climb into her cheeks. Instinctively, before she realized just how telling the gesture was, she started to reach for the overlapping neckline of her robe to check to see how low it was. But his gaze followed the movement and with a silent curse, she dropped her hand and forced herself to not fidget.

"Actually, I was just going to read for a while before I went to bed," she replied, standing stiffly in front of him. "If you'd like to come in, I'll change into something more suitable and make some coffee—"

"I'm not staying that long," he said quickly, stopping

her before she could push the door wider. "I just wanted to let you know that I've been thinking about your proposal all evening, and I've decided to accept it."

Stunned, Summer blinked, unable to believe she'd heard him correctly. "You have?"

Nodding grimly, Gavin could well understand her surprise. He hadn't realized he'd made a decision until he'd found himself pulling up in front of her house. "I have to admit, I've had my suspicions of you. I don't know why you offered to do this—or why you believe I'm innocent when no one else does. But I don't have time to worry about whether you've got some kind of hidden agenda or not. My only concerns are clearing my name and getting my daughter back. I have a better chance of doing that with you as my wife than I do standing alone. So if your offer is still good, I'd like to accept."

For a second, he thought she was going to say she'd changed her mind. She hesitated, and he couldn't say he blamed her. Their arrangement—if she went through with it—was strictly a business one, but he was the one who stood to gain the most. If things worked out the way he hoped, he'd get not only his life, but his daughter back. All Summer was getting out of the deal was a hired hand at her clinic for a year.

"Summer? If you've changed your mind—"

"No," she said quickly, silently cursing the betraying color in her cheeks. It wasn't that she'd actually changed her mind—she'd just had her own share of self-doubts. But that wasn't something she intended to share with him, not now that he'd decided to accept her offer. It would only cause misunderstandings and awkwardness, and there was enough of that already. "I'm just surprised, that's all. When you said earlier that you needed some time to think about it, I really thought you were going to turn me down."

"So did I," he replied. "But to be perfectly honest, you're the only chance I've got. And if we're going to carry this off and convince people that you trust me enough to fall in love with me, we've got to get busy."

"You mean, we've got to start dating."

"Not just dating," he corrected her. "If we're going to get married before the trial starts, this has to be a whirlwind courtship. Fortunately, we've known each other all our lives, so there's a history between us that should make it easier for people to believe we've suddenly found each other. Now we just have to give them some public displays of affection and every romantic in town will think we've really fallen in love."

He made it sound so easy. They'd hold hands, gaze into each other's eyes, and fool the world. For another woman that might have been a piece of cake, but Summer's experience with men was practically nil. Oh, she'd dated some when she was in college and medical school, but she'd never met a man who made her heart turn over, so there'd been little hand holding, let alone romantic evenings where she gazed into someone's eyes over a candlelit table for two. She didn't have a clue how she was going to pull it off.

She didn't, however, tell Gavin that. She was the one who had come up with this idea in a moment of madness, and she'd find a way to hold up her end of the bargain. After all, how difficult could it be? They had a world of things in common—medicine, their Native American heritage, hospital politics. They could spend hours talking about those things and anyone who saw them together would think they were totally wrapped up in each other.

Telling herself she could do this, she faced him squarely, all business. "Then I guess tomorrow night is as good a time as any to start. I'm usually home from the clinic by six unless I have an emergency. Just to be on the safe side, why don't you pick me up at seven?''

As pragmatic as she, he nodded. "Wear something nice. We'll go to the Wild Boar. We should cause quite a splash.''

They would do that just by walking in the door, Summer thought privately. The Wild Boar had just opened and was one of the nicest places in town. She hadn't been there herself, but she'd heard the decor was rich, the wine list extensive, and the clientele the upper crust of Whitehorn society. The second they stepped foot inside the place, they'd set tongues wagging.

Which was exactly what they wanted, Summer reminded herself. The sooner people noticed they were dating and started talking, the quicker the locals would hopefully change their opinion of Gavin and look at him in a different light. "Then I guess I'll see you at seven," she said simply, and prayed she wasn't getting into something she couldn't handle.

When Gavin rang her doorbell promptly at seven the following evening, Summer thought she was prepared for their "date." She'd spent most of the day psyching herself up for the part she had to play, and she was sure she could get through it without making a fool of herself. After all, how difficult could it be? They were just going to share a meal together in public, and they'd already done that at the Hip Hop.

But the man she opened her door to looked nothing like the one she'd approached that day in the diner. Dressed in a navy-blue suit that emphasized his broad shoulders, he was incredibly handsome. Caught off guard, Summer let her gaze slowly travel from his shoes to his freshly shaven square jaw to his neatly trimmed black hair, and felt her breath catch in her lungs. She'd never seen him in a suit before. She had to admit, he was something to see.

Standing in front of him in a dress that was at least three years out of date, she felt decidedly frumpy and old-fashioned. And she had no one to blame but herself. Her aunts had been telling her for months that there was more to life than medicine and she needed to update her wardrobe and get out in the world more. She should have listened.

Smoothing the skirt of her red silk dress, she said self-consciously, "I hope I'm dressed all right. I don't go out very often, so I didn't have much to pick from."

"You look fine," he replied roughly. "Just fine."

She did, in fact, look fantastic. He'd always thought that she was an attractive woman, but she did her best to hide it. She usually wore her black hair pulled back in a severe bun that wasn't the least bit flattering and she wore glasses that were the wrong shape for her face and hid her eyes. Tonight, however, her glasses were nowhere in sight, and she'd left her hair loose so that it fell past her shoulders in a waterfall of black silk that his fingers itched to touch.

For the first time in recent memory she was wearing makeup, and he was amazed at the difference in her. He'd never noticed before how beautiful her brown eyes were or just how sexy her mouth was. Unable to drag his gaze away from her, all he could think of was that red was definitely her color. With the red silk sensuously draping her slender, lithe body, she looked as though she'd just walked out of a dream.

But she wasn't *his* dream, he reminded himself grimly. Just the woman he was going to give a year of his life to, hopefully in exchange for a not-guilty verdict at his trial. Their arrangement was strictly a business one, and he'd do well to remember that.

"If you're ready, we should be leaving," he said coolly. "Our reservation is for seven-fifteen."

"Of course," she replied in a voice as cool as his. "Let me get my purse."

They walked out of her house like two strangers who didn't know what to say to each other, and without a word, Gavin opened the door of his Chevy sedan for her and helped her into the passenger seat. Moments later, he buckled in beside her and headed for the Wild Boar. The drive took all of ten minutes, but neither of them spoke the entire way.

Then, before Summer was quite ready to play the role of Gavin's infatuated girlfriend, he braked to a stop under the restaurant's portico. A valet was there to park the car for them, but before he could open Summer's door for her, Gavin was there first. Taking her hand in his, he closed his fingers around hers and gave her a slow, intimate smile as he helped her from the car. Reeling from the kick of that smile, she'd hardly recovered when he linked his fingers with hers.

She'd known that they would hold hands, that he would touch her when the opportunity presented itself, and it was all for show. But it didn't feel like much of a show when his hand squeezed hers as they stepped inside and the maître d' showed them to their table. Heat climbing in her cheeks, Summer felt the touch of dozens of pairs of eyes on them and knew Gavin had to feel it, too. But he gave no sign of it. Not sparing a glance for anyone but her, he seated her at their table, then took the chair across from her. In the glow of the candle that burned between them on the table, he gave her a smile that was slow and intimate and should have been outlawed in all fifty states.

Hit with the full impact of his sex appeal, Summer forgot to breathe. All around them, people began to whisper, but she never noticed. Her heart pounding in her breast, all she saw was Gavin.

"Miss?" Standing at her side, the waiter cleared his throat. "Would you like a menu?"

Transfixed, Summer hardly heard him. Then Gavin smiled in amusement, and the spell that had fallen over her broke and she realized she'd been staring at Gavin like a star-struck teenager who'd just stumbled across her favorite rock star. That was, of course, exactly what she was supposed to be doing. The problem was, she'd completely forgotten it was the role she was playing when Gavin smiled at her. And that horrified her.

"Miss?" the waiter said again, this time with exaggerated patience. "Your menu?"

Jerking back to awareness, she blushed. "Yes, of course. Thank you." Ignoring Gavin, she grabbed the oversize menu and quickly buried her hot cheeks behind it.

Chuckling, Gavin ordered champagne—to celebrate, he informed the waiter. When Summer finally lowered her menu, he was there waiting for her with a heart-stopping smile. "See anything you like?"

How was she supposed to answer that? she wondered wildly. When he forgot to brood and turned on the charm, he was a very attractive man—which every woman in the place had already noted, if the feminine glances he was getting were anything to go by. And that was exactly why they were there, she reminded herself. To have people look at him in a new light.

Remembering her role, she forced a smile that didn't come nearly as easily as his did. "Actually, I do. How about you?"

"Oh, yeah," he drawled, leering at her teasingly. "But it's not on the menu."

"It could be," she replied, flirting for the first time in her life. "If you're lucky."

Chuckling, Gavin reached across the table for her hand, and that set the tone for their evening. They touched and flirted and made no attempt to keep their voices down or to be discreet. And they accomplished just what they set out to do. By the end of the meal, everyone in the restaurant thought they were falling in love.

Exhilarated, exhausted, stunned that she'd actually been able to pull off her role, Summer didn't know whether to laugh or to sigh in relief as Gavin escorted her outside and they left their audience behind. Grinning as he took her hand, she said in triumph, "We did it! Did you see the way people were looking at us? I can just hear the gossip tomorrow."

"So can I," he replied. "Especially after everyone hears about this." And with no more warning than that, he stopped and tugged her into his arms for a hot, sizzling kiss in full view of the diners sitting by the restaurant's large picture windows.

Caught off guard, Summer could do nothing but close her eyes and helplessly kiss him back. And all the while, her heart was slamming against her ribs. Dizzy, her knees weak, she tried to cling to the knowledge that this was just another act of the little play they were putting on, but her mind had a tendency to fog over with pleasure and she found it impossible to think straight. Unable to stop herself, she melted against him, boneless in his arms.

Later, she couldn't have said how long he kissed her. It could have been mere seconds or hours. She just knew that when he finally let her up for air, she could do nothing but stare at him in bemusement. Why hadn't anyone ever told her that the man could kiss like that?

"Smile," he said huskily.

Still standing in his arms, her thoughts all jumbled, she frowned up at him in confusion. "What?"

"Smile," he said again. "Everyone in the restaurant can see your expression."

Disgruntled, she immediately turned the corners of her mouth up in a slow, sultry smile, but inside she was more than just a little miffed. He'd practically knocked her out of her shoes with that kiss, but he didn't seem to be affected at all.

"How's that?" she asked through her teeth, gazing up at him like an infatuated teenager.

"Perfect." Chuckling, he released her, but only long enough to take her hand. "I think we've done enough damage for one night. C'mon, I'll take you home."

Any fears she had that he might try to kiss her goodnight ended the second they reached her house and he followed her inside. Refusing the coffee she offered, he immediately began analyzing the evening. "Did you see the mayor? His eyes nearly popped out of his head when he saw the two of us together! It was great. By lunchtime tomorrow, everyone in city hall will be talking about that kiss in front of the Wild Boar. But that's just the start. Tomorrow, I'll order you flowers and have them delivered to you at the hospital. That'll really get the gossips going. Then we'll go out again tomorrow night."

She'd expected as much. "How about the movies? It's bargain matinee night, and there's bound to be a crowd."

"Good idea," he agreed. "We'll grab a burger first, then go see something romantic."

Not surprised, Summer said dryly, "Of course."

Lost in his musings, he never noticed. "You know, it was really clever of you to join me for lunch that day at the Hip Hop. It started people wondering about the two of us, and now, less than a week later, we're going out and kissing in the parking lot.''

Pleased with himself, he impulsively hugged her. ''This is great. Just great! I don't know how to thank you for all your help.''

''Don't thank me yet,'' she cautioned. ''We just started, and we still have to get through the trial. We might be able to convince everyone in town, but that doesn't mean the jury will return with a not-guilty verdict.''

''They will,'' he said confidently. ''I'm sure of it.''

Satisfied that he had everything worked out, he promised to pick her up the following evening at six, then wished her a quiet good-night and left. And he never knew that the real reason she'd joined him at his table at the Hip Hop that day wasn't because she was trying to be clever but because she'd thought he needed a friend.

Summer had never dated much. But even if she'd had a wealth of experience with the opposite sex, she didn't think anything could have prepared her for dating Gavin.

Over the course of the next week, they went out every night, and she had to give him credit. When he set out to show a woman a good time—even if it was all a pretense— he spared no effort. He sent her flowers and brought her gifts that he made a point of giving her in public. Sweet, inexpensive romantic gifts like a book of sonnets, a pair of heart earrings, a ceramic frog for her kitchen windowsill. And even though she knew it was for show, she couldn't help but wonder what it would be like to receive such attention from a man who really cared about her.

For a while, though, she could pretend, and she had to admit, she enjoyed herself. They went dancing and roller skating and had a candle-lit picnic at the town park in full view of anyone who chose to drive by. Anywhere there were people, they showed up, and everywhere they went, whispers followed them.

For a woman who considered herself an introvert, she should have been extremely uncomfortable. She wasn't used to being on public display, and there were times when it was awkward. But they were causing a stir, which was the whole point of their going out, and she couldn't help but be pleased. When she overheard people questioning her sanity, she knew they were making progress.

"I think she's lost her mind."

"Maybe it's one of those midlife crisis things. Though come to think of it, she's not that old, is she? Maybe she's having a breakdown from working so hard."

Stopping in at the Hip Hop for a quick sandwich before heading out to the reservation, Summer inadvertently stepped right into the middle of a gossip session in which she was the main topic of conversation. And not surprisingly, Lily Mae Wheeler, holding court in her booth, was leading the discussion. When she saw Summer, she did have the grace to lower her voice, but only to a hoarse whisper that carried the length and breadth of the café.

"The girl obviously needs therapy. Any woman who would voluntarily spend any time alone with that murderer after what he did to that poor Montgomery girl can't be all there. I think she needs her head examined."

Taking a seat at the counter instead of in one of the booths, Summer didn't so much as wince, but Janie Austin shot Lily Mae a reproving frown as she set a glass of water and the menu in front of Summer. "I'm sorry about that, Summer," she said quietly. "Don't pay any attention to Lily Mae. You know how she is."

Summer did, indeed, know how the old battle-ax was, but in this particular instance, she couldn't take offense—

not when Lily Mae's criticism generated just the response she was hoping for.

"Well, I don't know about that," Meg Reilly said with a frown from the booth where she sat with her soon-to-be stepdaughter, Hope Baxter Kincaid. "Maybe the girl's just got more sense than most of the folks around here who are so quick to judge. Better yet, maybe all this time everyone's been mistaken about Gavin. Summer's smart and kind and nobody's fool. She wouldn't go near any man she thought was capable of murder."

Surprisingly, a few more diners nodded in agreement, but Lily Mae only sniffed in disdain. "You always were a dyed-in-the-wool romantic, Meg, seeing hearts and flowers everywhere you looked. And that's fine when you're putting together one of your fancy weddings at your flower shop. But you need to take off the rose-colored glasses when you're out in the real world. The man's guilty as sin and we all know it. If Summer can't see that, she's the one who'll pay. If I was one of those aunts of hers, I'd take out a big life insurance policy on her because any day now she could turn up as dead as Christina Montgomery."

Just last week, practically everyone in the café would have agreed with Lily Mae, but there'd been a subtle shift in attitude over the last couple of days. No one other than Meg spoke up in Gavin's defense, but more than a few people were frowning in silent disagreement with Lily Mae. Pleased, Summer quietly ordered a chicken salad sandwich.

Three

Seated at the very back of the café, Audra Westwood quietly listened to the conversation skipping back and forth between Lily Mae and Meg and told herself she had nothing to worry about. What did Meg know about anything, anyway? She was a wedding consultant and a florist, for God's sake! She saw romance everywhere she looked. Well, life just wasn't that way, and anyone with any brains in her head knew that. Just because Gavin looked at Summer with goo-goo eyes and wined and dined her all over town didn't mean people were suddenly going to think he was some kind of choirboy. Nobody was that stupid.

But as she furtively studied the other diners, Audra had to admit she didn't like the doubt she saw on some people's faces. She tried to take solace in the fact that most of them were hicks from the sticks, but she was still worried. Her appetite dwindling to nothing, she pushed away the meat loaf she'd ordered and signaled the waitress for her check. Five minutes later she hurried out the door and headed for the nearest phone booth to call Lexine.

Every time she talked to her birth mother, Audra's stomach knotted with nerves. She hated the day Lexine Baxter ever contacted her and informed her she was her real mother, hated the day she'd pulled her into her scheme to regain the sapphire mine that had once belonged to the Baxters. But most of all, she hated the day Lexine had tricked her into confessing that she was the one who'd killed Christina Montgomery. From that day forward, she'd been under Lexine's thumb in spite of the fact that she was locked away in prison.

She didn't want to tell her that there'd been a shift in attitude about Gavin, even if it was, as far as she was concerned, an insignificant one. But Lexine had her sources, and she wouldn't be happy if she heard the latest news from someone other than her daughter.

If it had been anyone else but Lexine, Audra wouldn't have given a damn about keeping her happy. But her dear birth mother had all the information she needed to blackmail her and could, if she chose, make her life a living hell. Digging for change, Audra stepped inside the phone booth, slammed the door shut so she wouldn't have to worry about anyone overhearing her conversation, and punched in the number to the prison.

When Lexine finally came on the line, she was all sweetness and concern. "Darling, thank God you finally called! I haven't heard from you in a while, and I was beginning to wonder if something had happened to you."

Not fooled in the least by the loving-mother routine, Audra just barely swallowed a snort of disbelief. Underneath the sweetheart image Lexine presented to the world was a bitch who would say or do anything to get what she wanted. And right now, there were two things she wanted more than her next breath—the sapphire mine and a way—either legal or illegal—out of prison. With her scheming mind, it was, Audra figured, only a matter of time before she found a way to get both.

"There's been some new developments," Audra said by way of a greeting. "Gavin Nighthawk's got himself a girlfriend, and the whole town's talking about it."

"Summer Kincaid," she said flatly.

Not surprised that Lexine knew, Audra didn't even

bother to ask where she'd gotten her information. Lexine loved playing I-know-something-you-don't and wouldn't give out her source of information until it was to her advantage. "A few people are starting to wonder if they may have misjudged him, but I don't think we have anything to worry about. Lily Mae is telling everyone who walks through the door at the Hip Hop that Summer's in the middle of a midlife crisis and taking her life in her hands every time she goes out with Gavin."

Chuckling, Lexine practically purred in satisfaction. "Good ole Lily Mae. With her in our corner and all the evidence against him, Gavin hasn't got a prayer. Let him have his little fling with the Indian doctor. He could kiss up to Mother Teresa herself and it wouldn't help. He's going down."

Audra hoped so. Then maybe she could sleep at night without waking up at all hours with panic attacks. "I just wish the trial would hurry up and get here and be over with," she muttered. "I'm tired of looking over my shoulder every time I step outside."

"I told you to just act normal," her birth mother reminded her sharply. "Nobody's going to suspect you of anything if you act like you've got nothing to hide."

"I do!" she snapped. "But that doesn't mean I like it."

"It won't be for the rest of your life," Lexine assured her. "Just a few more weeks, a month at the most. Once Gavin's convicted, we'll be home free. The police won't have a reason to visit the murder site anymore, so you can start looking for the sapphires again."

Lexine was gloating, and with no trouble at all, Audra could see her rubbing her hands together in greedy satisfaction. That was all Lexine cared about, finding the sapphires and getting revenge on the Kincaids for taking Baxter land they had no claim to. But just thinking about returning to the spot where she'd killed Christina Montgomery turned Audra's blood cold. She hadn't been back there since that awful day, but she could picture it all too clearly in her mind.

Shivering, she desperately searched for a reason to put Lexine off. "Maybe we should hold off on that a while. The police could still be watching—"

"Don't be ridiculous. Once there's a conviction, no one's going to give a damn about the murder site."

"There'll be curiosity seekers—"

"Why do I get the feeling you're trying to chicken out on me?" Lexine asked silkily. "You wouldn't do that to your dear old mother, would you?"

Her heart jolting with fear, Audra stuttered, "N-no! Of c-course not!"

"Good," her mother said in satisfaction. "Because I'd really hate to turn in my own daughter to the police for murder. Think of how people would talk. It would be a painful thing for me to do, of course, but what other choice would I have? You killed an innocent baby's mother. For that baby's sake, you'd have to be punished."

She would do it, Audra thought, sick with terror. She'd do it in a heartbeat and laugh while she did it. Not because she gave a damn about Christina Montgomery's motherless baby, but because she could. Because power turned her on and there was nothing she loved more than wielding that power and squashing someone under her heel. No wonder she'd been handed back-to-back life sentences without parole when she'd been convicted of killing her husband and father-in-law. Lexine was vicious and didn't deserve to be let loose on the streets with decent people.

At least when she'd killed Christina, she hadn't enjoyed it, Audra thought self-righteously. But that, she knew, wouldn't keep her out of jail if Lexine played her trump card and turned her in. Stuck between a rock and a hard place, she had no choice but to do as she was ordered.

"All right," she said grudgingly. "I'll start looking for the mine again as soon as the trial's over."

Delighted, Lexine laughed triumphantly. "That's Mama's good little girl."

One week after their whirlwind dating, the announcement of Gavin and Summer's upcoming marriage came out in the paper, stunning Summer's family and friends and the entire community. And although Summer had broken the news to her aunts ahead of time and they tried their best to appear happy for her, she knew them too well. They were devastated by the news and more than a little confused. They, more than anyone, knew how little she had dated and couldn't understand how she could rush into marriage with anyone, let alone someone who'd been charged with murder.

There was no question that they were worried about her, but they only asked her if she was sure marrying Gavin was what she really wanted to do. Summer's two best friends—who just also happened to be her aunt Celeste's daughters—weren't nearly as restrained, however. As soon as they read the announcement in the paper, they called and demanded that Summer meet them for lunch at the Hip Hop.

She would have rather gone anywhere else but there, but she knew Lily Mae and the rest of the gossips would be there, having a field day over her and Gavin's announcement; and this was her chance to play the part of the wildly happy bride-to-be. So she reluctantly gave in and promised to meet them at the café at noon.

Not surprisingly, her cousins, Cleo and Jasmine Monroe, were already waiting for her in a booth at the back of the café. The minute they spotted her, they waved, and Summer couldn't help but grin. She couldn't remember a time when they hadn't been in her life. The three of them had been raised together at the Big Sky Bed & Breakfast, and it had been wonderful. With Frannie and David, their aunt Yvette's children, also growing up on the same property, but behind the B and B in a home built by their father, they truly had all been one big happy family.

"All right," Jasmine said the second Summer slid into the booth with them, "I want to know what kind of medication you've been prescribing for yourself at that clinic of yours. And don't tell me I'm imagining things. I know you, Summer Kincaid, and there are only two reasons why you'd even consider marrying a man you hardly know. You've either got a problem with prescription drugs or an alien from outer space has invaded your body. So which one is it?"

Chuckling, Summer was far from offended. "I haven't seen an alien in weeks."

"Then why are you rushing into marriage like a damsel in distress in one of those Gothic romance novels you used to read when you were a teenager?" Cleo demanded. "What's the hurry?"

Aware that everyone in the café was listening, she just shrugged and smiled dreamily. "We love each other. Why wait?"

Her two cousins exchanged a worried look. "To give yourself time to think about what you're doing," Cleo replied somberly. "You're not pregnant, are you?"

Truly shocked, Summer gasped, "No, of course not!"

"Well, I had to ask," her cousin said defensively. "That's the only reason I could think of why you were doing this."

Jasmine, the romantic of the two, pointed out practically,

"Even if you're absolutely nuts about him, do you think this is really the right time to get married? His trial starts next week, Summer. And there's a better than even chance that he'll be convicted—"

"You don't know that."

"*Everybody* knows it," she insisted. "I'm not trying to be mean, but if you go through with this, you're going to find yourself married to a convict. Is that what you want?"

"No, of course not—"

"Then wait. *Please!*"

Summer could well understand their concern—she'd feel the same way if one of them was rushing into what appeared to be total madness. And given the chance, she would have confided in them in a heartbeat. But if word somehow got out about the scheme she and Gavin had concocted to get him acquitted, he'd be convicted for sure. So all she could do was try to convince them that she knew what she was doing.

"I can't," she said quietly. "I love him and I want to be with him. I know what you're going to say," she continued, holding up her hand when they both opened their mouths to argue. "How can I be with him if he ends up going to prison? That's not going to happen," she assured them. "He's a good man and he didn't kill Christina Montgomery."

"But how can you be sure of that?" Cleo asked, frowning. "You hardly know him."

"I know how much he respects human life and that he could never, ever hurt a woman, especially the mother of his baby. He's not that kind of man. And I'm not just saying that because I love him," she said into the sudden stillness that suddenly engulfed the diner as everyone seemed to strain to hear what was being said at their table. "He's a gifted surgeon, a healer. I've seen him agonize when he loses a patient. He couldn't take a life—he saves them.''

In the silence that followed her speech, no one seemed to so much as breathe. Then Lily Mae muttered, ''Hogwash! You can't trust a woman in love.''

Just that easily, the spell that had fallen over the café was broken, and all around them conversations started up again. More than a few people nodded in agreement with Lily Mae, but not everyone did, and Summer couldn't help but be encouraged.

Her smile bright, she arched a brow at her cousins. ''So, can I expect you two to be my bridesmaids next Saturday.''

They exchanged a look, but it was the ever-practical Cleo who spoke for the pair. ''If this is truly what you want, you know we'll be there for you. Have you got a dress yet? And the reception planned? What about us? What do you want us to wear? Lord, I don't know how we're going to throw this thing together in a week. Have you talked to Mom and Aunt Yvette? We're going to need some help.''

Caught up in the excitement of a wedding, they talked about flowers and music and the reception, and Summer joined in with all the enthusiasm of a bride-to-be. But deep down inside, she had reservations that she wasn't admitting to anyone. Not about Gavin's innocence, she silently assured herself as Jasmine talked about a beautiful wedding dress she'd seen in the window of a bridal shop there in town. Summer didn't doubt for a minute that he was as innocent as the day was long. No, it wasn't Gavin she was worried about. It was herself. And her feelings for him.

It wasn't supposed to be this way, she thought as she and her cousins made plans to visit the bridal shop that very afternoon. She wasn't supposed to have any feelings for him except those she would have for anyone unjustly accused of a crime he didn't commit. But with just a touch of his hand, he could make her heart pound. And when he kissed her—always for the benefit of other people—it was very easy to forget they were playing at love.

And that worried her. She didn't know how this had happened. Their agreement was strictly a business one. Emotions weren't a part of the deal. They'd both agreed that the marriage would last for one year only and be in name only, but her heart seemed to have other ideas.

Another woman might have backed out while she still could. It was the only logical thing to do. But she couldn't go back on her word and leave him in the lurch, not after she'd already promised to help him. Which meant that she would become Mrs. Gavin Nighthawk on Saturday. God help her.

The week that followed was one of the busiest of Summer's life. She hardly had time to turn around, let alone sleep. But with the help of her cousins, aunts, and Gavin, she was able to put together a simple, hastily arranged wedding and reception that would be held in the garden at her aunt's bed-and-breakfast. It wasn't easy. With so much to do, one day ran into another, and she totally lost track of time. Then suddenly, before she knew it, it was Saturday morning, her wedding started at noon, and it was time to put on her wedding dress.

It was then that she suddenly missed her mother to the point of tears.

She told herself it was silly. She had no memories of her whatsoever, and even if she had, this wedding wasn't real. But as she slipped on her dress and her aunts oohed and aahed and couldn't help crying, the one person who was missing was her mother. She should have been there, with her daughter, with her sisters, even if the wedding was a farce.

And with the tears she struggled to hold back came an attack of nerves that made it impossible to sit still. She was doing the right thing—there wasn't a doubt in her mind about that—but she cringed at the idea of saying her vows in front of her minister in a religious ceremony. Given the chance, she would have insisted on a civil ceremony, but that wouldn't have convinced many people that she and Gavin were really in love. No, it had to be this way. She knew that and accepted it. But she still felt guilty as sin.

Then, before she was ready, she was standing at the entrance to her aunts's garden with her uncle Edward, Aunt Yvette's husband and a sweetheart of a man. He had graciously agreed to give her away, and as she clutched his arm, she tried to appreciate the beauty of the garden setting. Even as they stood there, waiting to begin the ceremony, an Arctic cold front was racing down from Canada and was scheduled to arrive later that evening, but for now, the day was a gorgeous Indian summer day, without a cloud in the sky, and perfect for a fall wedding.

The garden was awash with yellow and gold mums, and at any other time, Summer would have gasped in appreciation of the beauty of the flowers. But not today. Not when the garden was filled with guests who had come there for her wedding. Every chair was taken and an overflowing crowd stood along the sides and at the back. Anyone who was anyone in Whitehorn was there, just as she and Gavin had hoped.

She told herself she was pleased, and she was. But if the wedding had been for real and she and Gavin had been marrying for love instead of convenience, she would have chosen something far more intimate, with just family and very close friends.

Lost in her musings, she never saw Gavin take his place in front of the minister. Accompanying him were his two groomsmen—Mike, his college roommate, and Noah James, one of the few friends Gavin had at the hospital who hadn't deserted him. The music started, and her eyes flew down the aisle to Gavin.

What happened after that was a blur. Her cousins must have walked down the aisle in front of her, but she wasn't aware of it. All she saw was Gavin. Suddenly he was right in front of her, taking her hand after her uncle kissed her on the cheek, then they were both turning to face the minister. From what seemed like the distant end of a wind tunnel, she heard the minister begin the ceremony. If Gavin hadn't squeezed her hand when it was her time to repeat the vows, she wasn't sure she would have been able to do it. With every word she spoke, she half expected lightning to strike her dead.

It didn't, however, and all too soon the minister smiled at them and said, "By the power invested in me, I now pronounce you man and wife. Gavin, you may kiss your bride."

She'd known he would have to kiss her, of course, but she hadn't expected him to beam down at her like a man besotted with love. He reached for her and pulled her into his arms, and her heart started to pound in her breast. Then his mouth covered hers, and the passion that always seemed to be just beneath the surface whenever he was near set her senses humming. Aching, she wanted to melt against him and give herself up to his kiss, but she couldn't forget the crowd or the circumstances that had brought them together. And all she could think was that this was a farce. Nothing but a farce. Don't get caught up in it, she warned herself. You'll only get hurt.

But she'd set herself an impossible task, and when he finally let her up for air and smiled down into her eyes, it was all too easy to believe that he was her husband in fact as well as in name. He certainly acted as if he was. Tenderly tucking her arm through his, he turned with her to face their guests. Then they were hurrying down the aisle as though they couldn't wait to begin their life together. And for the next two hours, he didn't leave her side.

Anyone watching them would have thought he was absolutely crazy about her. A buffet had been set up under the trees to the right of the garden, and as the guests joined them there and came forward to congratulate them, there was no sign of the brooding Gavin Nighthawk who usually walked around with a scowl on his handsome face. Instead, he laughed and smiled and appeared to be on top of the world. Accepting people's handshakes and, in some cases, hugs, he kept Summer close to his side. And when he didn't have his arm around her waist, he was holding her hand, touching her, stroking her with his eyes.

The curiosity seekers who had come just to see if there was any truth to the rumors that they were suddenly, madly in love, had to be impressed. When they cut the wedding cake, they laughed into each other's eyes, then kissed as if it was the most natural thing in the world.

Standing by Gavin's side, Summer knew that in spite of the cloud hanging over their future, they appeared to be the happiest couple in the world. Keeping up that appearance, however, wasn't easy. Her smile felt as if it was plastered on her face, and inside, her stomach was churning. She had to force herself to eat the incredible buffet her aunts had prepared, and the wedding cake tasted like dust in her mouth. She didn't know how Gavin was feeling—he kept his true emotions carefully hidden from view—but deep inside, there was an aching loneliness in her heart that weighed heavy on her soul.

How she got through the rest of the reception, she never knew. At the most inopportune time, tears stung her eyes, and for the life of her, she didn't know why. She'd never been one of those girls who daydreamed about Prince Charming and when he would come for her—she'd been much too interested in medicine and her career. So it wasn't as though she were pining for love and romance or anything. It was just that—

"Hey, Summer, you're supposed to be happy," Mike Lincoln suddenly called out to her. "What's the matter? Change your mind already?"

Jerked out of her blue funk to discover all eyes on her as she and Gavin posed for the photographer, she quickly pasted on a smile. "No, of course not. I was just wondering when I was going to get my husband all to myself."

Everyone laughed, and it was then that she realized what was bothering her so. She'd thought it didn't matter to her, but this was, in all likelihood, the only time she was ever going to walk down the aisle. Why couldn't it have been for real?

"And I was just wondering the same thing about my wife," Gavin said, taking her hand and pressing a kiss to it. "So if you all will excuse us, we're going to slip away."

Her aunts came forward to hug and kiss her, and her cousins cried as if they expected never to see her again. And then it was time to throw the bouquet. Feeling like a fraud, Summer sent up a silent prayer that the flowers would bring someone luck, then tossed them over her head...right into the waiting hands of her cousin Cleo.

Stunned, Cleo stared at the bouquet as if it were something that had suddenly grown two heads. "Oh, my God!"

For the first time in hours Summer laughed naturally. She could well understand her cousin's horror. Cleo was smart and beautiful, but she'd never quite understood men. And for that reason, she'd made it a practice to steer clear of just about all of them. More comfortable with the children she took care of in the day care she owned and operated, she rarely dated.

"You don't have to look at it that way," Summer teased her. "It's not going to bite you."

Gorgeous and sexy in her mint-green silk bridesmaid's dress, she looked up in panic. "But this means I'm the next one to get married! Here—you take it," she told her younger sister. And to the amusement of everyone, she shoved the flowers into Jasmine's arms, who immediately began to hum "Someday, My Prince Will Come."

It was on that fitting note that Summer and Gavin left, rushing to Gavin's car in a shower of birdseed and good wishes. Sweeping her into his car, Gavin took time to kiss her in front of their guests one last time as he helped her buckle up, then rushed around the hood of the car to slide in beside her. Seconds later, they drove away and only then discovered that some enterprising soul had tied tin cans to the back of Gavin's car.

They both laughed, but the laughter quickly died as they found themselves alone together for what seemed like the first time in days. It was only then that it hit them. They were, in the eyes of God and man, married.

Silence fell like a rock. Face grim, Gavin stared straight ahead, focusing on his driving, and tried to ignore the tension that had crawled between them. Over the past two weeks, whenever they'd been together they'd always been able to talk to each other without any effort at all. But that was before they were married. What did a man say to a woman who was his wife, but wasn't, at least not in the biblical sense, and never would be?

"Do you regret it?"

Out of everything he could have said, *that* was the last thing he should have said, but the words just popped out on their own volition. Disgusted with himself, he said quickly, "You don't have to answer that—"

"It's okay," she assured him. "It isn't that I regret it— I don't. It just feels…weird. You know, it's like when you're all dressed up to go somewhere fancy and you know you look your best, but you forgot to brush your teeth? It doesn't matter how many people tell you how great you look, you know something's not quite right. That's how this feels. It looks right, thankfully, to everyone else, but we know it's not."

"And you can't help feeling guilty even though you know that there's nothing wrong with what you're doing," he added, understanding perfectly.

"Yeah," she said with a smile. "That's it exactly."

And she was feeling that way because of him. Because she'd gone out of her way to help him in a way that no other woman he knew would, and he hadn't even thanked her. "I should have said it before now," he said huskily, "but I really do appreciate what you've done for me. I know it wasn't easy for you. Your family must have thought you were out of your mind."

Smiling, she didn't deny it. "Naturally, they were worried. I've never done anything so spontaneous before. But my aunts have always been very supportive of me and would never try to stand in the way of my happiness—or what they thought was my happiness," she amended. Suddenly noticing that they were headed across town instead of to his house, she frowned. "Where are we going?"

"To Jack and Rachel Henderson's house," he said somberly. "Since you're going to be my wife for the next year, I think it's time you met my daughter."

After their marriage last winter, Jack and Rachel had bought the old Tucker place on the north side of town and completely renovated the wonderful Victorian house into a home for themselves and the children they hoped to one day have. It was there that Gavin had visited his daughter as often as he could after he revealed he was Alyssa's father.

To their credit, the Hendersons had always been decent to him, which was, according to some people, more than he deserved since Christina had been Rachel's younger sister. And he appreciated that. If Rachel had chosen to be vindictive, she could have made it nearly impossible for him to see Alyssa, but she wasn't that kind of woman. She hadn't judged him; she hadn't condemned him. Instead she'd told him about her own childhood and how her father had been too wrapped up in his business, then later in politics, to have much time for his children. She wanted more than that for her niece.

Because of that, she'd always welcomed him when he'd come to visit Alyssa, but Gavin had to wonder if that might change now that he'd married Summer. For almost the last ten months, Rachel had, for all practical purposes, played the role of Alyssa's mother. And while Gavin appreciated that, he'd held out little hope that he would ever have custody of his daughter again. Until now.

Summer had changed everything. Besides giving him hope that he just might escape conviction, her position as his wife made it possible for him to hope that one day in the not too distant future, he would regain custody of his daughter. If that happened, it wouldn't be easy on Rachel. She and Alyssa had grown very close, and anyone seeing them together would think they were mother and daughter. The one saving grace, however, was that Rachel was now pregnant with her own child. Hopefully, knowing that she had her own baby to love would make it somewhat easier for her to let go of his.

They reached the Hendersons's place, and it was once again time to play the part of the head-over-heels newlyweds. Opening Summer's door for her, Gavin took her hand as she joined him on the sidewalk and gave her a rueful smile. "Last performance of the day. Ready?"

Her heart pounding, Summer nodded. He didn't have to tell her the significance of this meeting—she saw it in the tense set of his jaw, felt it in the way his hand gripped hers. He loved his daughter; there wasn't any doubt in Summer's mind about that. And aside from the clearing of his name, there wasn't anything he wanted more than to get her back. That was just one more thing that she admired about him. He could have taken the easy way out and left her to the care of her aunt—Summer knew plenty of men who would have run for the hills at the thought of being responsible for an infant. But right from the beginning, Gavin had been involved in Alyssa's life. He'd not only delivered her, but he'd spirited her away to Lettie Brownbear for safekeeping on the reservation, where he'd visited her for months before anyone discovered the baby's whereabouts or his relationship to her.

Alyssa's welfare had always been of utmost importance to him, even when he should have been focusing on his own safety before he was arrested, and Summer intended to do whatever she could to help him get his daughter back—including stand by his side during a custody battle.

She prayed it didn't come to that as they approached the Hendersons's front door, but she couldn't be sure. Although Jack and Rachel had allowed Gavin to see Alyssa as much as he liked up until now, that didn't mean they would always be so accommodating, especially if it meant losing a baby they'd come to love. The situation could turn nasty very quickly if they didn't want to let her go.

Gavin had called Rachel to notify her that he and Summer would be stopping by after the wedding to see the baby. She'd obviously been watching for them. The second Gavin knocked on the front door, Rachel pulled it open.

Summer didn't know her personally—Rachel had been two years behind her in school—but in a town the size of Whitehorn, it was impossible not to know everyone on at least a speaking acquaintance. She'd known Rachel was pregnant, but she hadn't seen her in a while, and she had to admit that pregnancy agreed with her. With deep blue eyes, shoulder-length dark brown hair and delicate skin, she'd always had a quiet prettiness, but now she was glowing.

Her smile slow and a tad shy, Rachel pulled the door wider at the sight of them. "You both look wonderful! Please…come in."

Just as she showed them into the entrance hall that ran the length of the old Victorian, her husband Jack stepped into the hall with Alyssa in his arms. The second the little girl caught sight of Gavin, she let out a squeal of delight and held out her chubby little arms to him.

"Da-da!"

A big, handsome man with a hard edge that was a by-product of years of working the streets of Los Angeles as a cop, Jack Henderson handled Gavin's one-year-old daughter as tenderly as if she were made of spun glass. "Hold on now, short stuff, before you fall. Gavin, I could be wrong, but I think she's happy to see you."

Alyssa was, in fact, thrilled. Her blue eyes dancing and dimples flashing, she launched herself at Gavin the second he held out his arms to her, then laughed happily when he swung her up and down in front of him. His grin a replica of his daughter's, Gavin looked as happy as Alyssa.

Watching them together for the first time, Summer felt something shift in the region of her heart. If ever she'd seen a father and daughter who loved each other, it was Gavin and his little girl. At just a little over a year old, Alyssa was only just learning to talk, but she and Gavin had only to look into each other's eyes to communicate. Summer envied her that. She'd never known her father, so she'd never had the chance to look into her father's eyes, to laugh with him, to throw herself into his arms and know that he would be there to catch her. What must that feel like?

Standing at her side, wearing a half smile tinged with just a trace of sadness, Rachel, too, watched the man and little girl. Then her husband came to her side and slipped an arm around her waist to give her a reassuring hug.

It was an intimate gesture, one that Summer felt awkward noting, but before she could look away, Rachel turned to her with a bright smile. "Summer, I don't believe you've met my husband Jack."

Introductions were made, handshakes exchanged, congratulations offered and accepted. Nodding at Gavin and Alyssa as they played together, he said quietly, "They're quite a pair, aren't they? She'll walk around the house an hour after he leaves looking for him."

Just the thought of that made Summer want to cry. They were father and daughter—they belonged together. But she could hardly say that to either Jack or Rachel when they had opened their home and their hearts to the little girl. Feeling awkward, she said simply, "He's very devoted to her."

Gavin joined them then, with Alyssa still in his arms, and she was more than content to be there. With one arm slung around his neck, it was obvious she had no intention of going anywhere. Grinning at Summer, Gavin said, "I guess I don't have to tell you this is my daughter. I'd offer to let you hold her, but I don't think she'd let you right now."

"Maybe later," Summer replied, reaching out to soothe the toddler's straight black hair. "She's beautiful."

"Give her a little time," Rachel suggested with a smile, "and she'll be crawling all over you."

True to her prediction, Alyssa was playing peekaboo with Summer and giggling merrily minutes later. His heart expanding at the sound of his daughter's laughter, Gavin didn't want to upset Rachel, but he wanted no misunderstandings about his intentions. "I brought Summer by because it's important that she and Alyssa establish a relationship as soon as possible. Once I'm acquitted, I will want Alyssa back."

Later, he should have realized that he didn't have to worry about Rachel giving him a fight about custody of his own daughter. She had more class than that. Her smile understanding, she said quietly, "I'm not your enemy, Gavin. And I'm certainly not Alyssa's. We both love her and want what's best for her. If it's possible for her to be with you, I want that for her as much as I do for you. A child needs her father."

Four

For appearance's sake, they should have gone on a honeymoon, preferably in some wildly exotic place frequented by newlyweds, where they could have lain on a private beach, soaked up the sun, and supposedly made love all hours of the day and night. That would have been the perfect ending to the farce they were playing, but Gavin was out of jail on bond until the trial began and not allowed to leave the county. So after visiting with Alyssa, they had no choice but to head to Gavin's house, where they would spend the next few days secluded together like two lovers who couldn't get enough of each other.

Gavin had no intention of touching her or taking advantage of the situation after everything that Summer had done for him. But when he pulled into the driveway of his house and saw several neighbors peek out their windows, he realized that there was one last chore required of the groom before he and Summer could disappear inside and be themselves for a while.

Cutting the engine, he turned to Summer with a smile that was little more than a rueful grimace. "The neighbors are looking out their windows, so we're not going to be able to just walk in the door like nothing out of the ordinary happened today. I have to carry you over the threshold."

Summer hadn't even thought of that. "You're kidding."

Chuckling, he grinned. "Nope. If you don't believe me, look over at Mrs. Peabody's place on your right. See that curtain rustling upstairs? She's the biggest gossip in the neighborhood. If I don't carry you inside like I'm supposed to, it's going to be all over town by sunset that we walked through the front door like a couple of strangers and something is obviously wrong between us.''

Surreptitiously glancing up at the second-story window of the house next door, Summer saw the curtain move and silently swallowed a groan. The wedding had been much harder on her than she'd expected. She was emotionally wrung out, and the visit with Alyssa and the Hendersons hadn't helped matters. Seeing Gavin with his daughter, seeing the love they shared, had touched a void in her heart, and she'd been fighting tears ever since. Tired of the game they'd played all day, all she wanted to do was to go inside and shut out the world. But they couldn't do that until they put on one more performance.

Resigned, she arched a dark brow at him. "Sure you can manage not to drop me? I must weigh a ton in this dress."

The idea of her weighing a ton in anything was ludicrous—five-six and slender as a wand, she could have easily gained a good fifteen pounds and still blown away in a stiff wind. "I think I can manage," Gavin said dryly, and came around to open her car door for her.

Aware of the interested eyes on them, Summer flashed the same smile she'd given him all day, the one that was bright and happy and excited—and never reached her eyes. Then he was sweeping her up into his arms for the benefit of the neighbors, and her heart turned over in her breast. Why did his arms have to feel so sure and strong around her? Why did he, out of all the men she knew, have to be the one who made her feel treasured? How had this happened? And what, dear God, was she going to do about it?

In full view of his nosy neighbors, there was, unfortunately, nothing she could do but play along with him. So she clasped her arms around his neck and laughed when he pretended to stumble. Then suddenly, they were at the door, and the laughter faded as he leaned down to kiss her.

He didn't have to say anything for her to know the kiss wasn't nearly as spontaneous as it appeared. But her heart didn't seem to care. He kissed her as if he couldn't get enough of her, and just that easily, he set her head spinning. Breathless, clinging to him helplessly, she kissed him back and never knew when he unlocked the front door and carried her over the threshold as if he were a knight returning to his castle with his prize.

The second he kicked the door shut behind them, however, he immediately set her on her feet and released her. Tumbling back to earth with a jolt, Summer couldn't have been more hurt if he'd slapped her. There were times when she was in his arms that it was hard for her to remember that they were playing a role. He didn't seem to have that problem.

The sting of tears burning her eyes, she quickly turned away, only to gasp softly as she suddenly got a good look at the entrance hall and stairway. There were flowers everywhere, and white bows and ribbons decorating the banister all the way up the stairs.

At her gasp, Gavin followed her gaze, only to swear. "What the hell! Where the devil did all this come from?"

Surprised, Summer said, "You mean, you didn't do it?"

"No! I wouldn't do that to you. We have a business arrangement. The rest of the world thinks we're in love, but that ends when we walk through the front door. We don't have to pretend when there's no one here to see."

"Then who…?"

But even as she asked, Summer had her suspicions. Before she could voice them, however, he growled, "C'mon," and started up the stairs.

Following the trail of white ribbon, he led her straight to his bedroom, where he took one look at the table that had been set up in front of the fireplace and once again started to swear. Her eyes wide, Summer couldn't blame him. Talk about a scene set for seduction! There was champagne on ice, a fire already crackling in the fireplace, and an intimate dinner for two laid out for them on the table, complete with china, crystal, and silver. And on one of the plates was a note informing them that dinner was in the warming oven downstairs in the kitchen and would be ready when they needed it.

There was no signature on the card, but Summer didn't need one to know who was responsible for this little tête-à-tête. She recognized all too clearly the handiwork of her dear, sweet cousins. Cleo and Jasmine, indignant over the fact that the authorities wouldn't allow Gavin to take Summer on a honeymoon, had obviously put their heads together to come up with a way to at least make their wedding night special.

Touched—and more than a little embarrassed—she said gruffly, "I'm sorry about this, Gavin, but I think I know who's responsible. My cousins."

"Your cousins! How the hell did they get in here?"

She hadn't thought that far. "I don't know. I certainly didn't loan them the key you gave me. Who else has a key?"

"No one. Except my cleaning service—"

Putting two and two together, she groaned. "Let me guess. You use Acme Cleaning Service."

"Yeah. How'd you know?"

"Because my aunts use the same one at the B and B and my cousins are friends with some of the maids. I'll bet they got the key from one of them." Wincing at the thought, she said, "I'm sorry. They stepped over the line. They should have asked me first, and they certainly shouldn't have used one of the maids to gain access to your place. They were just upset that we couldn't go on a honeymoon. I'll call them tomorrow and make sure they apologize—''

She started to stack the plates together, but he stopped her. "An apology's not necessary, Summer. They just wanted to do something special for you. And you don't have to pick everything up. Since it's all here and the food's already cooked, we might as well eat. Your cousins would be hurt if they found out we didn't appreciate their efforts."

Surprised by his consideration, she hesitated. "Are you sure? This is so awkward."

"It'll be fine," he assured her. "Why don't we both change, then we'll see what other surprises they left for us in the kitchen? I'll get your bags."

Using the guest bathroom down the hall from the master suite, Summer decided to go for comfort instead of style and changed from her wedding dress into jeans and a forest-green turtleneck sweater. When she rejoined Gavin in his bedroom, she discovered that he, too, had changed into his most comfortable clothes. Dressed in black corduroy jeans and a flannel lumberjack shirt, he'd already brought the food up from the kitchen and was waiting for her.

"There you are," he said as she tentatively stepped into the bedroom. "C'mon in. I hope you're hungry. We've got enough food here for an army."

Cleo and Jasmine had, indeed, outdone themselves. They'd cooked Cornish game hens, wild rice, stuffed mushrooms, and a squash casserole rich with cheese and cream. Then, to top it all off, they'd talked their mother into making her prize-winning cheesecake. Dripping in a chocolate-cherry sauce, it looked positively sinful.

Summer's mouth should have watered just at the sight of the feast Gavin had spread out in front of her. She'd had nothing but a dry piece of toast for breakfast, and with her stomach jumpy with nerves for most of the day, she'd barely eaten anything at their reception. But when she sat down across the table from Gavin, her attention kept drifting to the bed on the opposite side of the room.

It was a huge walnut bed with austere lines, but even here, Summer's cousins's touch could be seen. They'd turned back the comforter invitingly to display new sheets, and on the nightstands on each side of the bed were scented candles just waiting to be lit.

Knowing Cleo and Jasmine as she did, Summer could just see them humming to themselves as they fussed around the room, making certain everything was just right. Under other circumstances, she might have seen the humor in the situation, but she couldn't right now. Not when she only had to look at that huge bed to picture herself there with Gavin, making love by candlelight. She was, she promised herself, going to kill the two women as soon as she got the chance.

"Maybe this wasn't such a good idea, after all. You're just picking at your food, and you haven't eaten anything all day. Would it help if we moved everything downstairs to the dining room? It won't take any time."

Jerking her gaze from his bed, Summer cursed the blush that burned her cheeks and wanted to sink right through the floor. Had he noticed she couldn't stop looking at the bed? she wondered wildly, then wanted to kick herself for even having to ask. Of course he had!

"No, this is fine. Really," she said when he didn't look convinced. "I guess I'm just tired. The last two weeks have been pretty hectic. I'll feel better after a good night's sleep."

That brought the subject right back to the one she wanted to avoid, but she couldn't avoid talking about it for the rest of the night. Silently groaning in defeat, she forced a weak smile. "In fact, I think I'll just skip dinner, if you don't mind. I'd rather just unpack, then take a shower and go to bed."

"I'll show you where everything is."

"Oh, you don't have to do that," she said hurriedly, feeling guilty for interrupting his meal. "Finish eating. I can explore on my own."

"To tell you the truth, I'm not very hungry, either," he admitted with a wry grimace as he pushed away from the table and rose to his feet. "The master bath and closets are right through there," he said, nodding to the door behind her. "I've already cleared out space for you, so just put your things wherever you like."

"Space?" Surely she heard him wrong. She just looked at him. "What do you mean...space? I thought I'd be staying in the guest room."

It was his turn to blink in surprise. "There is no guest room. The house has three bedrooms, but I use one as an exercise room, and the other is Alyssa's room. The only bed in there is a crib."

Stunned, she felt as if he'd just pulled the rug right out from under her feet. Surely he didn't expect her to sleep with *him!* It would never work. Not after the kisses they'd shared. They'd both just be asking for trouble.

Don't panic, she told herself. There had to be another solution. "Then I'll bunk downstairs on the couch," she said desperately.

"For the next year? C'mon, Summer, be reasonable. I suppose I could buy a bed for the exercise room, but I've had the same cleaning service for the past two years, and they usually send the same maids every week. What do you think they're going to say about me buying a spare bed just days after I get married? When they clean that room, they're going to know you're sleeping there, and then it wouldn't take long for word to get out that our marriage is a sham. Then everything we've done so far would have been for nothing.''

He made it all sound so logical, so practical. He could have been discussing the weather for all the concern he showed. But it wasn't that simple. He was talking about sharing a bed with her for an entire year, sleeping side by side night after night, just like any other married couple. But they weren't married, not in the way she intended to be married one day, and her heart skipped at just the thought of crawling into bed with him. There had to be another solution.

"We should have discussed this more," she said half to herself. "I don't know what I was thinking of—"

"You don't have to worry," he said gently. "Nothing's going to happen. I haven't forgotten the terms of our agreement. Our marriage is in name only, and that's not going to change just because we share a bed. I can sleep with you without touching you.''

She should have been relieved—he was a man of his word, and she could rest easy knowing he wouldn't take advantage of her. But instead of reassuring her, his words struck her right in the heart. He might have had the best of intentions, but there was no misunderstanding his message. What he was really saying was that she didn't have to worry about anything happening between them because he didn't desire her. And although she knew that was for the best, it still hurt.

She would, however, have died before she told him that. After all, she had some pride. So hiding her pain behind a weak smile, she said, "I know I can trust you, Gavin. I didn't mean to imply that you were going to take advantage of the situation. I was just...surprised. I really hadn't thought that far ahead because I'd assumed you had a guest room. But this will be fine," she assured him, and tried to believe it.

But later, when she crawled into bed beside him and he switched off the light, she realized she'd only been fooling herself. Her heart slammed against her ribs, and every nerve ending she had seemed to be attuned to Gavin and his presence beside her. The bed was a king-size, thank God, so they could each lie on their own side and still have several feet of space between them, but she was still aware of every breath he took.

He moved—and her pulse jumped like a scared rabbit. Stiffening, she caught her breath, but he only turned onto his side away from her and settled into a more comfortable position. Within minutes his breathing lapsed into the slow, easy rhythm of sleep.

Wide awake and clinging to the very edge of her side of the mattress, she stared at the darkness and didn't know if she wanted to laugh or cry. This was just their first night of marriage, and she was already a basket case. How, dear God, was she going to stand a year of this?

In spite of the fact that they couldn't go anywhere for a honeymoon, they'd decided they could still give the appearance of loving newlyweds by devoting the next week totally to each other. So Summer had taken leave from her job at the hospital and arranged for a friend to take over for her at her clinic. With nothing but time on her hands, she'd expected to lie around the house, read and relax and catch up on some much needed sleep. But after their awkward dinner the night before and a nearly sleepless night, the morning dragged and it became obvious to her that she wasn't going to be able to relax. Not when Gavin was right there in her line of vision every time she turned around.

Reading her mind as he watched her try and fail to concentrate on a murder mystery that was supposed to be the latest bestselling page turner, he said, "You know, we don't have to hide away like we're under house arrest or anything. If you'd like to change anything in the house, we could go shopping, do some redecorating. People would probably expect that, anyway."

Glancing up from the blurred pages of her book, she cringed at the idea of stepping out in public again and playing the role of loving wife so soon after the ordeal of yesterday. Granted, that was the sole reason for their marriage, but just once she wished that everything they did together in public wasn't so orchestrated. She just wanted to be herself again.

Still, she had promised to help him, and she was quickly running out of opportunities to do that. The trial started next week. "All right," she said, "that works for me. We could look at window treatments—"

That was as far as she got. The phone rang, and they'd both been doctors too long to ignore it. Gavin picked it up. "Hello?" A split second later he was handing the portable to Summer. "It's for you."

She took it, only to frown when she recognized the voice of Laurie Mills, an intern from the hospital. "What's wrong?" she demanded, instinctively knowing there was a problem.

"I'm sorry for bothering you, Summer," she said, "but I didn't know what else to do."

"It's okay," she assured her. "What's wrong?"

"Do you know anyone named Bryan Gray Eagle? He showed up here a little while ago asking for you. He said his grandmother was dying, but when I asked where she lived so we could send an ambulance for her, he wouldn't tell me. He just said to tell you, then he ran off.''

Shock hit her first, then the pain, but she didn't so much as flinch. "I'll take care of it," she said quietly. "Thanks for calling, Laurie.''

She thought she had her emotions under control, but the second she hung up, Gavin said, "That was about a patient, wasn't it? Someone you care about.''

She nodded, her brown eyes dark with sadness. "Grandmother Gray Eagle's dying. I have to go to her.''

Gavin didn't have to ask who Grandmother Gray Eagle was. A tribal elder who was wise in the ways of healing, she was an institution on the reservation, the one everyone went to when they were hurt or sick. And if Gavin remembered correctly, she was the one who'd taught Summer the ways of tribal medicine when she was just a girl.

She had to be hurting right now, but she seemed to have herself well in hand, so he followed her lead and was all business. "You'll need your boots and coat," he told her. "It's a nasty day. I'll drive you to the hospital—''

"Oh, but she's not in the hospital.''

"Someone from her family called an ambulance, didn't they?" he asked sharply. "Or were they waiting for you to do it?''

"She wants to die at home, Gavin," she replied. "The two of us agreed a long time ago that when her time came, she would get word to me, and I would come to her home and help her make the transition to the other side. It's what she wants. So there'll be no ambulance, no life support, no white man's medicine. She's going to do this her way, and I'm going to help her.''

Her eyes locking with his, Summer had known he wouldn't like the sound of that, so she wasn't surprised when his expression closed up tight. He'd never been interested in anything but traditional modern medicine, never wanted anything to do with the healing ways of his ancestors or the spiritual side of his nature. He might be Native American on the outside, but on the inside he was white and had no tolerance for any kind of medicine that wasn't spelled out in a medical book.

And she found that incredibly sad. He was a man with an incredible gift for healing, but there was so much he was missing, so much he would never truly know, because he practiced medicine with his head and not his heart.

"If you'll warm up my car for me while I change, I'll be right down," she said as she started to turn toward the stairs. "Oh, and I'll need my medical bag. It's in your study."

"The Gray Eagle place is back in Bear Canyon, isn't it? I'm not letting you go all the way out there by yourself on a day like today," he said stubbornly. "I'll drive you."

She wanted to argue, but one look at his chiseled jaw and she knew better. "This could take a while," she warned him. "She's a strong woman. She may not let go easily."

"We'll stay as long as it takes," he retorted. "I'll warm up the car." Without another word, he headed for the garage.

It was a miserable day to die.

Seated next to Gavin in her four-wheel-drive Jimmy, Summer looked out at the desolate countryside and shivered. Overnight, the weather had turned horrible. Just yesterday, it had felt like summer, but now it was wet and icy, with a chilling wind out of the north that cut to the bone. And for the life of her, Summer couldn't understand why Grandmother Gray Eagle had chosen this day of all days to die. She would have expected her to go in the spring, when the weather was warm and the wildflowers were in bloom and the birds would sing a song to the Great Spirit when she passed. Instead, she had chosen today, when the world was cold and raw.

And there wasn't a doubt in Summer's mind that *she,* not the Great Spirit she believed in, had chosen her time to die. A woman of strong faith in the power of the spirit, Grandmother Gray Eagle had always controlled her own destiny and held the forces of life and death in her hands.

Her heart heavy at the thought, Summer dragged her eyes away from the weather and focused instead on Gavin's driving. "You do remember where she lives, don't you?"

It wasn't something Gavin was likely to forget. He'd been in his first year of medical school when his parents had died within six months of each other—his father first, of a heart attack, then his mother of pneumonia. They both might have been saved if they'd let him take them to the hospital, but they'd refused and insisted he take them to Grandmother Gray Eagle instead. At the hours of their deaths, after a lifetime of instilling in him the belief that the white man's ways—and medicine—would be his salvation, they'd abandoned their own teachings and put their trust in the primitive medicine of their childhood. And because of that, he was convinced that they'd died before their time. To this day, he'd yet to forgive them—or Grandmother Gray Eagle—for that.

"Yes, I know," he said grimly. "The road hasn't changed."

Little on the reservation ever did, which was one more reason why he made it a point to avoid the place if at all possible. He found the all-consuming poverty and hopelessness more than he could deal with. If he lived to be a hundred, he'd never understand how the people who lived there got through the day knowing that tomorrow—and the day after that and the one after that, ad infinitum—would be exactly the same, with no expectation or optimism. They could get out—he had. But most of them seemed perfectly content.

Grandmother Gray Eagle lived in a remote area on the northwest side of the reservation, in a house that was little more than a shack. But it was clean, and when Gavin and Summer arrived, it was filled with the old woman's relatives, who were gathered around her bedside, chanting softly.

Swearing softly under his breath, Gavin would have liked nothing better than to turn around and walk out. The haunting sounds of the chanting grated against his nerve endings, taking him back to his childhood and a place he didn't want to be. But he'd married Summer with the promise to help her with her clinic for a year, and he couldn't go back on his word just because the work took him to places that made him feel uncomfortable.

So he followed her to the old woman's bedside and wasn't surprised that Grandmother Gray Eagle had changed little since the last time he'd see her seven years ago. For as long as he could remember, she'd been old. Small and shrunken, with wrinkled skin like leather and twin braids of thick gray hair that fell to her waist, she was nearly lost among the bedclothes.

Obviously weak and waiting to meet her maker, she shouldn't have been an imposing figure. But as Gavin watched her greet Summer, he couldn't help but be impressed. She still had her power, that aura of strength that had made her a leader among her people all of her life.

Her faith in the ancient ways had always been unshakable, and it was that, Gavin realized now, that had made her so powerful. She'd believed in herself and the Great Spirit, and she'd made everyone around her believe, too.

And he knew from his own experience with medicine that most of the time, that was all it took to heal someone. You had to make them believe that they were going to get better.

So how was the healing that Grandmother Gray Eagle had done all of her life so very different from what he practiced?

The question came out of nowhere to hit him right in the face. Stunned, he immediately tried to reject the idea, but he couldn't. And for the first time he understood why his parents had had such faith in an old, uneducated Indian woman who'd never, as far as anyone knew, ever stepped foot off the reservation. They'd believed in her more than they'd believed in the care they would have received in a cold, sterile hospital, and even though she hadn't been able to save them, their trust in her had given them a peace that they never would have found with traditional medicine. And for that, he was thankful.

After years of blaming her, Gavin realized that he needed to tell Grandmother Gray Eagle that, but when he moved to her bedside and his black eyes locked with hers, he realized that no words were necessary. With a nod of her head, she silently acknowledged that she understood everything he wanted to say. She didn't have to hear the words to know how he was feeling. All resentment was understood and forgiven.

Amazed that *she* was giving him comfort when she was the one who was dying, Gavin marveled at how strong she appeared to be even as she faced death. Then Summer took her hand, and he realized that up until then, the old lady hadn't been nearly as fearless as she'd appeared. She'd put on a brave front, but the second her gnarled hand closed tight around Summer's, relief flashed in her eyes and a peace unlike anything Gavin had ever seen on anyone's face before settled over her.

Murmuring quietly to her in their native tongue, Summer gave Grandmother's hand a reassuring squeeze, then went about the business of gathering her most important possessions. Her prayer stick, a sacred stone, the medicine bundle that her mother's mother had used nearly a century before. Visiting the reservation as a child, learning tribal medicine from Grandmother Gray Eagle, Summer had always loved it when the old woman had let her hold the things that were closest to her heart. But now, touching them, bringing them to her in quiet ritual, gave Summer little joy.

Grief pulled at her heartstrings, but she couldn't give in to it. Grandmother was depending on her to be there for her, to help ease her into the world of the Great Spirit, so there was no time for personal feelings. Later, she would cry, but not with sadness. Just knowing her, loving her, having the benefit of her teachings, had been such a blessing that any tears she shed would have to be ones of joy.

So as the hours dragged by and the day gave way to twilight, then darkness, Summer kept her emotions at bay and softly repeated the ancient prayers and songs that she had, over the years, seen Grandmother perform for hundreds of other dying people. And in the rituals that she knew as well as her own name, she found the strength she needed to finally sing the last song and watch Grandmother take her last breath with a soft smile of peace on her face.

It was, Summer knew, the way people were meant to die and so often rarely did. And Grandmother's family knew it, too. They thanked her with hugs and kisses, but she knew she was the one who had reason to be grateful. She was the last one who'd been able to do something for Grandmother Gray Eagle, and that gave her a peace that nothing else could.

Caught up in offering comforting words to the family, Summer had completely forgotten Gavin's presence until he tapped her on the shoulder as she was talking to Grandmother's eldest daughter about the burial arrangements the family had already made. "I hate to interrupt, Summer," he said huskily, "but the weather conditions are worsening. I didn't know how much longer you want to stay, but I just thought you should be aware of that."

She'd not only forgotten about him, but she'd forgotten that he'd insisted on coming with her because of the icy roads. Far back in the reservation, where roads were little more than dirt paths, it didn't take long for them to become impassable.

"I'm sorry. I completely forgot," she told him. "Just give me a few more minutes and I'll be ready."

It was, in fact, another thirty minutes before she said her final goodbyes to everyone. Standing patiently by the door, Gavin didn't rush her. These people were like family to her, and she needed this time with them. In spite of the fact that she'd been as steady as a rock throughout the day and evening, Gavin knew she wasn't nearly as unmoved by the old woman's death as she appeared.

Oh, she put on a good front, but she was hurting. Gavin could see it in the deep shadows in her eyes, in the wisp of the smile that kept disappearing from her face. She'd been strong up until now, but that strength had a limit, and any minute now she was going to reach it.

She seemed to realize that at about the same time he did, and within minutes she'd collected her purse and coat and reached his side. "I'd like to go now," she said quietly. "There's nothing more I can do here."

Without a word he opened the door for her and a cold, icy wind hit them right in the face. Muttering a curse, Gavin swept an arm around her shoulders and rushed her out to her truck, which he'd parked under a tree to protect it from the weather. The doors weren't iced shut, and with a sigh of relief, he helped Summer inside, then quickly joined her. Within seconds he had the motor running and the heater on high. It was still another ten minutes before the defroster was warm enough to melt the ice glazing the windshield.

And during that entire time Summer didn't say a word. She just sat there, in utter silence, staring out the windshield at the cold darkness of the night.

Gavin almost asked her if she wanted to talk about the pain he knew she had to be feeling, but one look at her grief-stricken face and the words died unspoken on his tongue. She'd talk when she was ready, without any prompting from him. In the meantime he needed to get her home while he still could. So without a word, he headed south toward Whitehorn and home.

Later, he couldn't have said how far he'd driven before he realized she was crying. She didn't make a sound, didn't make a move to wipe away the tears that silently trailed down her face. It was the saddest thing Gavin had ever seen in his life.

Later, he realized he should have let her grieve, but he couldn't stand seeing her in such pain. Making a snap decision, he pulled off to the side of the road, threw the transmission into park, and turned to take her into his arms.

"It's all right," he murmured. "Everything's going to be all right."

The second his arms closed around Summer and pulled her against the hard wall of his chest, what was left of her control just snapped. With a sob, she buried her face against his neck and let the tears fall.

Held tight against him, she never knew how long she cried. It could have been minutes, hours. There was so much sadness in her heart that it actually ached, and once she gave in to it, a dam just seemed to burst within her. She cried and cried and cried.

When she finally ran out of tears, she was still safe within the security of his arms. Spent, she could have stayed just where she was for the rest of the evening. That was when she realized she was playing with fire.

She wasn't a woman who was used to leaning on a man—that just wasn't her nature. Strong and independent, she took care of her own problems, and when she cried, she did it in private. Or she had up until now. But Gavin made her feel as if it was all right to drop her guard, to give in to her emotions, and that made him very dangerous indeed. Because when she was in his arms, she tended to forget that she needed to be cautious. And that could only lead to trouble.

Their marriage, she reminded herself, had nothing to do with love. She had to remember that or at the end of the year when they filed for an annulment, she'd be crying again, this time from a broken heart.

Stiffly pulling out of his arms, she wiped at her wet face and choked, "I'm sorry I cried all over you. Believe it or not, I don't usually do this. It's just that Grandmother and I were so close. I can't believe she's really gone."

"She lived a long life," he said huskily. "She was ready to go."

"I know. And I thought I was ready to let her go. But I wasn't." Forcing herself to concentrate on her grief instead of the remembered feel of his arms around her, she shifted on the seat as if she was trying to get more comfortable, but used the move to put more distance between them. It helped, but not nearly enough. Aware of every breath he took and the touch of his eyes on her, she desperately tried to cling to the subject of Grandmother Gray Eagle, but he didn't make it easy for her. All she wanted to do was to melt back into his arms.

Not daring to, she blurted, "Did I ever tell you about the time she taught me how to analyze dreams? I was twelve..."

Five

LINDA TURNER

that deadline, she hinged. "But I overall you about the
house … I hadn't the time to … balance of money I was
owed…"

Five

Pulling back onto the road, Gavin tried to focus on his driving as Summer rambled on beside him about her summers on the reservation and all she had learned from Grandmother Gray Eagle. But all he could think about was the feel of her in his arms. When had touching her, holding her, begun to feel so right?

Scowling at the thought, he tried to convince himself he was imagining things. There was no attraction between them—there couldn't be. Their marriage was a business arrangement, nothing more or less, and even if it hadn't been, he wasn't looking for a relationship. He hadn't had much luck with women over the past few years—his affairs with Patricia Winthrop and Christina Montgomery had both ended—one disastrously. So the only female he was interested in was his daughter, and even then, he didn't have a clue how she was going to fit into his life.

But knowing that, he was discovering to his disgust, and remaining indifferent to Summer were two different things. Touching her, kissing her, had become a habit over the past few weeks as he'd pretended to court her, one that he had to admit he'd enjoyed more than he should have, considering their agreement. And breaking that habit was turning out to be more difficult than he'd anticipated. Every time he turned around, he found himself wanting to reach for her.

She's the only person who's stepped forward to help you

out of the mess you're in, a voice in his head snapped. *Would you really betray her trust that way after all she's done for you?*

He had his faults, just like every other man, but he liked to think he wasn't that big a bastard. Scowling, he vowed to keep his hands to himself from that moment on, and just that easily, he set himself an impossible task. Because now that he'd decided not to touch her, she only had to shift slightly in her seat beside him for him to want her. It was, he decided grimly, going to be a long year.

By the time they left the reservation behind, Summer had run out of conversation and a deep silence fell between them that neither of them was inclined to break. Physically and emotionally exhausted, Summer just wanted to go home—to *her* house—where she could be alone, among her own things, to grieve in private. But even if she hadn't already had a renter lined up, that was out of the question. What would people say if she left him the day after they got married and went back to her place by herself?

As soon as they stepped inside Gavin's house, she knew she had to have some time to herself. "I think I'll go up and take a hot bath," she said huskily. "I feel like I'm chilled all the way to the bone."

"That's a good idea," he said. "While you're doing that, I'll heat up some soup and make some sandwiches."

She wasn't hungry, but she'd hardly eaten breakfast, they'd missed lunch completely, and it was already well past dinner. "I'm going to soak for a while, so go ahead without me if I'm not down by the time everything's ready."

She escaped upstairs and quickly filled the tub in the master bath with her favorite bubblebath, hoping that when she slipped into the steaming water and closed her eyes, the familiar scent would remind her of home. But when she lay back and the hot water closed around her shoulders, it wasn't home she thought of. It was Gavin.

The scent of his cologne lingered faintly on the air, teasing her senses, and even the clean smell of the soap in the soap dish reminded her of him. All too easily, she remembered that same scent when she'd buried her face against his neck and cried her eyes out in the car.

"Don't go there, Summer," she said out loud. "You're too shaky right now. Think about something else, anything else but that."

She tried—she honestly did. Focusing on Grandmother and the wonderful summers on the reservation, she soaked until the bubbles dissipated and the water cooled, but with every memory, her thoughts seemed to somehow always wind back to Gavin. With no effort whatsoever, she saw him as a child, his eyes dark and face somber as he stood on the sidelines at every tribal event, disassociating himself from who and what he was. He'd always looked so lonely that her heart had ached for him.

And that hadn't changed with the passage of time. In spite of the fact that he'd known everyone, he hadn't been comfortable at Grandmother Gray Eagle's. Whenever Summer had looked away from Grandmother and found him on the edge of the crowd, she'd caught a glimpse of that little boy from long ago.

Suddenly realizing what she was doing, she stiffened. She had to stop this. She couldn't afford to feel sorry for Gavin or to let herself get emotionally caught up in the loneliness of his existence. That wasn't why she was there. He didn't want her sympathy or concern. And she didn't need those things from him, either. There would be no more crying in his arms, no unburdening of her heart when she was hurting, no shared confidences. She would be polite, even friendly, but they couldn't be friends. Because to be friends, you had to drop your guard, and with a man like Gavin, that was just too risky.

Gavin heard her coming down the stairs and immediately began transferring the food to the dining room table. It hadn't taken him long to make grilled-cheese sandwiches and chicken noodle soup, then he'd spent the next fifteen minutes trying to keep everything warm.

Hearing her step in the hall, he turned with a smile. "You're just in time—"

That was as far as he got. The second his eyes settled on her, whatever he was going to say next flew right out of his head. There wasn't, he told himself, anything sexy about the gown and robe she wore. Every curve was hidden, and with her robe buttoned up to her throat and just about every inch of skin covered, she looked as pious as a nun. He shouldn't have been the least bit attracted.

But there'd always been something about a woman fresh from her bath that appealed to him. Maybe it was the lack of artifice, the face clean of makeup and pretense. With her hair hanging down her back and her bare toes peeking out from beneath the hem of her robe, she looked young and girlish and innocently sensual. And he couldn't take his eyes off her.

"Can I help you do anything?"

His brain in a fog, it was a long moment before he heard her—or realized he was staring like some kind of Neanderthal who'd never seen a woman in her nightclothes before. Hot spots of color burning his cheeks—he was blushing, for God's sake!—he quickly turned away. "No, thanks. I've got everything under control. Would you like milk or tea?"

"Milk."

"Have a seat," he called back over his shoulder as he disappeared into the kitchen. "It's coming right up."

What the hell was wrong with him? he thought furiously. He was acting like a teenager suffering from his first crush. If he didn't get a grip, she was going to wonder if she should have trusted him enough to marry him.

Ordering himself to straighten up, he poured them both a glass of milk, then defiantly returned to the dining room. After the way he'd stared at her, he half expected Summer to ask him what was wrong, but she seemed even less inclined to talk than he did. Silence stretched between them and was broken only by an occasional comment that could have been exchanged between two strangers.

Her stomach knotted with nerves, Summer had never eaten such an uncomfortable meal in her life. She'd thought last night, when they'd sat at the intimate table in his bedroom, had been awkward, but that was nothing compared to this. And for the life of her, she didn't know why. She'd thought she hid her feelings well—Gavin couldn't possibly know how obsessed with him she'd become—but every time she looked up, he was frowning at her as if he couldn't quite figure her out. Tension vibrated on the air between them, setting her heart pounding in her breast. She tried to eat, but her appetite was nonexistent, and all she could do was stir her soup and occasionally nibble at her sandwich.

They both decided at the same time that they'd had enough.

"I'm done."

"Me, too. Thanks for fixing everything. I'll clean up."

"Here, let me get that. You've had a rough day."

They came to their feet simultaneously, each moving to grab something from the table, only to find themselves face-to-face and kissing-close. Her heart pounding like a drum, Summer froze. With a will of their own, her eyes dropped to the sensuous line of his mouth. And with an ease that stunned her, she remembered the taste of him on her tongue.

Move! a voice in her head ordered sharply. *Move before you do something stupid.*

She should have. It certainly would have been the smart thing to do. But suddenly there was an ache low in her belly and a pain in her heart, and all she wanted to do was to step into his arms and to let him hold her. And why shouldn't she? she wondered resentfully. All of her life, she'd always followed the rules, always done what her head told her to do instead of her heart. Just this once, why couldn't she throw caution to the wind and just follow her heart? Could that really be so wrong?

Even as she questioned her own needs, she knew she wasn't like other women. It didn't matter what others were doing—she'd promised Gavin that their relationship would be strictly business, and she had no intention of going back on her word. Even if kissing him was all she could think of.

Considering that, there was nothing she could do but drag in a steadying breath and take a quick step backward. "You're right," she said huskily. "It has been a rough day, so if you don't mind cleaning up, I think I will go on up to bed. Good night."

Her heart pounding in her breast, she slipped past him and hurried up the stairs. She didn't glance back to see if he watched her, but with every step, she could feel his eyes on her. If he'd said just one word to call her back, she might not have been able to resist him. Before he could, she rushed into the master bedroom as if the hounds of hell were after her.

Long after Summer had escaped upstairs, Gavin found reasons to linger downstairs. He told himself that he wasn't sleepy, that he had chores to do that he'd let slide and this was just as good a time as any to take care of them, but a man could only lie to himself for so long before he was forced to face the truth. And when the mantel clock in the living room struck midnight and he realized he was putting off going to bed so he could organize the supplies in his study, he knew he was in trouble and that trouble had a name.

Summer.

What was he going to do with her? he wondered in frustration. He'd been so sure he could do this. After all, how difficult could it be, living with someone you weren't involved with? There were no emotional ties to tangle things up—it was like having a roommate. You lived under the same roof but you lived different lives.

But you don't share your bed with a roommate, a caustic voice in his head reminded him. *And you certainly don't hug and kiss one. Not if you want them to remain* just *a roommate.*

And therein lay the problem, he thought grimly. Every time he touched her, every time he wrapped his arms around her, it was harder to let her go. And he didn't know what the hell to do about it. They were caught in a trap of their own making. When they were in public, they had to act like newlyweds. But the situation wasn't much better at home. With the cleaning service coming in twice a week, they might as well have been living with half the town. They couldn't even bring in another bed without it being commented on, so they were forced to continue to sleep together.

Which was why he was rearranging the supplies in his study at midnight.

Suddenly imagining the maid's face when she found not

only the office supplies, but the spice rack in the kitchen, arranged alphabetically, he couldn't help but grin. She'd think either he or Summer had lost their mind, and he couldn't say he blamed her. It was a little screwy. And so was putting off going to bed. He couldn't stay up all night for the next year, so he might as well learn to deal with the situation now.

Resigned, he locked up and turned out the lights, then made his way upstairs. Just as he'd hoped, Summer was already asleep. Sprawled on her stomach, with her face turned away from him, she was out cold. Moving quietly across the room, he turned out the light she'd left on in the bathroom, then undressed and slipped into bed without making a sound. She never budged.

Gavin released the breath he hadn't even realized he was holding and grinned triumphantly in the darkness. This wasn't going to be so difficult, after all, he thought, congratulating himself. He could do this every night, wait until he was sure she was asleep before he came to bed, and everything would work out just fine.

It sounded good, but the thought had hardly registered when Summer's dreams suddenly grew restless. Muttering under her breath, she whimpered, and in the next instant she turned and before he quite knew how it happened, she was pressed up against him and crying softly in her sleep.

It happened so fast, he didn't have time to do anything but slip his arms around her. She was crying! What else could he do? Just lie there like a board and do nothing to comfort her? He had his faults, but he wasn't a monster. After everything she had done for him, he reasoned, the least he could do was try to soothe her when she had troubled dreams. After all, it wasn't as if he hadn't held her before while she cried.

But, he soon discovered, holding her in her sleep—in

bed—was a heck of a lot different from holding her in her truck. Asleep, with her defenses down, she snuggled against the length of him as her tears gradually dried, and she didn't have a clue what she did to him. Every nerve ending in his body screamed with awareness at her closeness, but he couldn't have pushed her away to save his soul. Not when she felt so fantastic in his arms.

She shifted into a more comfortable position, and it was all Gavin could do to hold back a groan. If she'd awakened then, he didn't know where he would have found the strength to let her go, but she only sighed softly against his chest and drifted into a deeper sleep. A muscle clenching in his jaw, Gavin reminded himself that he wasn't the kind of man who would take advantage of a sleeping woman. If he had been, Summer would have been in serious trouble. As it was, it was still a very long time before Gavin was able to relax his guard enough to fall asleep.

With less than a week left before the trial began, Gavin and Summer quickly became Whitehorn's most visible couple. Going everywhere hand in hand, they went to a play at the local theater, danced at a country-western nightspot, shopped for things for the house at the mall in Bozeman. And everywhere they went, they made an impression.

The problem was, they weren't sure it was the impression they wanted. People stared and whispered behind their backs, and the diehards who refused to even consider the possibility that Gavin might be innocent cut them dead. While there was no question that some of the locals were beginning to wonder whether Gavin was actually capable of murdering the mother of his little girl, the vast majority still treated him as though he were some sort of amoral monster who'd been let loose among them.

Summer didn't know what else they could do. They'd

even gone out to dinner with her family to show people that Gavin had been accepted by the Kincaids, but it seemed to have done little good. With time running out, there appeared to be a very real possibility that Gavin would be convicted.

Seated across from him at the Hip Hop the day before the trial was scheduled to begin, Summer tried to paste on a bright smile, but it was a weak attempt at best, and just about everyone in the place saw through it. "I'm sorry, Gavin," she said quietly. "I really thought this would work."

"Don't give up yet," he replied. "We don't know that it hasn't."

"But you heard that DJ on the radio talking about the poll the radio station did. Three out of five people think you're guilty."

"So two out of five don't," he countered logically. "We just have to have faith that whoever gets picked for the jury will keep an open mind until they hear all the evidence."

"And if they don't?"

"Then it doesn't matter what we do. I'm screwed."

Seated at the booth behind Gavin, Micky Culver had to agree. Most people had already made up their minds one way or another, and things didn't look good for Nighthawk. Unless something drastic happened pretty damn quick, the good doctor was going to prison for a murder he didn't commit.

And that infuriated Micky. Damn Audra! How could she do this? How could she sleep nights knowing that an innocent man was going to spend the rest of his life in prison for something she did? Did she even care? She certainly didn't act like it. She'd been flirting around town as if she didn't have a care in the world, adding her voice to the rest of the judgmental jackasses who were so quick to condemn a man down on his luck, and he'd even heard she was taking bets on how many years Nighthawk would get. The word on the street was she was betting on life without parole.

And it sickened Micky. When she'd moved out last week, claiming she couldn't stand living in his dump of a trailer any longer, he hadn't said a word to stop her. He loved her, God help him, and his gut knotted at the thought of losing her, but there was a part of him that hated what she was doing to Gavin Nighthawk. Another man might have turned her in in a heartbeat, but he just couldn't bring himself to do that. Not yet. She was his Audra, his beautiful blond princess, and he adored her. He had to believe she would do the right thing—he just had to give her time.

It wasn't easy, though, to stand back and watch what she'd become. She wasn't the Audra he'd first fallen in love with. She'd been sweet and loving and all she'd cared about was having fun. Then Lexine had come into her life and everything had changed.

He told himself that Audra's mother had her so screwed up, she just didn't realize what she was doing. That was the only explanation. He had to talk to her, had to make her understand that if she let Gavin Nighthawk take the rap for her, her conscience would haunt her for the rest of her life. She'd never be able to live with herself.

She'd do the right thing, he assured himself as he left fifty cents on his table for the waitress, then paid his bill and went looking for Audra. Once he made her understand that she really didn't have any other option but to tell the truth, she'd come clean and finally break the hold Lexine had on her. Maybe then, he'd have his old Audra back and life could return to normal.

But when he spent the rest of the day and evening searching for her at all her favorite haunts, he couldn't find her anywhere. Then he figured out where she was—out in the woods, looking for that damn sapphire mine Lexine was so obsessed with.

Just thinking about it gave him the willies. He'd gone out there to the old Baxter spread a couple of times to help her search for the lost mine, but the place had spooked him. The entire time they were there, he'd kept looking around, half expecting to see Christina Montgomery's ghost watching their every move. Audra had laughed at him, but he hadn't seen anything funny about the situation. She'd killed the woman there, for God's sake! He didn't care what anyone said—the dead did come back to haunt people who'd done them wrong. If he'd been Audra, he wouldn't have gone within a hundred miles of those damn woods.

She, however, couldn't stay away, and it was all because of Lexine. The bitch was blackmailing her—he knew, because Audra had told him all about it—and Audra was scared to death she was going to expose her. He had to find her, had to make her understand that if she'd just come clean and tell the police what happened, Lexine could never threaten her again.

After the last search for that damn mine, he'd sworn he'd never go near the place again, but he'd do anything for Audra. Including tramp around in the dark where the Montgomery chick had been murdered just so he could find Audra and talk some sense into her. So ignoring his fear, he headed for the last place on earth he wanted to go.

He didn't find her. After searching the woods for hours and calling her name until he was hoarse, he finally gave up and went home in defeat. Worried about her—it wasn't like her to just disappear like that—he was up at dawn and out on the streets, determined to find her. This time, he didn't have to look far. Her car was parked in front of her new apartment.

Relief washed over him—thank God, she was safe—then the anger hit him. Damn her, she knew how much he loved her. If she was going to disappear for a while, the least she could do was call him and tell him what she was up to so he wouldn't worry!

Furious with her, he parked in an empty spot reserved for another apartment, then stormed over to her front door. Banging on it loud enough to raise the dead, he doubted that she even heard him. She was a deadhead in the morning and usually slept until noon if she could. Well, not today. He'd stayed awake most of the night worrying about her, and by God, she was going to hear about it!

He had the speech all worked out in his head—it was time she grew up and quit being so self-centered!—but he never got the words out. Without warning, the door was jerked open, but it wasn't Audra who stood in front of him. It was Buck Simpson, one of the bikers who hung out at the Leather Spoke, a bar on the southside of town that catered to the motorcycle crowd. And he was wearing nothing but a pair of dirty, unsnapped jeans.

Stunned, Micky sputtered, "What the hell are you doing here, Simpson?"

Not the least bit concerned that he'd practically been caught with his pants down, Buck grinned mockingly. "I always did think you were a dim bulb, Culver. God knows what Audra saw in you, but she's finally wised up. Take a hike. The lady doesn't want you anymore."

He started to slam the door in Micky's face, but Micky snapped his hand up just in time and sent the door crashing open just as Audra stepped into the living room. Dressed in nothing but a T-shirt that fell to mid-thigh, she turned pale at the sight of Micky forcing his way into her living room like an angry bull. "Micky!" she gasped. "W-what are y-you doing here?"

"'Micky,'" he mimicked. "'What are you doing here?' You little two-timing bitch!" he snarled. "What the devil do you think I'm doing here? I was worried about you. Stupid me, I spent most of the night looking for you, thinking you might be in trouble. And all the time you were with a piece of lowlife trash."

"Hey!"

Distraught, Audra didn't even spare Buck a glance. "No, honey. I wasn't *with* him. Not that way. How could I be? You're the one I love—"

"Don't lie to me!" he roared. "Do I have 'stupid' tattooed on my forehead or what? You don't *love* me. If you did, you never would have done this!"

"That's not true!"

"You just used me," he said flatly. "That's all you've ever done, right from the very beginning. I knew it, but I didn't care. I just wanted to be with you. And I thought that if I gave you enough time, you'd finally love me the way I love you. But you were just saying what I wanted to hear. Because I knew your secret, and you were protecting that pretty little ass of yours."

What little color there was left in her face drained away. "No, Micky! That wasn't it at all. You know I've always been crazy about you."

"Yeah, right," he snorted. "Tell it to someone who doesn't know you so well. The only one you're crazy about is yourself. Do whatever you have to, say whatever you have to to keep Audra safe, and to hell with the rest of the world. That's your motto."

"It is not!"

"Oh, no? So who's going on trial tomorrow for Christina Montgomery's murder? It sure isn't the murderer, is it, Miss Westwood? And you're just thrilled. Well, here's a news flash for you, sweetheart," he sneered. "I'm sick and tired of listening to you gloat. I think it's time I did Nighthawk a favor."

He made a move to step past her, and her heart jumped into her throat in alarm. "Where are you going?" she cried, grabbing his arm.

"To the police," he retorted, shaking her off as if she were a pesky fly. "If I were you, I'd get the hell out of Dodge while I still could."

Not sparing her another glance, he stormed out, slamming the door after him and leaving behind a silence that was deadly. A scream of denial echoing in her head, Audra stared dazedly at the closed door. No! He couldn't. He wouldn't!

"What the hell's going on, Audra?" Buck growled. "Why's Culver going to the police? What does he know about the Montgomery murder?"

"The police," she muttered to herself, ignoring him. "He's going to the police. Oh, God!"

"Damn it, Audra, quit mumbling and tell me what you know about Christina Montgomery's murder!"

He yelled at her as if he had the right to, as if she was some simpleminded female who was supposed to jump when he snapped his fingers just because they'd had sex. Well, he could think again. "Get out!" she screeched. "Get out of my apartment. Now! Before I kill you, too!"

She didn't give him time to argue, but literally pushed him out the door, and he was only too happy to go. "Crazy bitch," he snarled as she threw his shirt at him and hit him in the head with it. "I hope Culver does go to the cops. You need to be locked up!"

Audra hardly heard him. She had to get out of there, she thought wildly as panic raced through her bloodstream like some kind of high-priced designer drug. Out of the apartment. Out of town. Out of the country. It was the only way.

Christina's murder had made national headlines. There was nowhere she could run to that people wouldn't have heard of it...except maybe Canada.

A sob welling in her throat, she couldn't think of what to do next. Clothes. She'd need clothes. And her suitcase. No, she'd hocked it. Damn! She'd have to use a garbage bag.

Her thoughts in a whirl, she rushed into the kitchen and jerked open the door to the cabinet where she kept the garbage bags, only to remember that she'd used the last one just yesterday. She'd use a pillowcase instead.

She snatched the one off the pillow on her bed and started stuffing it with whatever she could find until it was full. Panties, a strapless bra she never wore, a blouse she'd tossed on the floor because it was missing a button. And all the while, only one thought ran through her head. *Run!*

Sobbing, the overflowing pillowcase clutched to her thin chest, she grabbed her keys and ran for the door, uncaring that she'd forgotten her jacket and it was colder than hell outside. She could buy a coat when she got to Canada.

Tossing everything into the car, she threw herself into the front seat and jabbed the key into the ignition with a shaking hand. She told herself to calm down, she'd never be able to drive if she didn't get control of herself, but she couldn't. Her heart slamming against her ribs, she looked wildly around for the cops, half expecting them to come screeching up behind her at any second and cut off her only avenue of escape.

But the street was deserted, and with a sigh of relief, she turned the key...only to cry out in alarm when the motor tried halfheartedly to start, then died. "No! Start, damn you!"

Horrified, she tried the key again, but this time all she got for her efforts was a painful groan, then nothing but silence as her battery gave up the ghost. Dear God, why hadn't she gotten a new one? She'd known it was going out—Micky had been jumping it for her all week.

"A jump," she muttered to herself. She just needed a jump. Old man Eastman, the drunk next door, would help her. She'd seen those cable things like Micky used in the back of his truck, and he was always giving her the eye. She'd promise to go out with him, and he'd do anything she wanted. Hell, he'd probably drive her to Canada himself if she asked him.

No, she told herself as she rushed over to his door and pounded on it like a madwoman. She didn't want any company on this trip. She'd travel faster alone. "Jim! Open up! It's Audra. I need help."

It seemed as though she banged on his door forever before she heard him moving around inside. When he finally unlocked the dead bolt, she pushed the door open herself and sent it flying back on its hinges. "Thank God," she breathed in relief as he stumbled backward and she grabbed his arm. "C'mon. I've got an emergency and I can't start my car. You have to give me a jump."

Hungover and not quite focusing, he frowned in confusion as she tugged him toward the door. "What? Wha'swrong? Damn, what time is it?"

"Time for me to be getting the hell out of here," she retorted as she grabbed his keys from a hook near the door and literally dragged him outside with her. When he just stood there, still trying to get his bearings, she swore under her breath. Damn it, why did he have to be drunk this morning of all mornings? She didn't have time for this!

But she wouldn't get anywhere with him by swearing at him, so she gritted her teeth and forced a smile as she batted her eyes at him flirtatiously. "Jim, honey, you're the sweetest thing for helping me this way," she purred, tracing a finger down his misbuttoned shirt. "I've got to go out of town for a little while, but when I get back, the two of us are going to go out and have a really good time. Okay, sweetie?"

He grabbed at her finger and missed. "You mean it, Audra?"

"I certainly do. But first you have to help me get my car started." Pressing his keys into his hand, she closed his fingers around them. "I'm in a hurry, Jim. If you help me now, I promise I'll be very, very nice to you when I get back. But you've got to help me *now*."

Finally he moved, and with a sigh of relief, Audra got in her car and waited impatiently for him to hook up the jumper cables. If he hooked it up wrong and blew up her battery, she swore she was going to kill him.

Holding her breath, she cringed as she turned the key at his signal, half expecting smoke to come spilling out from under the hood. Instead, the motor fired to life with a roar. Stunned, she laughed. "Yes! Thank you! Thank you!"

She would have hugged him, but she didn't have time. The second he disconnected the cables, she threw the transmission into reverse and went flying out of her parking spot. Before Jim could do anything but wave, she was racing down the street.

So Micky thought he was going to turn her in, did he? she thought gleefully. The bastard. Let him try. The cops couldn't catch her now—they didn't have a clue where she was going. They'd expect her to take the interstate, but she wasn't that stupid. She was sticking to the back roads and keeping a low profile. If she was lucky, she'd be in Canada by that afternoon, and then she'd be home free. She'd change her name, head east to a big city, maybe Montreal, and never be heard from again.

She had it all worked out in her head, but then she

thought to look at her gas gauge and gasped. Empty. Damn it to hell! Why did everything have to happen to her?

Swearing, she pulled into the first gas station she came to and almost turned off the motor before she remembered that her battery was still low. If she cut the engine, it might not start again. Grinding her teeth on an oath, she was left with no choice but to leave the damn car running while she filled it with gas.

"Hurry," she muttered, glaring at the pump as it ticked off the gallons. Why the hell was it so slow? She had to get out of here.

Caught up in the panic eating at her, she never noticed the two police cars that turned into the gas station until one braked to a screeching halt in front of her car and the other blocked her from behind. It all happened so fast, she couldn't do anything but gasp before she found herself trapped and staring down the barrel of two guns.

"Put your hands in the air and step away from the car, Miss Westwood. You're under arrest for the murder of Christina Montgomery."

Six

When she'd come to town at the request of Garrett Kincaid to represent Gavin, Elizabeth Gardener had rented office space in a redbrick building several blocks from the courthouse. Although formally decorated with burgundy carpet and antiques, the office wasn't cold. And that was due to Elizabeth herself. She softened the decor with fresh flowers and always welcomed Gavin into her office as if she were inviting him into her home.

Because of that, Gavin was usually able to relax there. But not the morning that his trial was scheduled to start at ten. Dread rising like bile in his throat, he could feel the walls of a cage closing in on him and it took all his self-control not to bolt. Seated beside him in front of Elizabeth's desk, Summer offered her steady support, and he appreciated it. But there was little she or anyone else could do to help him at this point. He didn't like to think of himself as a pessimist, but there was no escaping the inevitable. The situation didn't look good.

Elizabeth didn't appear concerned, however. One of the best criminal defense attorneys in the country, she was confident and fearless, and that never ceased to amaze Gavin. Didn't she realize that most of the citizens of Whitehorn had already tried and convicted him?

Seated at her desk with her notes spread out in front of her, she looked over the top of her half-moon glasses and read his mind. "This isn't a popularity contest, Gavin. It's evidence that wins a case, and the D.A. doesn't have what it takes to slide this one past a jury."

"But the DNA—"

"Doesn't prove anything other than you're Alyssa's father. That isn't a crime."

"But I admitted I was there that night," he argued. "I delivered the baby."

"That doesn't make you a murderer." She spoke in that tone that Gavin had labeled her lawyer voice, the one that warned she was a force to be reckoned with when she stepped into a courtroom, even if she was a sixty-three-year-old grandmother with more gray in her hair than blond. She fought to win, and nine times out of ten, she did.

But what if she didn't this time? Worry eating at him, he said, "I need to know my options."

It was the wrong thing to say to a woman who didn't like to lose. Shooting him a hard look, she growled, "You're not thinking of copping a plea, are you?"

His stomach clenched at the very idea, but just the thought of being convicted turned his blood cold. "Just give me my options. I know we went over it all before, but tell me again."

Left with no choice, she said, "You can take your chances and hope the jury will see things your way. If they do, you're cleared of all charges. If they don't, you could be facing life—or the death sentence."

"Unless I cop a plea."

Her mouth pressed tight in disapproval, she nodded. "If the D.A. is agreeable, you could plead guilty to a lesser charge, such as manslaughter. At the most, you'd probably get twenty years and we could push for an early release with good behavior. If you're lucky, you'll be out in ten."

Stunned that he actually seemed to be considering that,

Summer cried, "You can't be serious about this! You're innocent!"

"I have to consider the risks," he said stubbornly.

"But you'd be giving up ten years of your life—maybe twenty—for something you didn't do! Elizabeth, tell him!"

"Just the thought of an innocent man pleading guilty goes against everything our justice system is supposed to be about," Elizabeth said flatly. "I don't like it. It stinks, and I certainly wouldn't advise Gavin to do such a thing. I'm going to fight for him with everything I have, and I plan to win. But I can't stop him, Summer, if he doesn't want to risk a trial. Granted, it's not something either of us would choose for him, but it does give him some say over his own destiny. Twenty years in jail is better than life. Or death."

Put that way, Summer had to agree. Anything was better than the death penalty. She knew that, accepted it. But everything inside her cried out in protest at the thought of him spending even a single day behind bars, let alone twenty years, for something she knew he hadn't done. Damn it all, how could this happen to an innocent man?

"You're right, of course," she said huskily. "It's just so frustrating."

And if it was frustrating for her, she could just imagine what it must be like for Gavin. Suddenly realizing that while she'd been carrying on about the injustice of the situation, he hadn't said a word, she turned to him in contrition. "I'm sorry, Gavin. This has to be horrible for you, and here I am, acting like a whiny baby because life's not fair. You're the one who should be raging. If I were you, I'd have been screaming and pulling my hair out long before now."

"Trust me, if I thought it would help, I'd be bald by now," he retorted. "But I learned a long time ago that that only makes the situation worse. So I pretend this is all happening to somebody else, and sometimes I actually believe it.''

He would have said more, but the phone rang and Elizabeth snatched it up. "Yes?"

"Mrs. Gardener? This is Mr. Corwin. I hope I'm not interrupting anything.''

Surprised that the D.A. was calling her less than an hour before the trial was scheduled to start, Elizabeth didn't fool herself into thinking he wanted to make any kind of a deal. He wouldn't do that unless he felt he had a weak case, and he knew as well as she did that the evidence he had against Gavin was damning.

"No, of course not, Mr. Corwin," she said, shooting Gavin a speaking glance. If he wanted her to try to get the charge reduced in exchange for a guilty plea, this was their opening. "What can I do for you?"

"There's been a new development in the Montgomery case."

Surprised, she stiffened, wondering how things could get any blacker than they already were. "What kind of development?"

"A new witness came forward less than an hour ago and implicated Audra Westwood—"

"What?"

"I know—I was surprised as you are. According to Micky Culver, Audra went into the woods on the old Baxter property that night to look for that lost sapphire mine everybody's been talking about for months now. Micky followed her and was hiding in the trees when she stumbled upon Christina right after she'd had her baby. Apparently Audra panicked and was afraid Christina would turn her in for trespassing, so she hit her in the head with a shovel and killed her.''

"So why did it take Culver so long to come forward?"

"He's in love with her," he retorted. "Or I should say, he was. He blackmailed her into living with him until last week, then this morning, he found her with another man."

"So he turned her in for spite," Elizabeth concluded. "Are you sure Culver didn't do it himself?"

"No, ma'am," he said. "He's telling the truth. In fact, when the police picked up Audra, she was leaving town. She confessed to everything, including the fact that Lexine Baxter became involved after the fact."

"Lexine Baxter? How did she get tangled up in all this?"

"Are you sitting down?" he said dryly. "Believe it or not, she's Audra's real mother. She's the reason Audra was out in the woods in the first place, looking for that damn mine. She convinced her they were both going to be rich, then when she learned about the murder, she threatened to turn Audra in if she didn't keep looking for the mine."

"And what about my client?" she asked bluntly. "I assume all charges have been dropped."

"Of course," Corwin assured her quickly. "I would have called you sooner, but we had to get Audra's statement first and make sure this wasn't some kind of twisted joke. She signed a confession, though, so Gavin is free to go. Please extend my apologies to him. I'm glad it worked out this way."

Elizabeth thanked him, then hung up, still shaking her head in disbelief. But when she looked up at Gavin, there was a smile as broad as Texas on her face. "You must be living right, Gavin. All charges have been dropped against you. You're free to go."

Stunned, Gavin just looked at her, his dark eyes narrow with suspicion. "Is this some kind of a joke? Because if it is, I don't like it."

After everything he'd been through, Elizabeth could well understand his distrust. If she'd been in his shoes, she would have been just as leery of a fairy-tale reprieve. "It's no joke," she assured him kindly. "Micky Culver went to the police this morning and implicated Audra Westwood. She confessed to everything."

Rising to her feet, she walked around her desk and held out her hand to him. "It's over, Gavin. For good. Congratulations."

Gavin stared at the hand Elizabeth held out to him for what seemed like an eternity, unable to believe he'd heard her correctly. But then his gaze lifted to hers, and there was no doubting the sincerity he saw in her eyes.

It hit him then. The nightmare really was over.

Emotions pulled at him, tearing him in a thousand different directions. He'd been braced for the worst, sure that he didn't have a chance in hell of escaping conviction. And now it was all over, like a bad dream. Not sure if he wanted to laugh or cry, he surged to his feet and the next instant ignored Elizabeth's outstretched hand and snatched her into his arms.

"Thank you!"

At his hoarse cry, Summer, too, stood, hot tears stinging her eyes. It was true. Dear God, it was true! Just when she'd begun to think all hope was lost, an angel stepped forward in the form of an ex-biker named Micky Culver, and Gavin was saved.

Unable to stop smiling, she laughed as Gavin released Elizabeth, only to turn to her for a fierce hug. "I still can't believe it," she choked, smiling through her tears as he held her as if he'd never let her go. "All this time, Micky Culver knew and he never said anything. Why now? What happened?"

Elizabeth told them the whole story. "When Micky

found her with another man this morning, that did it. He wanted revenge and he got it.''

''Thank God, he did,'' Summer said as Gavin released her. Grinning, she cocked her head at him. ''So how does it feel to know you're a free man?''

''I can't even begin to describe it,'' he said simply. ''I just want to get in the car and drive and drive and know that I can go as far as I want to without answering to anyone.''

''Then do it,'' Elizabeth urged. ''After everything you've been through, you deserve some freedom. Go! Run away and have some fun and forget all of this for a while.''

She didn't have to tell him twice. Thanking her again for all her help, Gavin took Summer's hand and hurried outside, feeling as if he were walking on air.

In spite of the fact that it wasn't even ten o'clock in the morning, the news spread through Whitehorn like a forest fire devouring dry timber. Fifteen minutes after Elizabeth Gardener was notified that all charges against Gavin had been dropped, the gossips started gathering at the Hip Hop like buzzards circling roadkill.

Emma Stover Harper struggled to take the rush of orders, but as she was about to enter her third trimester, it wasn't easy. Maddeningly short snippets of conversation flew all around her, and it was some time before she was able to piece together the story that would no doubt have all of Whitehorn talking for some time to come. Everyone had been wrong about Gavin Nighthawk. Just as he'd claimed, he hadn't murdered Christina Montgomery, after all. The real culprit was, of all people, Audra Westwood. The same Audra Westwood, it turned out, who was Lexine Baxter's daughter.

And her twin sister!

Reeling from the news, Emma hardly heard anything after that. She'd known she'd had a twin sister ever since *she* had been accused of killing Christina and DNA testing had revealed that she and the murderer had the same DNA composition. But she'd never dreamed that Audra was her twin. And Lexine had never told her. She'd kept that news to herself, and for the life of her, Emma didn't know why. She must have had some plan in her twisted mind, but Emma doubted that she would ever know what it was.

Lost in her thoughts, she never noticed that she'd given Lily Mae someone else's order until the old woman snapped her fingers under her nose. "Hey, girl, is anybody home inside that head of yours? You know I can't eat eggs. My doctor'd have a stroke if I ate all that cholesterol. Bring me one of those cinnamon rolls, the kind with a lot of icing. All this talk of murder's given me a sweet tooth this morning."

Repulsed, Emma hid her feelings well and did as she was told, but she couldn't help thinking that the gossips were talking about *her* twin. She'd been looking for her for months in the faces of everyone she'd met, desperate to help her. If only she'd known who she was, she could have talked to her and convinced her to do the right thing and turn herself in before things got out of hand. Or at least she could have tried. But Lexine hadn't given her that opportunity, and she'd never forgive her for that.

Drowned out by the buzz of excited conversation, the phone rang behind the counter, but Emma never noticed until Janie answered it, then yelled to her, "Emma! Phone!"

Assuming it was her husband, Brandon, calling to make sure she was all right after hearing the news, she rushed behind the counter as quickly as she could and turned her back on the crowd in the dining area as she picked up the phone. "Hello? This is Emma."

"Hi, sweetheart. This is your momma. How are you and that grandbaby of mine?"

Her blood running cold at the sound of Lexine's voice, Emma stiffened. It was bad enough that Lexine referred to herself as her "momma," but it was downright outrageous that she actually thought she was going to be a grandmother to her baby. That, Emma assured herself fiercely, was never, ever, going to happen!

But that wasn't something she intended to get into with her on the phone. "I'm fine," she said coolly, not even mentioning the baby. "But it's very busy here this morning. I don't have a lot of time—"

Not a slow-witted woman, Lexine didn't have to ask if she'd heard the news—she could hear the resentment in Emma's voice. Normally, she wouldn't have given a rat's ass. Of her two daughters, Audra was the one who took after her mother, the one she could twist around her finger to do her bidding, but thanks to that tattletale boyfriend of hers, she was out of the picture. Which meant she had to make do with what she had, which was the stiff and cautious Emma.

Playing the role of the contrite mother to the hilt, she said sadly, "You found out about Audra, didn't you? Look, I don't blame you for being hurt, honey. I should have told you. She's your twin and you had a right to know, but I had to protect her. I was afraid if I told anyone, even you, word would get out and she'd end up in jail, just like me. And no mother wants that for her daughter. Why, I'd incriminate myself in a heartbeat before I'd let something like that happen to one of my precious girls."

"I could have helped her," she said stiffly.

"I know, honey, and I'm sorry about that," Lexine said

sorrowfully, lying through her teeth. "I should have talked to you about it. You always were the smart one, the one I knew I could depend on when things got tight. Which is why I called. I need your help with something."

"What?"

A deaf woman couldn't have missed her wariness, but Lexine wasn't concerned. The girl had come looking for her in the first place because she wanted a relationship with her birth mother, and Lexine knew just how to use that to her advantage. "It's something that's very close to my heart and a part of your heritage, honey. If it hadn't been lost years ago, I wouldn't have had to give you and poor Audra up when you were born. When I think of the years that were lost and all the time I wondered where you girls were and if you were okay, I just want to cry. I loved you both so much, but I just couldn't support you. And you must hate me for that."

"I wouldn't use the word hate," Emma said.

"Oh, sweetheart, you don't know how grateful I am to hear that," she gushed, smiling gleefully to herself. Now she had her right where she wanted her! All she had to do was push the right buttons, and she'd fall in line just like Audra. "I want us to be a family. There's so many things I want to give you to make up for all the years I missed with you, but I'm stuck in this hateful place for God knows how long and can't do anything. You could help me, though, by looking for the old sapphire mine for me.

"And I know you could find it, a smart girl like you," Lexine hurried on before Emma could say anything. "Audra came close, but like I said before, sweetheart, she just doesn't have it upstairs the way you do. If you'd go out there and start digging around, I bet you could find it in no time. Whaddaya say? Will you do that for your old mom?"

Taken aback by the request, Emma couldn't believe she

was so cold. One of her daughters had just been charged with murder—a murder that had, by the way, been committed when she was out looking for that same sapphire mine—and all Lexine could think about was the mine. She didn't care about Audra or that she could spend the rest of her life in prison. The only thing that mattered to her was the sapphires and finding them before somebody else did.

All this time, Emma thought she'd missed something by not growing up with her birth mother's love. Now she realized that she'd actually been blessed. Lexine had done her a favor when she'd given her up to the foster care program. At least she'd finally ended up with the Stovers, who'd taught her what love was really all about. If she'd been raised by Lexine, God only knew how she would have turned out.

Silently sending up a prayer of thanks that she didn't feel an ounce of affection—or guilt—for the monster who'd given birth to her, she said, "No, Lexine, I'm afraid I won't. As far as I'm concerned, my mother died a long time ago, so I guess you're going to have to find someone else to help you. Oh, and one more thing," she added when the older woman gasped in outrage. "In the future, I'd appreciate it if you wouldn't call me here at work—or anyplace else, for that matter. We really have nothing more to say to each other. Goodbye."

Hanging up before she could do anything but screech at her, Emma felt as if a huge weight had been lifted from her shoulders. Finally, she was free of the shadow that Lexine had cast over her life from the moment she'd met her! She'd never have any kind of hold on her again.

The same, however, couldn't be said of Audra. She was her twin; there was a bond between them that they shared with no other person. There was nothing she could do to help her—it was too late for that—but she had to at least see her and to let her know she wasn't completely alone in the world.

Hurrying over to her boss with her pregnant stomach leading the way, she said, "Janie, I hate to ask this of you when we're so swamped, but I need to leave—"

Alarmed, Janie grabbed her by the arm. "Oh, God, are you all right? Is the baby—"

"No. We're fine." She chuckled as the usually calm Janie nearly self-destructed in panic. "This has nothing to do with the baby. Honest. I just need to go see Audra. I think I should, don't you?"

Janie hesitated. "I don't know. Maybe you should talk to your doctor first. And Brandon."

Her smile faint, Emma shook her head. "Not if I want to go. If he even suspected that I wanted to talk to Audra, he'd be over here in a heartbeat to talk some sense into me. I can just hear him now. 'All this stress isn't good for the baby. You need to get off your feet and not worry about people who aren't your family.'"

"Well, I can see why you wouldn't want to claim Lexine," Janie said dryly, "but Audra's your twin. Even though you weren't raised together, I wouldn't imagine you could just turn your back on her, especially when she's in trouble."

Thankful that she understood, Emma sighed in relief. "I have to at least see her, Janie. I know the timing stinks but—"

"You're not supposed to be working this hard anyway," the other woman said with a rueful smile. "Go on. Take a break. You need one."

Tears flooding her eyes, Emma gave her an impulsive hug, then turned and grabbed her purse and rushed out to her car. Five minutes later, she pulled up in front of the stark confines of the jail and parked. Regret squeezing her heart, she sat there for what seemed like five minutes, hating the thought of going inside. Ever since she'd learned her twin was out there somewhere, she'd pictured the moment when they first met. Not once had she imagined it would be in the grim setting of a jail.

If she'd known about her sooner, maybe she could have changed things, she thought. But then again, they'd both been set on different paths a long time ago, and they'd each had choices to make in life. Audra had made hers, and Emma had to believe that nothing she could have said or done would have changed anything. Resigned, she went inside to meet her sister.

Thankfully, the jail wasn't quite the nightmare Emma had imagined it would be. It was clean, modern, and bright, and the cells were equipped with all the amenities—TV with a remote, a private bath, a bunk with covers that looked new. Despite that, Emma found nothing appealing about the place. There was just something about being locked behind bars like an animal that sickened her.

Her stomach twisting into knots as she was escorted to Audra's cell, Emma shifted forward when the guard stepped in front of a door, only to stop in her tracks when she found Audra sitting on her bunk and staring right at her. Stunned, she couldn't believe she hadn't seen the resemblance sooner. It was right there in both their faces for the entire world to see. Granted, Audra was thin as a rail and had bleached platinum-blond hair, but they had the same hazel eyes, the same bone structure and chin. If she'd let her hair grow out and stripped the bleach job, then added a much needed fifteen pounds, they couldn't have hidden the fact that they were twins from anyone.

For what seemed like an eternity, neither of them said a word, but they didn't have to. Audra knew she was her sister—the knowledge was there in her eyes. Emma wouldn't have been surprised to discover that Audra had known it a lot longer than she had.

"I had to come," Emma said huskily. "I hope you know why."

"You had to satisfy your curiosity," Audra retorted. "I guess I can't say I blame you."

She shrugged indifferently, as if she couldn't have cared less that Emma was there, but Emma wasn't fooled. There was a connection between them that they shared with no other person on earth, and Audra felt it, too. Emma could see it in her eyes. "I wish I'd known sooner. Maybe I could have helped."

"Don't beat yourself up over it. It was too late years ago."

A pang of regret squeezed Emma's heart at that. "Don't!" she cried. "It doesn't have to be that way…"

But even as she protested, she knew her sister was wiser than she. Separated not only by bars, but by a lifetime of different influences, there was little they had in common but their shared DNA. And any chance they'd had of developing a relationship had died with Christina Montgomery.

Tears stinging her eyes, she wanted to reach out and touch Audra, just once, but she couldn't. "If things had been different…"

She couldn't finish, but Audra understood. "Yeah," she said huskily. "If things had been different…"

But they weren't and never would be. Accepting that, Emma said quietly, "I wish you luck." And with a somber nod, she turned and walked out without once looking back. With the closing of the door, Emma closed the door on her past.

* * *

With a simple phone call, Gavin's entire world had changed. He didn't know how the word had spread so quickly, but by the time he and Summer left Elizabeth's office and stepped out onto the street, the news had already broken. People who would have cut him dead just an hour before nodded in embarrassment and couldn't quite look him in the eye. A few of the bolder ones even lied and called out to him that they'd always known he was innocent.

Yeah, right, he thought cynically. Then his eyes met Summer's and they both burst out laughing. What difference did it make? The nightmare was over. He was free and would soon have his daughter back. Nothing else mattered.

But they soon discovered that that freedom didn't come without a price tag. By the time they reached Gavin's house, the phone was ringing off the wall. Every reporter within a two-state area wanted to talk to him. At first, he took the calls as they came in, but the second he finished one interview and hung up, the phone immediately rang again. Then two reporters from the local newspaper, the Whitehorn *Journal*, pulled up in front of the house. Scowling, Gavin recognized them immediately. The shorter one, called Dutch for some obscure reason, had interviewed him right after he was charged with Christina's murder and twisted everything he'd said. Tuttle, his partner in crime, was just as bad. By that evening, Gavin imagined others from around the state would be camped out in his front yard, acting as if they'd believed all along that he would be vindicated.

"C'mon," he told Summer as he let the answering machine take the next call. "If we don't get out of here, we're going to be trapped, and I refuse to spend my first real day of freedom talking to the press."

At that very moment the two reporters out front banged loudly on the front door. "C'mon, Dr. Nighthawk," Dutch called in a wheedling voice. "We know you're in there. Just answer a few questions for us and we'll leave you alone."

"Yeah, right," he muttered. "And I bet you've got a map to the lost Baxter sapphire mine you can let me have cheap, too. Thanks but no thanks."

"But won't they just follow us?" Summer pointed out logically as he urged her to the garage.

"Not where we're going," he assured her grimly. "Go get in the car. I'll be right there." His dark eyes glinting with purpose, he stepped over to the front door and said loudly, "Give me a few minutes, fellas. My wife and I are celebrating with a bottle of champagne. Then I'll answer all your questions. Okay?"

Thrilled at the thought of getting an exclusive before the big city boys from Butte and Helena arrived in a couple of hours, they neatly stepped into the trap. "Sure thing, Dr. Nighthawk," Tuttle called back, pleased. "Take your time. There's no hurry. We'll be here when you're finished."

Gavin doubted that, but he wisely kept that to himself. Grinning, he hurried out to the garage to find that Summer had already opened the garage door and started the motor. With the garage located at the back of the house, the reporters didn't even know they were about to be duped.

Quickly slipping behind the wheel of his Chevy, he buckled up, then glanced over at Summer and grinned. "Ready?"

"When you are," she replied, chuckling. "Let's go."

Putting the car in gear, he eased quietly out of the garage, then followed the drive around the side of the house. Still standing in the walled-in entry by the front door, Dutch and Tuttle didn't hear them until they reached the street, and by then, it was too late. Shouting in outrage, they rushed to their cars, but before they could reach them, Gavin turned the corner at the end of the street and was lost to view. Outsmarted, there was nothing the two reporters could do but curse.

Gavin didn't have a clue where he was going—he just wanted to get away. So he made sudden turns, U-turns, and doubled back half a dozen times before Highway 17 beckoned him west. It had been months since he'd been allowed to leave the county, and suddenly a nice long drive with no particular destination in mind sounded incredibly appealing. He just wanted to go somewhere where nobody knew him, nobody stared, and the local reporters wanted nothing from him.

Glancing over at Summer, he arched a brow at her. "You're not in a rush to get back, are you? I thought I'd drive a while."

Summer, too, had no desire to go back anytime soon. "Are you kidding? I can't remember the last time I went for a drive in the mountains. Take the whole day if you like. You deserve it."

"Thanks," he said with a grin. "I just might do that."

He turned on the radio, only to wince when he tuned into a news report about Audra's arrest and his own release. With a grimace, he quickly turned off the radio and shoved in a CD instead. Instantly, low, mellow jazz engulfed them, and they both sighed in relief.

Later, Summer couldn't have said where they went. On a whim, Gavin turned off onto a side road that twisted and turned and eventually came back to Highway 17 again. He could have headed home then and she wouldn't have said a word, but once again, he turned west. Pleased, she settled back to enjoy the music and the scenery, content to go wherever he wanted to take her.

Neither of them noticed the passage of time or remembered how long it had been since they'd eaten breakfast that morning until Summer's stomach suddenly growled loudly. Startled, she pressed a quick hand to her midsection, hot color burning her cheeks. "Oh, God, I'm sorry!"

"No, I should be the one apologizing." Gavin laughed. "I should have fed you hours ago. There's an inn up ahead that has great steaks. We'll stop there."

High up at the top of a mountain pass, the Gas Light Inn sat back in the pines and had the kind of charm that only came with age. Built in the style of an old English inn, it had gas lights, diamond-paned stained-glass windows, and dark, rich wood everywhere. Just as Gavin pulled into the parking lot of the inn's restaurant, it started to snow, and that only added to the atmosphere.

Entranced, Summer took one look at it and fell in love. "Oh, this is beautiful!"

"Wait'll you see it inside," Gavin told her as he came around the car to open her door for her. "The owners are English and decorated it with antiques from all over Europe. It's the food, though, that brings people in. I don't know what they do to their steaks, but they've got this incredible flavor. And they're so tender, you can practically cut them with a fork."

Summer's stomach growled just at the thought, and they both burst out laughing. Grinning, Gavin took her hand. "I'd say we've come to the right place. C'mon."

In spite of the fact that it was well after lunch but too early for dinner, the restaurant was doing a brisk business. Gavin would have preferred a table by the fieldstone fireplace, where a roaring fire was crackling merrily, but they were all occupied, so they had to settle for a booth in the corner. Not that they really paid that much attention to their surroundings once the waiter brought their menus. All they could think about was eating.

"We're celebrating," Gavin told Summer when he saw her wince at the prices. "The sky's the limit, so get whatever you want. I don't know about you, but I plan to have Cherries Jubilee and the praline cheesecake for dessert."

Shocked, Summer glanced up from her menu and laughed in disbelief. "You're going to have two desserts? Plus dinner?"

"You're damn straight," he retorted, grinning. "I've got a hell of a lot to celebrate. If the D.A. hadn't called Elizabeth when he had, I was going to insist Elizabeth let me plead guilty in exchange for a manslaughter plea."

"Oh, Gavin, no!"

"I would have lost in court, Summer," he said huskily, his smile fading. "You know I would have. At least by copping a plea, I would have had a chance to see my daughter again."

He would have done it, she thought, shaken. He would have agreed to a guilty plea and years in prison for something he hadn't done rather than take his chances with a prejudiced jury. And as much as she'd argued against that with Elizabeth, she couldn't say she'd have blamed him for making that choice. She probably would have done the same thing if she'd had a daughter to think of.

"All I can say is God bless Micky Culver," she replied, lifting her water glass in a toast. "He saved your bacon."

"Which is why I plan to enjoy life from now on and not take anything for granted," he replied. "If you want two desserts, have them. If champagne and strawberries sound good for breakfast, then go for it. We don't have a clue what tomorrow's going to bring, so live for today. It's all we've got."

When she thought about just how close he had come to disaster, she had to agree there was a lot to be said for living in the moment. She was too pragmatic to do that on a regular basis—if you didn't want any nasty surprises when you reached retirement age, you had to think about the future now—but sometimes you just needed to let go and forget about the consequences. This was one of those times.

"Okay, then I think I'll try the grilled pork chops," she said with a smile, "and the duck á l'orange. *And,*" she added when the waiter started to turn to Gavin for his order, "Chocolate Delight for dessert."

Her eyes sparkling, she turned to Gavin with a challenging look that dared him to top that. Not to be outdone, he ordered his desserts first, then lobster thermidor and a rib eye cooked to perfection. When the waiter walked away, shaking his head over the fact that they'd ordered enough food for four people, they only laughed. So they had enough for a snack later. What was wrong with that?

The service wasn't fast, but the Gas Light Inn wasn't the kind of place you went to for a quick hamburger. Instead, the staff prided itself on serving excellent food and wine at a leisurely pace that allowed its patrons to not only enjoy the meal without being constantly interrupted by the wait staff, but each other.

And that's exactly what Gavin and Summer did. For the first time Gavin could actually discuss the future and know that he had one. He told Summer about his plans to become the best surgeon in the western part of the country, how he wanted to spend a year in Boston working with Dr. Miles Agold, a legendary brain surgeon at Massachusetts General who made history in the operating room on a regular basis. And Summer told him about her own dreams to improve medical care not only on the Laughing Horse Reservation, but on every reservation in the country.

And while they talked and ate, they never noticed that the restaurant was filling up with customers or that outside, the snow that had started to fall when they'd arrived at the inn had turned into the first blizzard of the season.

Their waiter quietly appeared at their table and unobtrusively cleared his throat. "I'm sorry to interrupt, but management has asked me to inform you that the weather has taken a turn for the worse and the highway department has started to shut down the roads."

"What?" Gavin said sharply, surprised. "When did this happen?"

"Over the last few hours, sir," the waiter replied. "All the other patrons have already booked rooms for the night, but we could still have some late arrivals. We only have one room left, and if you'd like it, you need to reserve it now."

Rising to his feet, Gavin was already pulling his wallet from his pocket. "Thanks. We'll do that. Is it a double?"

"No, sir," the younger man said. "It's the honeymoon suite."

Seven

"The honeymoon—" Breaking off abruptly, Gavin swore under his breath and didn't dare look at Summer. "That's all you have?"

"Yes, sir, I'm afraid so. If you'd like to reserve it, I can bring you a registration card and you can do it here at your table."

He wanted to tell the waiter there was no way in hell he was taking that room, but unless they wanted to spend the night in the car and freeze to death, they were stuck. But the honeymoon suite, for God's sake! Even a broom closet would have been better than that!

Beggars, however, couldn't be choosers, and with a muttered curse, he arched a dark brow at Summer. "Is that all right with you?"

Summer would have loved to have been sophisticated enough to shrug and act as if she couldn't have cared less, but she'd never spent a night in a hotel with a man in her life. Just the thought of sharing the honeymoon suite with him sent heat climbing into her cheeks, but what other choice did they have?

Her heart pounding like a drum in her breast, she forced a smile for the waiter's sake and nodded. "I'm sure it'll be fine."

Pleased, the waiter took the credit card Gavin held out to him and said, "Then I'll take care of that for you right now."

He hurried away to the hotel registration desk, leaving behind a silence between Summer and Gavin that was as thick as the snow blowing outside the windows. The easy, relaxed mood they'd enjoyed before the interruption was now shattered, and there didn't seem to be anything they could do to get it back.

Her appetite nonexistent, Summer pushed her food around on her plate in a pretense of eating, but she only had to glance up to catch Gavin's eye to know that she wasn't fooling anyone, least of all him. With a grimace, she set down her fork. "I guess I shouldn't have ordered all this, after all. I seem to have lost my appetite."

"We'll ask for a doggie bag and take it with us to the room. You might get hungry later tonight and want your dessert."

When she was sharing the honeymoon suite with him? Her throat closed tight just at the thought. "Maybe," she said huskily. "But I don't think so."

The waiter returned then with the registration card for the room, and by unspoken agreement, that automatically signaled the end of the meal. What they hadn't eaten was packaged up for them, the bill and tip were paid, and before either of them was ready for it, they were headed for the honeymoon suite.

All but dragging her feet as she followed Gavin, Summer tried to convince herself it wouldn't be that bad. After all, it was just a room and couldn't be that different from the one the two of them had been sharing for the past week. They were already sleeping in the same bed and being quite civilized about it. So what was the big deal? All she had to do was act the way she usually did, and everything would work out just fine.

Or at least that was what she thought until she preceded Gavin into their room and stopped short. There was a heart-shaped Jacuzzi tub right next to the fireplace in the living room of the suite. To enhance the romantic atmosphere, someone—presumably a chambermaid—had thoughtfully lit a fire and all of the dozen or so candles strategically placed around the room.

Her eyes wide, Summer took in everything in a single glance, then found her gaze zeroing through the open doorway at the far end of the living room to the bedroom beyond. There, illuminated by more candles, was a tall antique poster bed with a feather mattress that was right out of a romantic's dreams. Summer took one look at it and felt her mouth go dry.

Without thinking, she turned and didn't have a clue where she was going except out of that suite. Gavin, however, was blocking the doorway and showed no inclination to move. Undaunted, she lifted her chin to a stubborn angle and looked him right in the eye. "Maybe this isn't such a good idea, after all. I think I'll just sit in the lobby all night."

"And do what? Sleep in a chair instead of a bed we've already paid for? C'mon, Summer, don't be ridiculous."

She opened her mouth to tell him, paid for or not, she would never be able to sleep in that bed, but before she got a chance, there was a firm knock at the still open door. Startled, they turned to find a young man from room service holding a silver ice bucket with a bottle of champagne. "I'm sorry to interrupt, folks, but management is providing a bottle of champagne to all the guests tonight with their compliments. Have a good night."

He was gone as quickly as he'd appeared, leaving the champagne with Gavin, who promptly set it on a nearby table with a grimace of distaste. "Don't pay any attention to this crap," he told her, motioning to the seductive setting with a wave of his hand. "It's all just window dressing. It doesn't mean anything—at least not to us, anyway. It's just a room, Summer. That's all. A room with a bed and a dresser and a bath, just like the master bedroom at my house. And we're going to do the same thing here we do at home—sleep. That's it, I promise. Okay?''

He was right—she knew that. The best thing they could both do was act as if their surroundings were nothing out of the ordinary and follow their regular nightly routine. But she usually took a bath at night while Gavin was reading in his study, then went to bed at least an hour before he did. That wasn't going to work tonight. It was early yet, barely seven. And the tub was in the middle of the living room!

So what were they going to do for the rest of the evening?

Silently groaning at the possibilities that sprang to mind, she forced a weak smile. "I know I can trust you, Gavin. It's not that. I just wasn't expecting...*this!* Talk about overkill. I guess we should be grateful the bed's not heart-shaped, too."

"There is a god," he said dryly, grinning. "Now that we've got that settled, what would you like to watch on TV? Presuming, of course, that there is a TV in this love nest."

There was, but it was well hidden in a cabinet next to the fireplace. Flicking it on with the remote, Gavin surfed the channels and finally settled on an old Bob Hope/Bing Crosby movie, *The Road to Morocco,* that they both agreed was perfect for a snowy night in the mountains. They'd seen it before, of course, but the jokes were still funny, and for a while, at least, they were able to laugh and forget where they were.

It couldn't last, however, and all too soon, it was over and a Cary Grant/Grace Kelly romance flashed onto the television screen. Summer stiffened, and beside her, Gavin swore softly under his breath and reached for the remote. A heartbeat later, he switched the channel to a sitcom, and Summer sent up a silent prayer of thanks.

Still, neither of them could relax after that. The sitcom held little humor, or maybe they were just no longer in the mood to appreciate it. Unable to laugh at any of the jokes, they just sat there and stared at the screen, wishing the torture would end and the evening would hurry up and be over. It was another hour, though, before the nightly news finally came on.

Relieved, Summer popped up like a jack-in-the-box. "Well, I think I've had enough TV for one evening. I'm going to bed. Good night." And without waiting to see if he would follow, she hurried into the bedroom.

Unprepared for an overnight stay, they had no luggage, no change of clothes, not even a toothbrush between them. And no pajamas, Summer silently acknowledged as she stepped into the bedroom and quietly shut the door behind her. And that was just fine with her. She intended to keep all her clothes on, anyway, and she expected Gavin to do the same. That way, nobody got into trouble. Satisfied that she had everything worked out, she pulled off her shoes and crawled into bed.

All she had to do, she reasoned, was get through the rest of the night. By morning, the blizzard would blow itself out, and the road crews would begin clearing the roads. They'd start with the highway through the pass first— which meant that by ten or so in the morning, she and Gavin could leave. As far as she was concerned, that couldn't happen a moment too soon.

Just go to sleep, and it'll be morning before you know it, she told herself. But that was easier said than done. When she closed her eyes, she found it impossible to relax in spite of the fact that she had the bed all to herself. Frustrated, she shifted into a more comfortable position and silently prayed for sleep. But when Gavin came to bed thirty minutes later, quietly letting himself into the darkened bedroom with barely a sound, she was still wide awake.

It wasn't until he eased under the covers onto his side of the bed, however, that she realized just what kind of trouble she was in. The mattress dipped, giving way to his superior weight, and gravity almost sent her rolling into him. Her heart thumping crazily in her breast, she grabbed for the side of the bed, convinced she'd never be able to fall asleep now.

It had, however, been a roller coaster of a day, and the emotional strain finally started to take its toll. Concentrating on not rolling to the middle of the mattress, she never noticed when tiredness overtook her. One second she was sure she was wide awake, and the next she couldn't keep her eyes open.

Beside her, Gavin knew the exact second she finally relaxed enough to fall asleep. A sigh whispered from her side of the bed, and the stiffness he could almost feel emanating from her body in waves gradually eased. Only then, when she let down her guard, could he let down his. His own sigh echoing hers, he fell asleep thinking of her, and never knew when they rolled against each other.

It was hours later when the power went off, killing not only the muted lights in the hallway, but taking out the electric heating system, as well. Sound asleep, neither Gavin nor Summer noticed. Then the temperature began to drop. At first, it was barely noticeable. A slight coolness that had them both blindly reaching for covers. But as the power outage continued and an icy north wind whistled at the windows and doors of the inn, searching for a way inside, the temperature took on a decidedly chilly cast. Already rolled up against each other, Gavin and Summer inched closer together in their sleep, seeking one another's warmth.

If the power had come back on then, they might have slept safely through to morning without ever knowing they had slept in each other's arms. But with no heat and the temperature outside continuing to drop, they turned in their sleep to face each other and huddled closer.

Gavin came awake abruptly with the realization that something was wrong, and wasn't surprised to discover Summer wrapped in his arms. Every night for a week now, she'd curled against him in her sleep and he hadn't been able to resist the unconscious need to hold her. Tonight, however, she had good cause. It was bitterly cold. Obviously the heat had gone off and there was no way to tell when it would come back on.

Holding Summer close, Gavin frowned in the pitch blackness of the night and considered their options. They needed more covers, but so, no doubt, did every other guest in the inn. If the heat stayed off much longer, he imagined the front desk was going to be flooded with calls for more blankets than the inn probably had. Which meant he and Summer would just have to find another way to keep warm.

Suddenly remembering the fireplace, not only in the living room of the suite, but in the bedroom, too, he eased Summer from his arms and slipped out of bed, then carefully tucked the covers back around her. The cold hit him full-force almost immediately, and with a softly muttered curse, he hurried over to the fireplace in the dark and fumbled with fresh logs and kindling from the wood box. Thanks to the gas starter, he had a roaring fire going within minutes.

Still, the room was bone-numbing cold, and it would be

a while before it warmed up. Shutting the door between the living room and bedroom to help hold in the heat, Gavin glanced over at the bed. In the firelight, he could see Summer shivering under the covers. Hurrying back to her, he slipped under the covers and took her back into his arms.

He just meant to hold her. Later, he swore to himself that that was all he meant to do. But as she snuggled trustingly against him and buried her face against his neck, he felt the heat of her breath against his skin and his arms instinctively tightened around her. He was, he knew, playing with fire, but she felt so damn good in his arms. And he was just holding her in her sleep, he reasoned. What harm could that do?

But his hands, with a will of their own, began to roam. Unable to resist touching her, they gently traced the length of her back, the curve of her waist, the breadth of her hips. And even through her clothes, he could feel how soft and delicate she was.

Entranced, he was totally lost to everything but the touch and feel of her when she moaned softly in her sleep. Suddenly realizing that he was doing a hell of a lot more than just holding her, he froze and sternly ordered himself to let her go before she woke up.

He had, however, waited too long. She stirred under his hands, and before he could release her to try to put some distance between them, her eyes fluttered open and met his in the flickering light cast by the fire in the fireplace. "Gavin?" she murmured in confusion. "I'm cold."

"I know," he said huskily. "The furnace seems to have gone out, but I've got a fire going in the fireplace. It should warm up here in a moment."

Even as he spoke, the heat from the fireplace began to take some of the chill out of the room, giving him the excuse he needed to release her immediately. But just then she suddenly noticed how close they were. She stiffened, awareness flaring in her eyes as they locked with his. "I'm sorry. I'm crowding you. This mattress is so soft—"

She started to pull away, and if he'd been thinking clearly, he'd have let her go. But his defenses were down and she was so soft against him. He wanted her, heaven help him, and right or wrong, he couldn't bring himself to let her go. Not yet.

"It's okay," he rasped softly, tightening his arms around her ever so slightly. "It's still pretty cool in here. We should share our body heat."

The fire was warming the room now, and they both knew it. Her eyes wary, she arched a brow at him. "It feels quite nice in here, actually," she replied. "If you're still cold, maybe you're coming down with something."

The only thing he was coming down with was a bad case of desire for her, but he didn't tell her that. That was something he was still trying to deal with himself. "I'm fine," he assured her huskily. "Just stay."

She shouldn't have. His arms felt too good around her, his lean, hard body too tempting next to hers. And snuggled together under a cocoon of covers, with a blizzard raging outside the windows of their suite, it was all too easy to imagine that they were the only two people in the world. There was no past, no future, nothing but the never-ending darkness of the night and each other and the feelings they stirred in each other.

Temptation slipped up on her unannounced and set alarm bells clanging in her head, but she could no more pull away from him at that moment than he could apparently bring himself to release her. Still, she had to offer a token protest. "Gavin, this isn't smart."

"You know it's what you want," he rasped softly. "It's what we both want."

She hesitated—and gave herself away. Murmuring her name, he leaned over and kissed her, and she was helpless to stop him. Just that easily, the need he stirred in her so effortlessly was back, impossible to ignore, even more impossible to resist. With a soundless sigh of surrender, she melted against him and gave herself up to the magic of his kiss.

He groaned, and in the time it took to gather her against him, they were both lost to everything but each other. One kiss led to another, then another, and Summer ached for more. Moving against him, she needed something she couldn't put a name to, and somehow he seemed to know. His hands snaked under the cranberry-colored angora sweater she wore, and with an expertise that robbed her of breath, he blindly unhooked her bra. Her breasts spilled into his strong, warm hands, and she cried out in surprise at the gentle wonder of his touch.

"Easy," he murmured against her mouth as his fingers gently stroked and kneaded and caressed. "It's all right, sweetheart. Just let me take care of everything."

His mouth covered hers in a languid kiss that seemed to go on and on even as his fingers tenderly played with her breasts, and she could only moan and kiss him back. And all the while, deep inside, the restless ache that had lodged low in her belly tightened like a fist.

She wouldn't have considered herself a bold or demanding woman, but a need she had no experience with was driving her and suddenly she seemed to have no more control over her hands than she did the storm raging outside the inn. She needed to touch him—all of him—now! Her hands raced over him, fumbling with the buttons of his shirt, the fastening of his slacks, tearing wildly at his clothes. Her fingers were far from steady, however, and she could only manage a button or two.

More frustrated than she'd ever been in her life, she felt
a sob well up in her throat, but then his hands were there
to help her, not only with his clothes, but hers, as well.
Buttons parted from button holes, zippers growled low in
the night, and with an ease that stole her breath, he stripped
them both. Then, before she quite knew what to expect,
they were skin to skin.

Suddenly shy, she went perfectly still in his arms, not
quite sure of herself in these new, uncharted waters. But
then, he touched her. His hands moved over her in a slow
dance of seduction, stroking her breast, the curve of her
hip, the soft skin of her belly, and the breath she hadn't
even realized she was holding escaped in a shuddering sigh
of pleasure. She reached for him, her hands unconsciously
following his example as she learned the angles and planes
of his lean, hard body.

She'd thought he was a man with iron-clad control, but
it didn't take her long to discover that she could snap that
tight hold he kept on his emotions with just a touch. Her
fingers only had to trail down his chest, and with a low
growl, he quite simply lost it.

Before she could do anything but gasp, he rolled her onto
her back and in the next instant was moving over her, ca-
ressing her, loving her with his hands and mouth and driving her out of her mind with need. Her senses throbbing
and her thoughts reeling, she clung to him helplessly, her
body moving with his in a dance she would have sworn
she didn't know the steps to.

At that moment the world could have stopped revolving
on its axis and she never would have noticed. Lost in the
wonder of his touch, there was just Gavin and the wild
magic of his loving. She couldn't think, couldn't catch her
breath to tell him that they needed to take it slower. Then,
just when she thought she knew what to expect next, he

surged into her, stretching her, filling her, and she cried out in a mixture of pleasure and pain.

At her first cry, Gavin froze, disbelief nearly knocking him back on his heels. She was a virgin? How? She was nearly thirty years old! He'd known she didn't date much—in a town the size of Whitehorn, it was impossible not to keep track of what other people were doing—but he'd never thought, never expected...

She'd been a virgin, and he'd just taken her like an animal.

Self-disgust filled him, along with regret. She'd given him so much—her trust, her support, not to mention the respect that went hand in hand with her family name—and now she'd given him her virginity without any expectations of getting anything back in return, not even tenderness.

Riddled with guilt, he said hoarsely, "I'm sorry, Summer. I didn't know."

"It's okay," she whispered tearfully. "There was no way you could know. I should have told you. I just didn't expect—"

She couldn't finish, and with a murmur, he leaned down and kissed her gently. "Let me make it better."

He didn't give her a chance to argue, but simply kissed her once, then again, soothing her with slow, languid kisses that were soft and tender and seductive. When she hesitantly kissed him back, he felt as if she'd just handed him the moon and the stars. Wrapping her close and holding her as if he would never let her go, he covered her mouth with his and took the kiss deeper, then deeper still.

This time he was determined to not rush her. Keeping a tight rein on his control, he let her set the pace, waiting until she moaned and lifted her hips to his before he moved ever so gently inside her. He half expected her to cry out in pain, but she clung to him and kissed him with a sweet hunger that nearly destroyed him. The whimper that vibrated low in her throat was from need, not pain.

He'd thought he was a man who was ruled by logic, not emotion, and for her sake, he needed to take things slow this first time they made love. But when her mouth turned eager under his and her hips caught his rhythm, he discovered, to his surprise, that he had very little resistance when it came to Summer. With a groan that seemed to come from his very soul, he could no more hold back his desire for her than he could stop the snow from falling out of the night sky.

Madness. What happened after that could only be described as sweet, sweet madness. Intoxicated by the feel and taste of her, he drove her wild with his hands and mouth, until her soft, panting cries swirled about them in the warmth of the dark silence that enveloped them. Then when she was shuddering and crying out for release, he took her over the edge.

Still hard with need, he felt his own body catch fire when she shattered. Groaning, he clenched his teeth and tried to hang on, wanting to draw out the pleasure, but he was fighting a battle he couldn't win. Not when he wanted her so badly. Deep inside, what was left of his control started to unravel, and he was helpless to stop it. Her name a harsh cry in the night, he followed her over the edge.

Summer never remembered falling asleep. One second she was wrapped in Gavin's arms, her body still humming from the wonder of making love for the first time in her life, and the next the sun was shining full in her face. Coming awake slowly, she rolled over, buried her face in her pillow, and started to drift back to sleep—only to realize she was naked under the covers.

Memories came rushing back then and hit her in the face

like a bucket of cold water. Gasping, she bolted upright in bed, the covers grasped to her bare breasts and her heart pounding crazily. She looked quickly around for Gavin, a blush already stealing into her cheeks, but she was alone. If she hadn't known better, she might have thought he'd never been there at all. Then she noticed he'd neatly folded her clothes before he'd left and laid them on the end of the bed, along with a note.

Snatching it up, she read it quickly and learned he'd gone to the dining room to scrounge up something for them for breakfast. He'd thoughtfully noted the time he'd left, and a quick calculation had her reaching frantically for her clothes. He'd be back any second, and she didn't intend to be sitting naked in the bed.

Scrambling into her clothes, she'd just zipped her slacks and pulled her sweater over her head when there was a quiet knock at the bedroom door and Gavin walked in. The second their eyes met across the length of the room, every touch, every kiss they'd shared during the night was suddenly there between them.

Flustered, Summer ran a hand through her disheveled hair and tried to remember what she'd been doing when he'd walked in. Then she noticed her shoes sitting on the floor next to the fireplace and realized that if he'd arrived five seconds earlier, he would have walked in on her half naked. Just thinking about that stole the air right out of her lungs.

He made love to you last night, ninny. He wouldn't have seen anything that he hadn't seen before.

Realizing how silly she was being, she had to laugh at herself. So she wasn't thinking straight. Who could blame her? She'd had the most incredible experience of her life last night, and her emotions were still bubbling up inside her like a fountain. She wanted to laugh and cry and walk right into his arms. But most of all, she wanted to talk about it, about them, to tell him everything she was feeling and know that he understood what she meant because he felt the same way.

But when a smile she couldn't control bloomed on her face and she stepped toward him, he didn't give her an answering smile. Hesitating, she said, "Good morning. Is everything okay?"

His expression grim and his manner cool and distant, he nodded. "The snow stopped about five this morning, and the plows have been at work ever since. The highway department opened the pass about a half hour ago, so we can head for home whenever you're ready."

He didn't slap her, but he might as well have. Stunned, Summer felt her smile fall and could do nothing to hide her hurt. Last night, she'd shared an intimacy with him she hadn't even come close to sharing with another man, and this morning, all he could talk about was the weather? Who was this man? Had she imagined the tenderness of his touch in the dark of the night? Had it all been just a dream? Or was he already regretting it and trying to forget it happened?

She wanted, needed to ask, but his face was set and closed and didn't encourage further intimacy. Hurt, not sure if she'd ever be the same again, Summer just barely resisted the need to hug herself. No, she wouldn't give herself away that way. If he wanted to act as if nothing had happened between them, then she certainly could, too. Even if she did feel as if he'd just ripped her heart out by the roots.

"I just need to put on my shoes and comb my hair and then we can go," she said stiffly, and turned toward the bathroom. "Just give me a second."

Gavin watched the proud way she walked away from him and wanted to throw something. She was hurting, and he was the one who'd hurt her, damn it! But last night never should have happened. They had a business arrangement, nothing more, and that hadn't changed just because the charges against him had been dropped. Granted, they were two consenting adults and they could have sex if that was what they both wanted, but they'd shared a lot more than sex last night. He'd let her get too close, and he couldn't let it happen again. Not if they were both going to walk away from their marriage at the end of a year with their hearts still intact.

So he let her go without offering any kind of explanation and wouldn't have blamed her if she hated his guts. But some things were for the best, even when they hurt like hell.

The drive back to Whitehorn was accomplished in virtual silence. Summer wanted to ask what was wrong, but the set of Gavin's jaw didn't encourage conversation and she didn't really need an explanation, anyway. He obviously regretted ever touching her. Well, he didn't have to worry, she thought with a sniff, staring blindly out the passenger window. It wouldn't happen again.

She was so miserable, all she wanted to do was to go off to cry by herself when they got back to the house, but Gavin didn't head directly home when they drove into town. Instead, he turned north. Not surprised, Summer didn't have to ask where they were going. Now that his name had been cleared, he would, of course, want his daughter back. Summer just hoped Rachel Henderson had meant it when she'd told him she wasn't his enemy. If she bucked him on this, she was in for the fight of her life, and Summer couldn't think of anything sadder. No one won in a custody battle, least of all the child.

Reading her mind, he broke the silence and said gruffly,

"I'll do whatever I have to to get my daughter back. You know that, don't you?"

She nodded. "I'd be disappointed in you if you didn't," she replied. "But I don't think it's going to come to that. Rachel and Jack know Alyssa belongs with you. They'll do the right thing."

He wanted to believe her, but after all the hell he'd been through over the course of the past year, his faith in the basic goodness of people wasn't what it had once been. He doubted that he'd ever trust anyone ever again to do the right thing.

Still, he was willing to be proven wrong. "I hope so," he said as they reached Rachel and Jack's and he parked at the curb. "I guess we'll know in a few seconds."

Ready for a fight, he escorted Summer to the Hendersons's front door and knocked boldly. He didn't doubt for a second that Rachel and Jack were expecting him—the second they'd heard that Audra Westwood had confessed to Christina's murder, they had to know he would come for Alyssa—but the welcome he and Summer got when Jack opened the door to them was nothing like what he'd expected.

The past few months, Gavin had thought he'd come to know Jack fairly well. Honest and hardworking, he'd spent years working the streets of L.A. as a cop, and it showed in his face. When he smiled, there was usually a cynical edge to it, and despite his happy marriage to Rachel, there was still a trace of disillusionment in his hazel-green eyes that came from dealing with the dregs of society on a daily basis.

Or at least there always had been in the past, Gavin corrected himself when the other man smiled broadly at the sight of him. He looked so damn happy that he almost looked drunk. Then it hit Gavin. "Rachel had the baby."

"Yeah! Can you believe it? I've got a daughter and she's beautiful. Just like her mother. Would you like to see her?"

"Oh, Jack, that's wonderful!" Summer said, stepping forward to impulsively hug him. "Of course we'd like to see her. And Rachel, too. When did all this happen? We've been kind of busy…"

"Yeah, we heard about Micky Culver turning Audra in," he replied. "That was too damn close. Congratulations, man," he said to Gavin, and held out his hand. "Rachel and I didn't believe you were capable of such a thing. If we had, we would have done everything we could to keep you away from Alyssa."

Instead, they had welcomed him into their home every time he had come to visit his daughter, and for that, Gavin would always be grateful. "I know that," he said gruffly, "and I appreciate it. I'm sure just about everyone you know warned you against me."

He didn't deny it. "We've never had much use for gossip."

"So when did Rachel have the baby?" Summer asked, changing the subject before it became awkward. "I thought she wasn't due for another couple of weeks."

"So did we, but the baby decided she'd waited long enough and put in an appearance three nights ago. She and Rachel just got home from the hospital this morning." Motioning them to follow him, he said, "Come on back to the family room. Rachel's there with the kids."

Considering that Rachel had only been home from the hospital a matter of hours, Summer realized they should have made their apologies and gotten out of there so the new mother could catch up on her rest. But this wasn't a social visit—they were there to collect Alyssa. Considering the circumstances, this probably wasn't the best time to do that, though Summer doubted that there would be a time that would be easy for any of them.

So she and Gavin followed Jack to the family room at the back of the house, where they found Alyssa sitting in Rachel's lap on the couch and talking about the baby, who was asleep in a portable crib next to the couch. At the first sight of Gavin, Alyssa grinned and pointed to the crib, talking excitedly, and the only word that was understandable was "Baby!"

Chuckling, Gavin strode over to her and picked her up, nuzzling her neck as they both peered down at that baby. "I know," he said. "You've got a new cousin. Isn't she pretty?" Looking over her head, he smiled at Rachel. "And how's the new momma feeling?"

"Tired but wonderful!" she said with an absolutely radiant grin.

Joining Gavin at the crib, Summer took one look at the baby and felt her heart melt. She was so tiny! "Oh, Rachel, she's so beautiful! You and Jack must be thrilled."

"It's funny—she's only three days old, but it seems like she's always been a part of us. Did Jack tell you what we named her? Phoebe. That was my grandmother's name. We wanted a family name."

A family name for a beautiful child that made them a family. Watching the way they watched every breath the baby took, Summer found herself envying them the happiness they had found and wondering if they knew just how lucky they were. "She's just beautiful," she said again. "We didn't even know you'd had her."

Her smile fading, Rachel glanced at Gavin. "With everything that's been going on, that's perfectly understandable. I'm happy for you, Gavin. Audra Westwood has a lot to answer for."

"Yes, she does," he said grimly. "If Micky Culver

hadn't given her up, I think she would have actually stood by and let me be convicted without saying a word.''

It was a daunting thought. ''Instead, she's the one who'll probably spend the rest of her life behind bars—with her mother.'' Grimacing at the thought, Rachel deliberately changed the subject. ''Since you didn't know about Phoebe, then I imagine you're here for Alyssa.''

When he nodded somberly, tears gathered in her eyes, but she quickly got herself under control. ''I'm okay,'' she said thickly when Gavin and her husband scowled and Summer stepped toward her in concern. ''This is just an emotional time for me. I knew it would be difficult when the time came for me to give her up. But having Phoebe has taught me so much in just the short time we've had her. I loved her the second she was born and would have fought the devil himself to keep her from being taken from me.

''I don't know how you stood being separated from Alyssa,'' she told Gavin. ''It must have been horrible.''

He didn't deny it. ''The only thing that made it halfway bearable was knowing that she was with family who loved her. But now that it's over, I need her with me.''

Tears still flooding her eyes, Rachel reached blindly for her husband's hand and held on to him tightly when he sat next to her and slipped his arm around her. ''We wouldn't have it any other way. The two of you belong together. I just hope you let us visit her once in a while.''

''Are you kidding?'' Gavin said, ''After everything you've done for her? You're her aunt and uncle, and now she has a new cousin. Of course you can see her. You're family,'' he assured them.

And just that easily, peace was made and bridges mended. His daughter was his again.

Eight

In spite of Summer's offer to pack Alyssa's clothes, Rachel insisted on accompanying her upstairs and helping her. "We don't need everything today," Summer protested. "You should be taking it easy. Just show me where her pajamas and play clothes are, and we'll come back in a couple of days to get the rest."

Laughing, Rachel said, "I'm not an invalid, Summer. I just had a baby, and that was three days ago. I'm fine. Really. And I want to do this. Anyway," she added as her smile faded, "I'm not sure bringing Alyssa back here that soon would be a good idea. We've gotten very attached to each other, and it just might confuse her."

Summer hadn't considered that. "Do you think she's going to have trouble adjusting to living with me and Gavin?"

"I don't know if I'd say trouble, exactly," she said as she collected Alyssa's favorite blanket and stuffed bear. "She loves Gavin dearly, but she's never actually lived with him. That's going to be an adjustment for all of you, and I just think it would be easier for her if Jack and I keep our distance until she gets weaned away from us and has a chance to bond with you and Gavin."

"But I don't know anything about babies except for caring for them when they're sick. What if she doesn't like me?"

"Are you kidding?" Rachel laughed. "Of course she'll like you. At least you've dealt with kids in your practice.

I had absolutely no experience when she came to live with us. I didn't even know how to change her diaper! I made so many mistakes, it's a wonder she didn't end up hating me. But I learned, and so will you. Just relax and enjoy her. She needs a mother to love her, and there's not a doubt in my mind that you can do that. She and Gavin are lucky to have you."

If her marriage had been a real one, Summer would have appreciated Rachel's vote of confidence more than she could say. But she and Gavin were living a farce, and considering how coolly he'd treated her all morning, she didn't think that was ever going to change. Not that she wanted it to, she quickly assured herself. Last night had been a mistake. She had to believe that.

Still, guilt tugged at her. They were living a lie. Rachel and Jack and everyone else thought they were in love and committed to a future together, when nothing could have been further from the truth. In less than a year they would go their separate ways, and once again Alyssa would be motherless.

And that, more than anything, bothered Summer the most. When she and Gavin had decided to get married, she'd never stopped to think of what their arrangement might do to Alyssa. She'd assumed it would take a court battle for Gavin to regain custody. It should have taken months to settle everything, then Alyssa wouldn't have had much time to get attached to her. Instead, there'd been neither a trial nor a custody battle, and nearly an entire year was left in their agreement.

Nothing was going as she'd expected and she didn't know what to do about it, but that was something she could hardly discuss with Rachel. Forcing a smile, she said, "I feel like I need one of those books called *Motherhood for*

Dummies. I'm so afraid I'm going to make a mistake and warp her for life.''

"Don't be so hard on yourself," Rachel chuckled. "And if you need some help, call me anytime. I mean that literally," she added, grinning. "Phoebe's still got her days and nights mixed up, so if you're having a meltdown in the middle of the night, don't hesitate to call. I'm sure I'll be up."

Laughing, they finished packing Alyssa's things, then went back downstairs to join the men and children. Then, all too soon, it was time to leave. Putting on a bright smile, Rachel tried to act as if it was nothing out of the ordinary for Alyssa to leave with Gavin, but she couldn't quite pull it off. Tears glistened in her eyes, and when she hugged the baby goodbye, she couldn't bring herself to release her until Alyssa squirmed in protest.

"I'm sorry," she said huskily, blinking back tears as Gavin took his daughter from her and settled her comfortably in his arms. "I know this is the best thing. It's just harder than I expected. She's so sweet. Take good care of her."

There was no question in any of their minds that he would do exactly that, so there really was no further reason to linger and draw out the pain of leaving. While the women had been upstairs packing the baby's clothes, the men had transferred her car seat from the family van to Gavin's Chevy, so all they had to do was buckle Alyssa in and they were ready to go. Alyssa, not realizing the repercussions of what was happening, thought she was just going for a ride. Waving merrily as they drove off, she never saw her aunt Rachel turn into her husband's arms and cry her eyes out.

Ever since he'd left Alyssa on Rachel's doorstep right before he was arrested for Christina's murder, Gavin had dreamed of the day when he could bring his daughter home where she belonged. He'd had her room decorated with all the things a little girl could want, from a crib with a canopy to a closetful of clothes and a toy box stuffed with the latest in educational toys. She should have loved it. And for all of two minutes she did. But then she lost interest and wanted to explore the rest of the house, which he hadn't thought to make child-safe.

"Uh-oh, gotta move that," Summer said, snatching up a vase in the family room when she set Alyssa down on the carpet and she went right for it. "I had no idea she could move so fast." Frowning, she eyed the glass-topped coffee table in front of the couch. "Maybe you should put that away for now, too."

Gavin grabbed his daughter and, to her giggling delight, swung her up into his arms. "Whoa there, Half Pint! It looks like we've got some work to do before we can let you run wild. Stay here with Mama while I get your play-pen and bring it downstairs."

Handing her over to Summer, he hurried upstairs to Alyssa's room, and Summer never saw him leave. *Stay here with Mama.* His words echoing in her ears, Summer stared down at the baby and couldn't stop herself from gently holding her closer. *Mama.* An arrow pierced her heart just at the thought of anyone calling her that. She'd never had the chance to call anyone mama—and she'd never realized how much she'd missed that until just now. Just the thought of a sweet baby like Alyssa thinking of her as her mother brought the sting of tears to her eyes. Dear God, what had she gotten herself into?

That was a question she was to ask herself time and time again for the rest of the day. With Alyssa safely tucked away in her playpen, she and Gavin went about the business of making the house childproof. For two people who had very little experience with children, it wasn't easy. Just when they thought they had locked away everything that could present a danger to her, they stumbled across an unlocked cabinet under the kitchen sink or a potted plant that was within easy reach of little hands. Worried, they went through the house again and again, until they were convinced they'd put childproof catches on every cabinet door and locked everything of danger away.

After that, they should have been able to relax. But by then, it had grown late, and Alyssa began to miss not only the only home she remembered, but Rachel, as well. Whining, she looked around for her aunt, and when she couldn't find her, she started to cry.

Summer's first instinct was to run to her to try to console her, but considering the circumstances of her and Gavin's marriage, she thought it was best that Alyssa bond with Gavin. So she held back and let Gavin try to distract the baby.

For a few minutes he almost succeeded. He teased her with her stuffed teddy bear and made her laugh, but only for a moment. She quickly lost interest and started to pucker.

Her heart breaking for her, Summer might have found the strength to keep her distance, but then Alyssa turned to her and held out her arms. Just that easily, Summer's good intentions crumbled. "What is it, sweetie?" she crooned, reaching for her. "Are you missing Aunt Rachel? You'll get to see her again, I promise. You've just got to get used to staying here first."

It was doubtful that the baby understood a word she said, but something in Summer's tone must have reassured her. Popping her thumb into her mouth, she snuggled against Summer's breast and within minutes she was asleep.

And with no more effort than that, she stole Summer's heart.

Watching the two of them together, Gavin smiled ruefully. "Well, I guess I know where I stand."

"Oh, but it's nothing against you personally," she said, startled. "She's just always been taken care of by women, hasn't she? First Lettie Brownbear, then Rachel, now me. You could bring Judge Judy in here, and she'd probably do the same thing."

She gave herself no credit, but Gavin wasn't buying it. He'd watched her all day with Alyssa and seen the way she'd tried to hold herself back, but she hadn't been able to do it. Every time Alyssa had smiled at her, she'd just melted. She might try to convince herself that the baby would have responded the same to any other woman, but he knew his daughter, and she didn't turn to just anyone for comfort.

"It's okay, Summer," he said gently. "It's important for her to love us both. I don't have a problem with her turning to you instead of me when she's upset."

"But you're her father! And she doesn't even know me."

"But she's already starting to trust you," he pointed out. "And that's what's important."

If Summer needed any proof of that, she got it when she carried the baby upstairs to her room to put her to bed for the night. Sound asleep, Alyssa still held tight to her, even in her sleep.

"What do I do?" she asked Gavin in a whisper as he adjusted the covers on the bed. "I'm afraid if I tug her loose, I'll wake her up, and she'll start crying for Rachel again."

She had a point, Gavin acknowledged. It had broken his heart to see her so upset and confused, and the last thing he wanted to do was to wake her up again. Poor baby, she was hurting, missing Rachel, and he'd do whatever he could to help her feel safe and happy. "The two of you can have our bed for tonight, and I'll sleep on the couch. Then I'll see about getting a cot in here tomorrow. It could take her a while to adjust to living here. If she needs you to stay with her again, we'll be prepared."

Their night of passion at the inn wasn't mentioned, but it was there between them as their eyes met, throbbing like an ache that wouldn't go away. And although they'd both sworn it wasn't going to happen again, Summer knew as well as Gavin that if the baby hadn't been their main concern, the temptation of reaching for each other in the dark of the night would have been impossible to resist.

"I think that's for the best," she said huskily, cradling the sleeping Alyssa close against her heart. "So I guess I'll see you in the morning. Good night."

Stepping around him, she headed down the hall for the master bedroom and felt his eyes on her all the way. It wasn't until she reached the bedroom and started to shut the door behind her, however, that she heard his quiet, "Good night." She'd never heard a lonelier sound in her life.

Half expecting Alyssa to have a troubled night, Summer was pleasantly surprised when she slept all night. But any thought she had of sleeping in the next morning ended at dawn. Full of energy and raring to go, the baby was up with the sun and made sure everyone else was, too.

"Well, I guess you're not a sleepyhead in the morning," Summer said with a grin as she nuzzled her playfully after she'd changed her diaper. "C'mon, let's go find Daddy, and he can watch you while I make breakfast."

Scooping her up, Summer carried her downstairs, only

to hesitate when she found Gavin still asleep on the couch in the den. Sprawled on his stomach, his hair standing on end and the quilt he'd used heaped on the floor, he looked as though he'd had an uncomfortable night on the too short couch.

"Uh-oh," she whispered to the baby, "it looks like Daddy could use a few more hours' sleep. Why don't we just have some cereal until he wakes up?"

Still murmuring to her, she headed for the kitchen, but Alyssa had other ideas. Squirming to get down, she cried happily, "Dada!"

Gavin, used to working long shifts at the hospital and being on-call at all hours, woke with a start. Pushing up abruptly, he immediately spied Summer standing in the doorway with the baby. "What's going on?" he growled in a gravelly voice.

"I'm sorry we woke you," Summer said quietly. "Alyssa seems to be an early riser. I was going to make breakfast for her."

Alyssa grinned happily at Gavin and chattered in a garbled baby language that, apparently, she fully expected the adults to understand. Laughing, Summer said, "I think she's asking you if you'd like to join us."

"I'd love to," he chuckled, and had no idea how sexy he looked with his stubbled jaw and sleep-tousled hair. "Just give me five minutes to shave and change and I'll be right there."

She opened her mouth to tell him not to, only to realize that the last thing she needed was to sit across the breakfast table from him with him looking as if he'd just rolled out of bed. She'd never be able to eat a bite, let alone keep her head about her.

"Then I'll put Little Bit in her high chair and start breakfast. Bacon and eggs okay for you? Good," she said at his nod. "Rachel said Alyssa loves scrambled eggs, so that should make her happy."

Alyssa was, in fact, happy as a clam at high tide when her father joined them a short while later and the three of them sat down to breakfast. Summer didn't fool herself into thinking that the baby had bonded with her or Gavin that quickly, but for now she seemed content. Seated between her and Gavin in her high chair, Alyssa hummed to herself as she ate and got her breakfast all over her. And that, according to what Rachel had told her, was a sure sign that she was enjoying what she was eating.

Laughing at her, Gavin was trying to wipe her hands when the phone rang. In the shattered quiet, he swore and almost ignored it. "It's probably a reporter," he said. "Someone must have been watching the house and realized we were back."

"Or it could be Rachel checking to see how Alyssa got through the night," she replied. "I'm sure she's worried about her."

They could have let the machine screen the call, but Gavin was afraid that Rachel would worry even more if he didn't immediately answer the phone. Pushing away from the table, he strode over to the wall phone in the kitchen. "Hello?"

"Gavin? This is Michael Preston."

Not surprised that his boss would call him now that his name had been cleared, he said coolly, "Hello, Michael. What can I do for you?"

"I just wanted to congratulate you. I heard the good news and was wondering when I could talk you into coming back to work."

Still bitter about the way his colleagues had refused to work with him, Gavin couldn't believe Michael's gall. After the way he'd forced him to take a leave of absence for something Michael had known damn well he hadn't done, he had a hell of a nerve.

"Really?" he drawled mockingly. "The last I heard, no one wanted to work with me."

That clearly wasn't the response he'd expected. Cold silence echoed across the phone line, and all too easily. Gavin could imagine the scowl on his boss's face.

"Look," Michael said with an impatient sigh, "I wasn't any happier with the situation than you were, but my hands were tied. What was I supposed to do? Fire everyone and hire people who would be willing to work with you? Damn it, man, this is Whitehorn, not L.A. Good medical help is hard to come by."

"So you let me go!"

"It seemed the only practical solution at the time," he retorted, stung. "And I knew it was only a temporary situation. Once you went to trial, your name would be cleared and—"

"And life would go back to normal like none of this had ever happened?" Gavin finished for him. "Is that what you're saying? That I'm just supposed to forget that most of the people I work with thought I was a murderer?"

To his credit, Michael did try to understand. "If I were in your shoes, I'd probably feel the same way," he said quietly. "I saw the way you were treated. You have every right to be bitter. But you were cleared and it's over with, Gavin. I know this will probably infuriate you, but maybe the best way to deal with this *is* to go on like it never happened. I'm not saying to forget what was done to you— you won't ever be able to do that, no one would—but you're going to have to find a way to let go of your anger or it's going to ruin your life."

He had a point, Gavin readily admitted. He did have to let go of his anger. But going back to work now, with people who should have known him well enough to know that he could never deliberately kill anyone, wasn't the way to do it.

"I appreciate the advice, Michael," he replied, "and the fact that you'd like me to come back to work. But the only person who really believed in me throughout this entire ordeal was Summer. She was there for me when no one else was, and she could use my help right now at her clinic on the reservation. So I'm afraid my leave of absence is going to have to continue for a while. I'm needed elsewhere. If the situation changes, I'll give you a call."

Not waiting for a response, he hung up, convinced he'd done the right thing, and turned back to the breakfast table to find Summer watching him with troubled eyes. Since he'd made no attempt to keep his voice down, she'd heard every word.

"You didn't have to do that," she said quietly. "I never intended for you to give up your job at the hospital to help me at the clinic. That wasn't part of our agreement."

"So I'm changing the agreement," he said with a shrug. "If Michael doesn't like it, tough. I did what he asked of me—I took a leave of absence. Now I'm doing what I want to do."

"Oh, really?" Summer said with a quirk of a brow. "So now you're saying you actually *want* to work at the clinic? After I had to practically twist your arm to convince you to accept my proposal?"

She had him, and they both knew it. A reluctant grin turning up one corner of his mouth, he said, "Okay. So maybe that was a stretch. I made a commitment and I will honor it. But if I can do that and pay Michael back for not protecting my position when I needed his backing, what's wrong with killing two birds with one stone?"

"Hey, you won't hear me complaining," she said, holding up her hands in surrender. "Not when it means I get your help at the clinic. So when do we start? I've only been able to keep it open three afternoons a week, and I was hoping to expand to five full days a week, if you're agreeable, of course."

Alyssa chose that moment to remind them of her presence by banging on the tray of her high chair with the plastic spoon Summer had given her to play with when she'd finished her breakfast. Chuckling, Gavin arched a brow at Summer and looked pointedly at his daughter. "We've got to decide what we're going to do with Little Bit first. We didn't just get her back home to stick her in day care all day."

Summer agreed. "What about Lettie? If she would agree to take care of her in the mornings while you opened the clinic and I worked my shift at the hospital, we could trade off the afternoons. That would give us each every other afternoon off to be with Alyssa, and she would only be at Lettie's for about twenty hours a week. The rest of the time, she'd be home with one or both of us."

All things considered, it was a doable schedule. It would take some effort on their part, but they could make it work. Of course, it didn't take into consideration what they'd do when Gavin eventually returned to work at the hospital, but they'd deal with that when it happened.

"Sounds good," Gavin said, leaning over to nuzzle Alyssa under her double chin until she giggled helplessly. "I'll talk to Lettie this afternoon."

Lettie was thrilled at the opportunity to take care of Alyssa again, but she'd fallen and sprained her ankle, so Summer and Gavin decided it would be better to wait a couple of days, until she was completely healed, before they left Alyssa with her. That meant they had to postpone expanding the operating hours of the clinic. In the meantime, however, Summer's leave was up and she had to return to work at the hospital.

Up well before dawn the following morning, she'd just finished dressing and was drinking a quick cup of coffee with Gavin when there was a sudden knock at the front door. Surprised, Gavin frowned. "Who the devil can that be? It's not even six o'clock in the morning."

Scowling, he strode out of the kitchen to the front door, only to return seconds later with Tony Little Deer, who was more than a little frantic. "Cindy's gone into labor," he told Summer the second he stepped into the kitchen. "You have to come."

Summer felt her heart stop. Cindy Little Deer was thirty-eight years old and pregnant for the first time in her life. She'd been trying to have a baby for years and was thrilled when she finally conceived. She hadn't, however, had an easy pregnancy. She'd had trouble from the very beginning and had almost lost the baby several times. Three months ago, her husband had been killed by a drunk driver. Another woman might have miscarried right then, but it was the thought of the baby that had helped her through her grief. If something happened now, after she'd been through so much, Summer didn't think Cindy would be able to bear it.

Already reaching for her medical bag, she frowned worriedly. "Is she sure? She's not due for another two and a half months—"

"She's hurting real bad, Doc. She really needs you to come."

If they'd been talking about any other first-time mother, Summer might have hesitated, figuring it was a false alarm, but Cindy was steady as a rock. Summer had never seen her spiral into panic, even when her husband was killed. If she said the baby was coming, it was a sure bet that it was.

Turning to Gavin, she said, "Will you call the hospital for me and tell them I've got an emergency?"

"I'll take care of it," he assured her. "Go on and go. It sounds like she needs you."

He didn't have to tell her twice. "Alyssa should be awake soon," she said hurriedly, already halfway out the door. "There's applesauce in the cupboard and cereal—"

"I'll handle it," he assured her calmly. "Go."

Her thoughts already jumping ahead to Cindy, she went.

The door had hardly shut behind Summer when a cry went up from Alyssa's room. "I'm coming, sweetheart," Gavin called, rushing up the stairs. "Hang on. Daddy's coming."

Standing up in her bed, braced to holler again, she broke into a broad smile at the sight of him. "Da-da!"

Grinning, he laughed. "Good morning to you, too, beautiful. I guess I don't have to ask how you slept. You're full of sass this morning. Are you ready for breakfast or do you want to wait a while? Let's change your diaper, then we'll go downstairs and see, okay?"

Talking to her as though she understood every word, he changed her diaper, then carried her downstairs, confident that fatherhood was going to be a piece of cake. And why wouldn't it be? It wasn't as if he was a stranger to her. He'd visited her as often as possible when Lettie had taken care of her on the reservation, then again when she'd been with Rachel. They'd become great friends, and she trusted him. How difficult could taking care of a one-year-old be?

"All right," he said brightly as he set her in her high chair and gave her a spoon to play with while he prepared her breakfast. "Summer said applesauce and cereal. I think I can handle that. How about you?"

Pleased with her spoon, she chattered in baby talk and set about seeing how much noise she could make. Twenty seconds later, however, she became disenchanted and dropped it on her tray. "Just hold on a minute, sweetheart," he told her when she started to fuss. "Let me mix this cereal and we'll be all set."

But when he made the cereal according to the directions on the back of the box, it looked like wallpaper paste. "That can't be right," he said to himself, then nearly jumped out of his skin when Alyssa suddenly began to squall. "All right, honey, I know you're hungry," he crooned, and quickly poured some milk into the cereal. Then it looked like gruel.

"Damn," he swore, then shot her an apologetic look. "I know. I'm not supposed to talk like that in front of you. It'd be just my luck that would turn out to be your favorite word and you'd say it in church."

Far from appeased, she let out a bellow that should have raised the roof.

"Okay, okay, so this isn't the time for jokes. Summer said you're supposed to like cereal, so here goes." Hurrying over to her, he dipped a small spoon into the pasty-looking mixture and held it up to her. She took one bite and spit it out.

"Well," he said ruefully, wiping her chin and the front of her pajamas, "I guess this means you don't like cereal, after all. Can't say I blame you there, sweetheart. I wouldn't feed that to cats. How about some applesauce?"

Before giving her a bite, he tasted the stuff himself and decided it wasn't half bad. Alyssa, however, wanted none of it. The second he held the spoon up to her mouth, she clamped her lips shut and refused to even try it.

"Aw, c'mon, Little Bit," he groaned. "I thought you were hungry. Just try a bite for Daddy."

For an answer, she threw the plastic spoon she'd been playing with earlier on the floor.

Patience, he reminded himself when she shoved her fist into her mouth and began to whimper. He was the adult here—he could handle this. She didn't want cereal or applesauce and couldn't talk to tell him what she did want, so it was up to him to find something she would eat. Rachel had sent all sorts of baby food home with her, and she, more than anyone, would know what she'd like. He'd just go through the jars and find something Alyssa wouldn't be able to resist.

It sounded easy, but ten minutes later, he had opened jars of baby food scattered all over the kitchen, and Alyssa was still an unhappy camper. Frustrated and on the verge of pulling his hair out, Gavin picked up the phone and called Rachel.

"I apologize for bothering you, especially so early," he said the second she came on the line, "but I don't know what to do. Summer had to leave on an emergency and the baby's hungry, but she won't eat any of the food you sent home with her. She spits out everything I give her, but she keeps crying and gnawing on her fist like she's starving to death—"

"Make her a piece of toast with jelly," Rachel said with a chuckle, "then she'll eat her cereal and applesauce. Your daughter has a sweet tooth, Gavin, especially in the morning, and she tends to get a teeny bit impatient. Didn't I tell Summer? I thought I did, but the day was emotional. I may have forgotten."

"Maybe not," he replied. "Summer was pretty distracted when she rushed out of here—one of her patients was in labor. She probably just forgot. Anyway, thanks, Rachel. You saved both our lives."

"I doubt that," she laughed, "but I'm glad I could help. Make her some toast and give her a kiss for me. She'll be fine."

"I'll do that," he promised, and popped a piece of bread into the toaster the second he hung up. Minutes later, he was scrounging through the refrigerator for jelly and could come up with nothing but peanut butter. "This is all we've got, sweetheart. If this doesn't work, we're making a run to the store."

At first, he didn't think she was going to touch it. Staring suspiciously at the peanut butter-slathered toast he laid on her tray, she hesitated. Then reaching for it, she brought it to her mouth...and began to hum.

"Thank God!" Gavin breathed, laughing, and kissed her.

All the way to Cindy's house deep in the heart of the reservation, Summer sent up a silent prayer that Tony had exaggerated the seriousness of his sister's labor. It was far too soon to have the baby, and though there were certainly cases of babies that premature surviving, Summer didn't want to put Cindy's baby in that kind of jeopardy if she didn't have to. After all that the poor woman had been through, she shouldn't have to fight for her baby's life once it was born, damn it! It just wasn't fair.

But if Summer had learned anything in medicine, it was, unfortunately, that life wasn't always fair. And there wasn't a damn thing she could do about it.

Hang on, Cindy, she prayed as she raced toward Cindy's with Tony buckled in beside her. She found it incredible that he'd ridden all the way to her house on his moped. It had to be thirty-five miles. But Cindy didn't have a phone or a car and he'd had no choice.

Please, please, God, let me get there in time to help!

Cindy lived with her elderly grandmother and her brother in a two-bedroom house that was hardly as big as Gavin's family room. Rushing inside, Summer never noticed the tightness of the quarters as Cindy's worried grandmother hurriedly showed her to her granddaughter's bedside. All she saw was Cindy. One look at her and she knew the baby was going to be born today and there was no stopping it.

"Dr. Kincaid, thank God you're here! The baby—" A contraction hit her then, and with a fierce grimace of pain, Cindy grabbed Summer's hand and held on until it passed. "It's too soon," she panted as tears gathered in her eyes. "Please… I can't lose this baby!"

As worried as Cindy, Summer smiled reassuringly and squeezed her hand, never letting her see her own fears. "You're not going to lose her. Everything's going to be fine," she promised her, and prayed that it was. "Let me examine you and see what's going on."

Giving her hand one more squeeze, Summer did a quick but thorough exam, and just as she expected, the baby was well on its way to being born. Here Summer had none of the things she needed to ensure the safe delivery of a baby two months premature. Cindy needed to be in the hospital, where she and the baby could be monitored at all times, but from the moment she'd first learned she was pregnant, she'd been adamant about having the baby at home.

Still, Summer had to try one more time to convince her of the seriousness of the situation. "Cindy, you need to be in the hospital—"

"No!"

"I don't have any of the equipment I need for a preemie. Let me call Airlife—"

"No. I promised Dave I would have her here at home,

on the reservation, just as we'd planned," she insisted stubbornly. "After she's born, then we can go to the hospital."

She set her jaw and refused to budge from her position, and Summer didn't have time to argue with her about a promise she'd made to her dead husband. Turning to Cindy's grandmother, who was hovering close by, twisting her hands together, she said quietly, "We're going to need a clean blanket to wrap the baby in and plenty of hot water and sheets. And I'll need your help when the baby arrives, so you'll need to wash your hands thoroughly and put on a clean smock or housecoat. The baby's lungs won't be as developed as they need to be, so we've got to keep conditions as sterile as possible to avoid infection. I'll also need Tony to use my cell phone to call Airlife when it gets close to the time for the baby to be born so we can get them both to the hospital as soon as possible."

"Yes, Doctor," the older woman said, and quickly began gathering everything Summer had requested.

Hurriedly washing her hands, Summer expected the delivery to be a quick one, within the hour, but the baby had different ideas. The contractions didn't stop, but they slowed, and three hours later, the baby was no closer to being born than when Summer had arrived. She didn't mind admitting to herself that she was worried. Something was wrong. The baby wasn't helping the way it was supposed to, which meant Cindy had to do all the pushing, and she was quickly running out of energy. If something didn't happen soon, she and the baby could both be in serious trouble.

Once again, she tried to talk her into going to the hospital. "I'm worried about the baby," she told her bluntly. "I know how much she means to you and that you would never deliberately put her in jeopardy. But that's what you're doing, Cindy. I think she's in distress, but there's no way to tell without a fetal heart monitor. Let me call Airlife.''

Exhausted, wincing with the pain of another contraction, Cindy hesitated, then shook her head. "Dave is here, watching over us. He's not going to let anything happen to our baby. She'll come soon. Let's give it another couple of hours.''

Summer wanted to argue with her, but Cindy was so convinced she was doing the right thing. Left with no choice, Summer had to go along with her wishes, even though she knew with a sick feeling of dread that they were headed for disaster.

One hour stretched into two, then three, and Summer lost all track of time. Then, just when she thought she was going to have to do a C-section to save Cindy, her contractions suddenly strengthened.

"Push, Cindy! That's it!" she cried. "It looks like your daughter's going to be born today, after all. Push!''

Groaning, Cindy gritted her teeth and pushed with the last reserves of her strength, and finally, the baby came sliding into the world. Summer should have laughed in exaltation, just as she always did when she delivered a baby, but the second she touched the baby, she knew something was horribly, terribly wrong. The little girl was perfectly formed and Cindy's last link with her dead husband. And she didn't have a breath of life in her little body.

Panicking, Summer quickly cleared her airway and breathed into her little mouth, working over her frantically, but her desperate efforts were too little, too late. The baby was stillborn.

Nine

Thanks to Grandmother Gray Eagle's teachings, Summer had learned at an early age that death was a part of life and as natural as breathing. She knew that, accepted it, and thought she dealt with it as well or better than most people. That didn't, however, mean that she ever got used to it. There was a quiet stillness that accompanied death that always chilled her blood. At the exact moment that life ceased to exist, death stole uninvited into the room when no one was looking and, with a total absence of sound, froze time itself.

It was eerie, unsettling, and, at times, frightening. And after years of practicing medicine, she could by now tell, without checking with a stethoscope, the second the soul left the body. In the hushed quiet, she could always hear the thundering of her own heart.

And this time was no different. For what seemed like an eternity, nobody moved or spoke or even seemed to dare to breathe. It was obvious the baby was dead, and Cindy had to know it. But she just lay there, numb, the light in her eyes gone, while Summer sat motionless at the end of the bed with the poor, lifeless baby in her hands. The only sound she heard was the roaring of her own blood in her ears.

Then, with no warning, something seemed to snap and Cindy realized what had happened. She cried out sharply, and the quiet stillness of death shattered. "No! Not my baby, dear God! Please don't take my baby!"

Her heart breaking for her, Summer tried to explain that there'd obviously been a problem from the very beginning, which was why Cindy had had such a troubled pregnancy. They would never understand why God had chosen to take this baby, but they had to trust that He knew what He was doing.

Summer truly believed that, but Cindy, in her inconsolable grief, didn't want explanations. She wanted her baby back and her husband, and she knew she could have neither. Brokenhearted, she sobbed in her grandmother's arms and begged God to take her, too.

And there was nothing Summer could do to help her. Wrapping the baby in a clean sheet, she pulled out her cell phone and made the necessary calls to the proper authorities, then did what she could to make Cindy more comfortable. It wasn't much. Nothing she could say or do would take the pain away, and in the end, all she could do after she made sure Cindy was physically all right was give her a sedative. But even as she fell asleep, tears trailed down her pale cheeks. Summer had never felt so helpless in her life.

An ambulance arrived thirty minutes later from the medical examiner's office, and as Summer went outside to greet the EMTs, she was shocked to discover that most of the day was gone and the sun was already low in the western sky. She'd been so wrapped up in Cindy and trying to save the baby that she hadn't even noticed the passage of time.

"This wasn't your fault," Sally Birdsong, Cindy's grandmother, said quietly as she joined her outside. "You did everything you could."

"Then why is the baby dead?"

"Because you aren't God. Because some things are

meant to be. Because we each have a destiny and this was Cindy's.''

Ruefully, Summer had to admit that the old woman was wiser than she. And right on all counts. That didn't, however, do much to ease the hurt that still squeezed her heart. She never liked to lose a patient, especially a baby. There was so much hope with the birth of a child. It was supposed to be a time of joy, not grief. And for Cindy, the grief was twofold. Because not only had she lost the baby, she'd also lost her last possible connection with her husband.

''I know,'' she said huskily. ''Sometimes, though, it's just hard to accept the fact that we really don't have the control over our lives that we think we do. That's a lesson I'm still trying to learn.''

''You're not alone,'' Sally said with a crooked grin. ''Go home, Summer. It's been a long day and you've done all you can do here. Only time can heal Cindy now.''

Just weeks ago, Summer would have thought of her own house whenever anyone mentioned home, but things had changed drastically since her wedding day. Now when she thought of home, she thought of Gavin and Alyssa. He wasn't her husband in the true sense of the world, and Alyssa would probably never be her little girl, but suddenly she was desperately lonely for both of them.

Just thinking about them lifted her spirits. Gavin had had the full responsibility of Alyssa all day for the first time since his daughter had been born. It had, no doubt, been an eye-opening experience for both of them.

A slow smile curling her mouth, she said, ''You're right. It's time for me to go home. Cindy should sleep through the night, but don't hesitate to send for me if she needs me.''

''She'll be fine.''

Impulsively, Summer reached over and hugged the older

woman. "Thank you, Sally. You don't know how much I needed your wisdom today."

Her emotions suddenly all over the chart, she was afraid she was going to break down if she didn't leave immediately. Hugging Sally one last time, she turned and fled—toward home, toward Gavin and Alyssa.

The night sky was in full bloom by the time she left the reservation behind and made her way to Gavin's house, but she never even looked at the stars as she pulled into his driveway. All her attention was directed at the house. Lit up like a Christmas tree, lights glowed from every window. She took one look at the place and felt her heart stop dead in her chest. Something had to be horribly wrong. Cutting the engine, she grabbed her purse and ran for the house.

"Gavin?" Throwing open the front door, she bolted into the house, only to find the TV playing in the family room and the entire downstairs deserted. Trying to remain calm, she told herself not to panic. Gavin had her cell phone number. If something had happened to Alyssa, he would have called her immediately. She was just tired and the slightest bit paranoid. There was nothing to worry about.

Why, then, a caustic voice in her head demanded, *are there open bottles of baby food all over the kitchen counter? And look at the house. It looks like it's been hit by a tornado. What the hell happened there that afternoon?*

Her imagination supplied all sorts of catastrophic answers, terrifying her, and all she could think was that kidnappers must have come in and snatched them both. It was the only logical answer. Or something had happened to the baby. Swallowing a sob, she sprinted up the stairs and raced down the hall to Alyssa's bedroom.

"C'mon, baby," she heard Gavin coax tiredly. "You

haven't had a nap all day. You've got to be exhausted. Don't you want to go to bed?"

Stumbling to a halt in the doorway of the baby's room, Summer searched the room and immediately found Gavin sitting in the rocking chair with Alyssa in his arms. At the sight of the two of them, she nearly went weak in the knees with relief. Thank God, they were all right! She'd been so worried.

Gavin's words suddenly registered, and she finally realized why the house was in such a state. Alyssa hadn't had a nap all day and must have run Gavin ragged. Watching them together, Summer felt a tearful chuckle bubble up in her throat. She didn't know if he realized it yet or not, but when it came to a battle of wills, he'd met his match in his one-year-old daughter. Loaded down with her bottle and her favorite blanket, he was obviously trying to rock her to sleep, but she was having none of it. Sitting straight up in his lap, she stubbornly refused to lie back and relax, and there wasn't a heck of a lot he could do about it.

Tenderness flooded Summer's heart. She didn't know how they had gotten past her defenses so quickly and become so dear to her, but all she could think of was that she was blessed to have this time with them. Alyssa seemed determined to not sleep tonight, but given the chance, Cindy Little Deer would have gladly traded a few hours' sleep for the chance to hold her baby in her arms and rock her to sleep. The next time she asked herself how her life had gotten so messed up, Summer promised herself she would remember this moment and count her blessings.

"It looks like somebody had a rough day," she said huskily, shattering the quiet. "Can I do anything to help?"

A delighted smile bloomed on Alyssa's baby face, and with a garbled greeting that Summer couldn't understand, she held out her arms to her. Her heart melting, Summer went to her and scooped her up for a hug. "Hi, sweetie," she said, kissing the top of her head as the baby cuddled close. "I thought you'd be asleep by now."

"I think she was waiting for you," Gavin said as he rose to his feet. Giving her his place in the rocking chair, he shook his head in disbelief when Alyssa popped her thumb into her mouth, laid her head on Summer's shoulder, and closed her eyes with a soft, contented sigh. Within minutes she was well on her way to being asleep.

"How did you do that?" he whispered incredulously. "I've been trying for the past hour to get her to lie back and close her eyes, but she wouldn't budge."

Her smile poignant, her thoughts on the baby Cindy Little Deer would never hold, Summer tightened her arms around Alyssa and would have gladly held her the rest of the night. "She still hasn't adjusted to the move yet and losing Rachel. She just needs a woman to make her feel secure. Give her some time. She'll come around."

She was right, Gavin knew. And when he thought about it, he had to laugh. The little stinker. He'd spent the day running after her, playing with her and trying to keep her happy. The house was in a shambles, but they'd had a grand time—until he'd tried to put her to bed. The second Summer took her in her arms, though, she'd zonked right out.

He started to tease her about somehow bribing the baby, but just then, he caught the glint of sadness in her eyes. Frowning, he studied her through narrowed eyes. "Are you all right?" he asked quietly.

Whatever he thought he saw in her eyes was gone in a blink. Her smile too bright, she cradled Alyssa closer. "Of course. It's just been a long day."

She had that right. It seemed as if he'd been on the go with Alyssa since the crack of dawn, which he had, but a closer look at Summer's closed expression told him his day must have been nothing compared to hers. He wanted to ask her about it, but not there in the baby's room where they had to be careful to keep their voices down so they wouldn't wake her.

"I bet you didn't have anything to eat today, did you? While you're putting her to bed, I'll go downstairs and make you something hot. You look like you could use it."

Just the thought of food turned her stomach, but before she could tell him she wasn't hungry, he hurried out and the moment was lost. Which was just as well, she told herself as she kissed Alyssa's dark hair. Life went on and the sooner she quit chastising herself for something that couldn't be helped, the sooner she'd be able to let go of the hurt and put it behind her.

Holding Alyssa helped more than anything. Sound asleep in her arms, she felt wonderful cuddled against her so trustingly. And even though she wasn't hers, she felt so blessed to have her, even if it was only for a year. Given the chance, Cindy Little Deer would have done anything to have that much time with her daughter.

That, however, wasn't meant to be, Summer thought with a sigh, and she had to accept that nothing she could have done would have changed anything. But, Lord, it was hard. In spite of all her best efforts to shake off the loss, all she wanted to do was cry.

She didn't, however. She didn't dare or it might be hours before she could stop. So she stiffened her resolve and carefully rose from the rocker to lay Alyssa in her crib. The baby only sighed and stretched out into a more comfortable position. Smiling tenderly down at her, Summer waited patiently by her crib until she was sure Alyssa had drifted back into a sound sleep before she quietly walked out, shut the door behind her and headed downstairs.

In the kitchen, Gavin began dishing up a bowl of soup

for her the second she appeared in the doorway. "I hope you like vegetable beef soup. It's canned, but it's quick, and there's grilled-cheese sandwiches to go with it. Have a seat and I'll get us something to drink."

Already in the process of pulling out a chair at the breakfast table, she arched a brow in surprise. "*Us?* You haven't eaten?"

"I was waiting for you," he said simply. "And worrying too much about finding something Alyssa would eat to think about myself. Though I guess you noticed," he said with a rueful grimace, motioning to the open jars of baby food everywhere. "Don't worry about the mess. I'll clean it up later."

Summer surveyed the disaster that had once been Gavin's neat-as-a-pin kitchen and had to laugh. "I don't even think I want to know what went on here today. The two of you survived, and that's all that matters. Though it looks like it might have been touch-and-go for a while."

"It was," he chuckled. "I love her dearly, but I never realized before how difficult it was to take care of a baby. And I know she must have been as frustrated as I was. I swear there were times that she looked at me like I was some kind of moron, then just shook her head and rolled her eyes."

Grinning, Summer said, "And she's only a year old. If she's doing that at this age, can you imagine how she'll be a sixteen?"

She laughed, then chatted about the baby as they ate, and anyone listening to her would have thought she didn't have a care in the world. But Gavin had gotten to know her fairly well over the past few weeks, and he wasn't buying it for a second. Biding his time, he let her talk—and noticed that she barely touched her food.

Finally, when it became apparent that she wasn't going

to eat anything, he said quietly, "Why don't you tell me what happened at Cindy's?"

For a long moment he didn't think she was going to tell him. She glanced away, avoiding his gaze, and what little color there was in her face drained away. In the sudden silence that fell between them, she didn't say a word.

If he hadn't caught a glimpse of the tortured pain in her brown eyes, he might not have forced the issue. But something was tearing her apart, and he didn't have to know the details to figure out that something had happened to either Cindy or the baby. And his gut clenched at the thought. He didn't think for a moment that Summer had been negligent—she was too good a doctor for that—but even the best of doctors lost patients, and it was never an easy thing to accept. You always questioned yourself, always blamed yourself, always examined what you'd done and wondered if there was something, anything, you could have done differently that would have changed the outcome.

"Summer, whatever happened, I know it wasn't your fault."

Tears welled in her eyes. "How can you know that?" she choked. "You weren't there."

"I know you," he said simply. "I know your reputation. You're not careless. You don't make mistakes. If something happened, it wasn't because of something you did wrong but because it was meant to be. Sometimes the hardest part of being a doctor is accepting that."

He was right, of course, but that didn't make the hurt that squeezed her heart any less painful. All she could think of was the baby. The poor little girl had never even gotten to draw a breath.

Suddenly the pain was more than she could stand and she couldn't keep it bottled up inside anymore. Tears overflowing her lashes, she whispered brokenly, "The b-baby w-was stillborn."

Horrified that she was coming undone right before his eyes, she pushed back her chair abruptly and surged to her feet, her only thought to get out of there before she completely lost control. But Gavin was quicker than she, and when she turned blindly away, she turned right into his arms.

"Let me go!" she cried. "I need to get out of here."

"Shh," he murmured, and swept her up into his arms. Gathering her close against his chest despite her frantic struggles to break free, he strode over to the couch and sat with her in his lap, talking all the while in a soothing voice. "It's okay, sweetheart. You don't have to pretend it doesn't hurt. Cry and let it out."

Stiff as a board in his arms, she told herself that she wouldn't do this. But Gavin's arms were strong and sure around her, and he made her feel so safe. Her heart bruised and hurting, she felt her defenses start to crumble and there was nothing she could do to regain control. Shuddering, she buried her face against his neck and let the tears fall.

"That's it," he said softly, huskily. "Let it out. Cry as long as you need to. It's okay."

Sobbing, she couldn't have stopped if her life had depended on it. Not when the pain she'd been trying to block out ever since she'd left Cindy's rolled over her like a tidal wave. For what seemed an eternity, she cried—for the baby, for Cindy, for the awful feeling of helplessness that engulfed her—and all the while, Gavin held her without a word of protest, letting her cry her eyes out until there were no tears left.

When she finally lay still in his arms, exhausted, he held her as if he would never let her go. "It's going to be okay," he said huskily. "Everything's going to be okay."

Murmuring reassurances to her, he stroked her hair and the length of her back, soothing her with a touch, a soft whisper, a gentle brush of his lips at the curve of her cheek, her mouth. And with every sweep of his hands, with every tender caress, the hurt that had closed like a fist around her heart eased ever so slightly.

Later, she couldn't have said how long he held her after that or when the feel of his hands on her changed. His touch was still light, still gentle, but his fingers began to linger sensuously. And it felt wonderful. With a soft murmur of pleasure, she stretched under his hands, loving the feel of them on her.

Another time, alarm bells would have been ringing like a fire alarm when his fingers moved to the buttons of her blouse, and with good cause. With just a few brushes of his hands against bare skin, he lit a fire in her that quickly threatened to blaze into an inferno. And he'd barely touched her! She needed to stop him, needed to roll out of his arms and give her head time to clear, but her defenses were down, her good intentions nonexistent. And any chance she'd had of fighting off the desire he stirred in her had died the second he touched her. Already throbbing for him, all she wanted was more.

Murmuring his name, she moved against him, reaching for him. Until she'd met him, she hadn't considered herself a sensuous person, but he'd changed her. Now she loved touching him, loved feeling the way he responded to her. If she'd gone blind at that moment, she thought she would have always known him after that by touch alone. There was something about the way his skin felt under her hands, the shape of his shoulders, the hardness of his muscles and the chiseled shape of his jaw, that struck a cord of recognition deep in her heart. With nothing but her fingertips, she skimmed her hands over his body and savored the wonder of him.

And with every touch, every stroke, the need inside her burned hotter. Restless, achy, needing the feel of skin against skin, she reached for the buttons of his shirt. "I need to touch you," she said huskily. "To feel you."

Groaning at the admission, Gavin knew just how she felt. She made him burn, and right then there was nothing he wanted more than her bare skin next to his and her slender body moving under his. Growling low in his throat, he surged to his feet with her in his arms.

Startled, his shirt forgotten, she threw her arms around his neck. "Where are we going?"

"To bed," he rasped, and carried her up the stairs as if he were Rhett Butler sweeping Scarlet off to the privacy of their bedroom.

And just that easily, he made her forget the pain of losing Cindy's baby and the hurt that had lodged deep in her heart. Dropping kisses across her face and neck, he didn't give her time to think of anything but him and the need that coiled tighter and tighter inside her. Kissing her hungrily as he let her feet slide down to the carpet, he finished unbuttoning her shirt, and before she could do anything but gasp, he'd peeled off not only her blouse, but her bra, as well.

Urgency firing her blood, she wanted him as bare as she, but now, as before when they'd first made love, there was just something about the buttons of his shirt that her fingers couldn't master. When he laughed, the rough, sexy laughter teasing her nerve endings like a caress, she gave in to her frustration and curled both hands into the material of his shirt. In the next instant, buttons went flying.

Later, Summer couldn't have said who was more surprised—Gavin or herself. For a stunned moment they both froze, startled. Then she realized what she'd done. Appalled, she blushed crimson. "Oh, God, I'm sorry!"

Far from upset, he only grinned down at her in the darkness of the bedroom. "For what? I've never had anybody rip my clothes off before. I think I like it. So why don't you finish what you started?"

His brown eyes glinting with devilment, he arched a masculine brow at her, boldly daring her to continue. Hesitating, caught in the snare of his eyes, her heart slamming against her ribs, she was sure she couldn't do it. She wasn't an aggressive woman; she never had been. Especially when it came to sex. But there was something in his eyes that told her she could be...and she just might like it. All she had to do was shed her inhibitions and take what she wanted.

And she wanted him.

She hadn't realized how much until just then. She wanted to touch him, to make love with him, to make him forget every other woman he'd ever touched. Giving in to the need, she lifted her hands to his buttonless shirt. She saw his eyes flare, felt him take a sharp breath, and was surprised by the sense of power that surged through her. She hadn't even touched him yet and he couldn't hide his reaction to her. Encouraged, she slipped her hands beneath the gaping front of his shirt and swept it off his shoulders. Before it hit the floor, she was tackling the snap of his jeans.

Groaning, Gavin didn't think he could have stopped her if his life had depended on it. Her fingers were gentle, unsure but determined, and they drove him wild. With just the brush of her knuckles against his belly as she worked at the fastening of his jeans, she made him so randy, he burned.

Torture. There was no other way to describe what she

did to him as she fought to pull off the rest of his clothes. Sweet, wonderful torture. She finally managed the snap, then turned her attention to the zipper of his jeans, and that was almost his undoing. Sweat breaking out on his brow and a muscle clenching in his jaw, he struggled to hang on to his self-control, but a man could only take so much.

And where she was concerned, he quickly discovered, he had no control whatsoever. Her fingers brushed against his hardness, and just that easily, his control shattered. Her name a rough growl low in his throat, he swooped down to cover her mouth in a hot, sizzling kiss and he grabbed her hand to press it against the hard length of him.

After that, there was no time for teasing, for dares, for anything but satisfying the hot, burning desire that raged between them like an inferno. Stripping off the rest of his clothes, then hers, he carried her with him down onto the bed and moved over her, into her, stealing her breath, her thoughts.

And with no effort whatsoever, he turned her into a wild, passionate woman she hardly recognized. Whimpering, her body starting to shake with the need for release, she moved desperately under him, clinging to him, feeling as if she was going to go up in flames any moment.

"Gavin!"

"I know, sweetheart," he groaned. "It feels good, doesn't it?"

Good didn't begin to describe it. Nothing had ever felt so perfect in her life. She wanted to tell him, to explain how wonderful he made her feel, but her breath was tearing through her lungs and she couldn't find the words. Her heart pounding, her head hazy with passion, she clung to him and all she could think was that she wanted more. She wanted more of him, more of the tenderness that brought tears to her eyes, more of the heated desire that held them locked together in a dance that was as old as time. She wanted it all.

But with every breath she took, the need gathering deep inside her coiled tighter and tighter until she sobbed from the wildness of it. Then, just when she thought she couldn't bear it a second longer, her startled cry pierced the heated darkness and she shattered in his arms.

Groaning, Gavin fought his own release, wanting to cradle her close and cherish her sweetness. But the battle was lost before it had begun. The storm they'd created together grabbed him and dragged him under, and just that easily, he gave himself up to the wild wonder of the moment.

Long after Gavin had fallen asleep beside her, Summer lay wide-awake, staring up at the darkness as the thunder of her heartbeat echoed in her ears. Her body still humming and her emotions far from settled, she tried to convince herself that what she and Gavin had shared had been nothing but sex. That was all it could be, all she could allow it to be.

Why, then, did it feel like love?

Shaken, she immediately shied away from that thought. No! She wouldn't let herself get caught up in the idea of hearts and flowers and happily-ever-after. She wasn't living in a romance novel—this was real life, and the only thing she and Gavin shared was a limited partnership that would end precisely in one year. You didn't love your business partner. She wouldn't. She couldn't.

She did.

How had this happened? she wondered wildly. When? She'd been so sure she had her emotions under control, that she wanted nothing more from Gavin than his help at her clinic for a year. She'd walked right into their arrangement with her eyes wide open, smugly confident that she could handle anything for a year.

So much for wishful thinking, she thought with a groan. They'd been married a little over a week, and already she was in love with him! She had to be out of her mind. That was the only explanation. Gavin didn't love her; she wasn't even sure that he liked her. He just wanted her. And that hurt. Because she wanted a heck of a lot more from him than that, and she didn't think she was ever going to get it.

Dear God, what was she going to do?

Three days later, Summer was still searching for answers. Thankfully, though, she didn't have time to brood about it. It was Gavin's first day of work at her clinic, and she'd taken the morning off from the hospital so she could show him the ropes and introduce him to the staff and patients. They had to be there at eight, and before that, they had to take Alyssa to Lettie's. That meant their day started early.

Summer liked to think she was a responsible person. She was seldom late for work because she planned her wardrobe the night before so that everything she would need the next morning would be right there at her fingertips. In the past, however, she'd never had to worry about getting anyone else ready but herself. It was a whole different ball game when you had a baby who also needed to be dressed and provided for for the day. Especially when that baby was up with the chickens and demanding to eat while both parents were trying to get dressed for work.

In the process of hurriedly drying her hair, Summer swore softly under her breath when Alyssa let out a sharp warning cry that she was quickly running out of patience. "I know, baby," she called out. "I'm coming. Just give me a second. I'll be right with you."

She didn't dare call herself mama to her yet, but it didn't matter to Alyssa. She wanted toast and jelly, not excuses. Held captive in her crib, she let out another frustrated cry, this one more miserable than the last.

Adjusting his tie, Gavin stood next to where Summer sat at the vanity and grinned at her in the mirror. "Somebody's getting impatient. I seem to be further along than you—I'll take care of Little Bit."

"I'll be right there," she promised, trying not to notice just how devastatingly handsome he was this morning. She'd seen him in a dress shirt and tie at the hospital more times than she could count, but never the morning after spending the night in his bed. That single factor changed everything.

By the time Summer made it downstairs, Alyssa had finished her toast and she had grape jam all over her. She took one look at Summer, gurgled happily, and held up her arms.

"Oh, no!" Summer groaned, laughing.

"The more she likes her food, the more she likes to wear it," Gavin chuckled as he dampened a washcloth and stepped over to clean the baby's face. "How are we doing on time?"

Summer glanced at her watch and winced. "Not good. I didn't realize it would take so long to get all of us ready."

"That's because you've never had to mess with this little monkey in the morning," he said as he snatched Alyssa from her high chair and made her giggle. "Tomorrow we'll get up earlier."

They had to hustle to get to the reservation in time. Lettie, who'd taken care of Alyssa from the moment she was born until Gavin left her with her aunt Rachel, was thrilled to have the baby back in her care. Love shining in her dark brown eyes, she couldn't stop talking about Alyssa and how devoted a father Gavin was. Fascinated, Summer would have loved to stay to hear more, but she had responsibilities at the clinic. Promising herself that she would sit down with Lettie one day soon to learn all about Gavin, she made sure the older woman had the clinic phone number, then kissed the baby and hurried to the clinic.

It was a minute to eight when they arrived, and there was already a stream of patients spilling out of the waiting room onto the front porch. Pushing her way through the crowd, Summer took the time to speak or nod a greeting to everyone, and all the while she was checking to make sure there were no emergencies that had to be dealt with immediately. Only when she was sure that the majority of the patients were there for the usual cold or flu symptoms did she step through the swinging door that separated the waiting room from the examining rooms to introduce Gavin to her three-member staff.

"Gavin, this is Mary Joe Hunter, our receptionist, and Terry Carter and Beth Fox, the two best nurses in the world."

Smiling, Gavin shook hands all the way around. "It's nice to meet you, ladies. It looks like we've got a full house this morning."

Mary Joe, who had a round face and easy smile, had the kindest eyes he'd ever seen. "We have a full house every day, Dr. Nighthawk. Out here on the reservation, we're the only game in town."

"Gavin's going to be working the morning shift and three afternoons a week," she told the other women. "Let me show him around so he'll know where everything is, and we'll get started."

Of all the things she'd done in her life, there was nothing Summer was more proud of than the clinic. But when she gave Gavin a quick tour of the place, she couldn't miss the dismay in his eyes when he saw the old-fashioned equipment in the examining rooms and shortage of supplies in the supply room.

"This is the best I can do with the money I was able to borrow," she said gruffly. "I've applied for a government grant, but it takes time to be approved, so I just do what I can until it comes through."

Shocked, Gavin said, "Are you telling me you're using your own money and funding this entire clinic by yourself?"

"The funding will come through soon—"

"But in the meantime, you're digging into your own pockets," he cut in with a frown. "How in the world are you getting by? I saw that crowd in the waiting room. I'll bet most of them don't have insurance or the money to pay for medication or their exams. You've got to be operating in the red."

She didn't pretend to deny it. "It's only a temporary situation, just until the funding comes through."

"But you said yourself that could take months," he retorted. "How can you afford to operate the place? At this rate, you'll be broke by the end of the year."

Just then Terry escorted a young woman with an infant in her arms and a toddler clinging to her skirt into one of the examining rooms. Meticulously clean, the young family was dressed in clothes that had been washed many times and it was obvious that their circumstances were strained. And all three appeared to be miserably sick with colds and in need of help.

Nodding to the trio, Summer simply said, "How can I not? These are my people and they need my help." Nothing else needed to be said.

Ten

They worked side by side all morning long, and the crowd in the waiting room never seemed to lessen. As soon as one patient was examined and sent home with a prescription that Summer paid for herself, there was another one to take his place, then another. If he hadn't known better, Gavin would have thought he was working an assembly line. The faces of the patients blurred, and at that time of the year, their ailments were all fairly universal. Flu, cold, allergies, with the occasional stomach virus thrown in for variation. Gavin hadn't seen anything like it since his days of working the emergency room in the county hospital when he was in medical school.

And with every patient that came through the swinging door to the examining rooms, Gavin's admiration for Summer grew. She knew just about everyone's name and treated them as if they were old friends. There may have been dozens of people in the waiting room, but she didn't let that rush her. She took the time to ask each person she examined about their families, school, the new baby or the new job. And they loved her for it. She received hugs of thanks from one patient after another, and she didn't hesitate to return each embrace, even when that meant being exposed to some obviously contagious viruses.

Concentrating on the patients and their needs, she worked tirelessly through the morning, taking only the barest of breaks, and those were few and far between. Amazed,

Gavin didn't know how she did it. He was a dedicated professional and liked to think he worked as hard as the next doctor, but she left him standing in her dust. Marveling at her stamina, he could only shake his head and try to keep up. Motioning to Mary Joe to call the next patient, he drank the last of the now cold coffee he'd been trying to finish ever since he'd come in that morning, then hurriedly washed his hands.

Stepping into the examining room, he checked the name on the chart and greeted the elderly woman who sat stiffly in a chair rather than on the ancient examining table Summer had bought at an auction. "Good morning, Mrs. Elkhorn. How are you doing today?"

She was eighty if she was a day, but behind the lenses of her bifocals, her nearly black eyes were as sharp as a cornered cougar's. "I don't like doctors," she said with quiet dignity. "There is nothing you can do for me."

Early in his training, Gavin had learned that many of the elderly patients weren't afraid of doctors, as most people thought, but rather the thought of getting sick and losing control of their lives. So they denied their illnesses and pretended nothing was wrong, and in the long run, they only ended up harming themselves and bringing about the very thing they were trying to prevent.

"I'm sorry to hear that," he replied. "It says here in your chart that your daughter brought you in because you've been having dizzy spells."

Refusing to even look at him, her chin went up a notch. "My daughter meddles in things that are none of her concern."

Gavin's lips twitched, but he only nodded sagely. "I'm sure that must be frustrating for you, but since you're here, I'd like to examine you—"

"No."

"It won't take long—"

"No."

She had the look of a woman who was prepared to sit there all day if she had to. Surveying her ruefully, Gavin knew when he was beaten. "Well, then, I guess there's nothing I can do to help you, but I think there's someone here who might. If you'll excuse me a moment, I'll be right back."

Not giving her a chance to argue, he left her in the examining room and went in search of Summer. He found her at the nurses's desk making last-minute notes in a chart before she called her next patient. "I need your help," he said as soon as she glanced up.

Surprised, she immediately closed the chart and jumped to her feet in alarm. "An emergency? No one told me—"

"No, it's Sharon Elkhorn," he said, blocking her path before she could rush into the other examining room. Quickly and precisely, he told her about his conversation with the other woman. "She's not going to let me come near her. Maybe you should talk to her."

Surprised by the request, Summer couldn't believe she'd heard him correctly. As most doctors, Gavin had a healthy ego. He wasn't as bad as some surgeons who thought they were right up there with God in the pecking order, but he didn't lack for confidence when it came to doing his job. For him to admit that he couldn't get anywhere with a patient was pretty amazing.

"Of course," she said. "I'm surprised that she's even here. As far as I know, she's never seen a doctor in her life. She always went to Grandmother Gray Eagle whenever she was sick."

But Grandmother Gray Eagle was dead now, and Sharon had to be scared to death. Traditional modern medicine was as foreign and frightening to her as X rays would have been

to the pioneers. "Let me get some things from my office
and I'll be right back," she promised Gavin, and hurried
away.

When she returned a few minutes later with an ancient
prescription stick that had belonged to Grandmother Gray
Eagle and several smooth, rounded rocks that had been
used by tribal healers for generations to treat everything
from impotency to upset stomachs to heart conditions,
Gavin eyed the primitive items in disapproval. "In all likelihood, she's either suffering from high blood pressure or
low blood sugar or both. Nothing you've got there is going
to help."

Not surprised by his reaction, she merely smiled.
"There's more than one way to skin a snake, Doctor.
Watch and learn." And stepping around him, she led the
way to the examining room where Sharon Elkhorn waited
stoically.

Greeting the older woman with the respect that the elders
of the tribe deserved, Summer said softly, "I'm honored
that you have come to me at this time when you are not
well. You need have no fear. Grandmother Gray Eagle
taught me well the healing ways of our people. I have
brought her prescription stick and sacred stones and want
only to help you."

Summer spoke straight from the heart, but for a moment
she thought the other woman was going to flatly reject her.
Through old, wary eyes that had seen far too much of life,
she studied her skeptically, not sure if she wanted to trust
her any more than she had Gavin.

Something in Summer's sure, steady gaze, however,
must have reassured her. With a nearly soundless sigh, she
relaxed ever so slightly and unbent enough to admit stiffly,
"My daughter is worried about me. My head is old and
tired and swims when I move too fast. I tried to explain

that I just did too much, but she would not listen and insisted that I come here. It is not where I wish to be.''

That much was obvious, but Summer didn't take offense. "I understand, but there is no reason to be afraid. These will help." Sitting beside her, she gave her the stones and softly began an ancient healing chant she had learned as a child.

The old words in their native tongue were as familiar to Sharon Elkhorn as the prayers of the rosary beads were to a Catholic, and closing her eyes, she quietly began to chant to herself as she worked the stones in her palm. And just that easily, her fear lessened.

Pleased, Summer would have liked to have slipped the blood pressure cuff around her arm right then and taken her blood pressure without giving her the chance to refuse. But that would have completely destroyed the trust she'd just earned. So instead she said quietly, "I'm just going to slip a cuff around your arm and check your blood pressure. Don't be alarmed when it tightens. It won't hurt you.''

Her eyes still closed as she softly chanted, Sharon never indicated by so much as a flicker of an eyelash that she heard her, but Summer knew she had. Encouraged, she carefully wrapped the blood pressure cuff around her upper arm and had to smile when Sharon's chanting increased slightly in volume. She didn't, however, stop or open her eyes and Summer took that as a sign to continue.

She wasn't surprised that her blood pressure was elevated, but she waited a few minutes more, letting Sharon softly chant, and this time, when Summer took a second reading, the numbers were better, though still higher than she would have liked.

Carefully putting the blood pressure cuff away and removing her stethoscope from her ears, she waited until the older woman stopped chanting and opened her eyes before she said softly, "Your blood pressure is up, which isn't good, but there are several things I'd like you to do to improve your condition. First I want you to use the stones every day—"

She immediately objected, "But these are yours—"

"They were Grandmother Gray Eagle's before they were mine," she cut in mildly, smiling. "She would have wanted you to have them. And I want you to take these," she added, pressing a prescription bottle of blood pressure pills into her hand and closing her fingers around them. "You have trusted me so far—trust me with this. Grandmother Gray Eagle, if she were here, would tell you that just because my way of healing is not always the old way, that doesn't mean it's a bad way. I would never do anything to harm you."

There was no doubting her sincerity—or the fact that much more than Sharon's health was on the line. As a tribal elder, the old woman had an influence that reached far and wide on the reservation. If she accepted traditional medicine as well as the ancient healing methods of their people, others who had yet to accept Summer would do the same.

For what seemed like an eternity, Sharon didn't so much as blink, let alone speak the words that Summer longed to hear. Then, just when Summer was sure she was going to reject her help, she closed her fingers around the prescription bottle and rose to her feet. "You must tell my daughter how I am to take these. She will worry if you don't."

If Gavin hadn't seen it with his own eyes, he wouldn't have believed it. He didn't know Sharon Elkhorn personally, but in spite of the fact that he had little involvement socially with anyone on the reservation, even he knew just how tightly she and the other old women of the tribe clung to the traditions of the past. If he'd been a betting man, he would have sworn that no one, not even Summer, would ever convince her to take the white man's medicine. That was obviously a bet he would have lost.

He couldn't help but be impressed. He'd known Summer was a gifted doctor, but he'd never realized before just how well she related to people. Granted, her methods weren't exactly orthodox, but was chanting so very different from meditation? The end result was that she'd convinced Sharon to meditate on a daily basis and accept a prescription for her high blood pressure, and that was all that was important.

The rest of the morning flew by after that, and when his shift was up, Gavin didn't know where the time had gone. When he went over the number of patients he'd seen, he was shocked. And exhilarated. He'd forgotten what it was like to practice down-in-the-trenches medicine. If the morning was an example of an average day at the clinic, he was going to enjoy his work there far more than he'd expected to.

Given the chance, in fact, he would have stayed and helped Summer with the afternoon shift. In spite of the number of patients that they'd both seen that morning, the waiting room was still packed. And Summer would have to see every one of those patients before she left at the end of the day.

Frowning as he watched her hastily wolf down the sandwich that was all she would have time to eat for lunch, he said, "Maybe I should stay another couple of hours. You can't handle all this alone."

Summer bit back a smile at that and didn't point out the obvious—that she'd been doing just that for months without any help whatsoever. She was just glad he finally realized how desperate his own people were for medical care right there on the reservation. Unfortunately, he'd done all

he could for the day. Alyssa was waiting for him to pick
her up at Lettie's.

"I'll get by," she assured him. "I'm used to it. And
Alyssa needs you. It's been a while since she stayed with
Lettie and she's probably wondering where you are."

She was right, and they both knew it. Still, he hesitated,
clearly not happy with the situation but unable to come up
with a different solution. "All right," he said finally. "But
you can't work a full shift at the hospital every morning,
then handle this kind of load every other afternoon here at
the clinic without driving yourself into the ground. We're
going to have to make some kind of adjustment in your
schedule."

If circumstances had been different and there'd been
nothing but friendship between them, Summer would have
been the first to agree with him. But she needed something,
anything, to distract her from the fact that she was falling
in love with him, and right now, the only thing that could
do that was work. The more, the better. If she could work
herself into exhaustion, maybe then when she crawled into
bed beside him at night, she'd be so tired that she'd immediately fall asleep before she could even think of turning
into his arms.

"We'll see," she said, and knew she would do nothing
of the kind. Not if she intended to leave their marriage at
the end of a year with her heart still in one piece.

They fell into a routine after that that worked surprisingly
well. Their days were full and busy, and although Summer
and Gavin usually only saw each other in passing, they had
much more time for Alyssa. Except for the mornings, which
she spent at Lettie's, she was at home with either her father
or Summer.

And the baby loved it. She adjusted quickly to her new

home and to the two adults who occupied it with her. She already knew and loved Gavin, of course, but she was a sweet child with an affectionate disposition and from that first night, when she'd turned to Summer for comfort, she'd accepted her. Secure in her world and the love she received from two adoring parents, Alyssa thrived.

With every passing day Summer found herself more and more drawn to not only the father but the child. And she didn't know what to do about it. When she'd proposed to Gavin, she hadn't anticipated that her emotions would become involved. Oh, she'd expected to develop a fondness for the baby—she'd always liked kids—but what she felt for Alyssa was becoming much more than fondness. It was maternal love, and that terrified her.

This wasn't supposed to happen! But Alyssa was so cute and funny and lovable. And when she snuggled up against her, popped that little thumb into her mouth, and fell asleep, Summer's heart just melted. How could she *not* love her?

And then there was Gavin. She'd thought she'd known him, thought she'd known exactly what living and working with him would be like. He would grudgingly put in his time at the clinic because he'd given his word, tolerate her presence in his life and home, and keep an emotional distance from her at all times so that at the end of their year together, they could go their separate ways and he wouldn't feel a thing.

That was the Gavin Nighthawk that she'd have sworn she married, but the man she found herself sharing her life with was nothing like that. He didn't just show up at the clinic every morning and go through the motions as some men might have. Instead he threw himself into the work with an enthusiasm that surprised her and got as involved as she did with the patients.

As for keeping an emotional distance and just tolerating

her presence in his life, that never happened. At night, when they were both home with the baby, they were just like any other married couple. They worked together to get dinner on the table, discussed their day as they sat down as a family to eat, then bathed Alyssa, put her to bed, and did all the little chores that had to be done before they were finally able to relax for the rest of the evening.

And no one knew better than Summer just how seductive those normal, everyday routines were. All too easily, she found herself falling into the trap that the lie they were living was real. They were raising a child together, working together at the clinic toward the same end, and that created an intimacy between the two of them that had nothing to do with sex.

When she realized that she was starting to think of Gavin as her husband and Alyssa as her daughter, panic nearly sent her running for the hills. She had to get out—*now!*— while she still could, before she completely lost her heart. She'd talk to Gavin, come up with some excuse—

But even as she tried to think of a logical reason for going back on her word, she knew she couldn't. The agreement she'd made with Gavin no longer affected just the two of them. Alyssa would be hurt, and so would all the patients who depended on the clinic for medical care.

She was well and truly stuck in a trap of her own making and there was nothing she could do about it—except find a way to somehow lessen the intimacy of their evenings at home as much as possible. So Friday night, after Gavin had worked at the clinic a week, she decided it was time for a night out. Dressed in black jeans and a red cowl-necked sweater, she had Alyssa's diaper bag packed and the baby dressed in a green corduroy jumper, white tights and the cutest little dress shoes she'd ever seen when Gavin walked through the front door after work.

Surprised, he took one look at the two of them and lifted a dark brow. "What's going on?"

"I thought we'd go out to dinner to celebrate your first week at the clinic," she said brightly. "Nothing fancy," she added quickly when she noticed how tired he looked. "Just the Hip Hop. It's Friday night and that means catfish. And Alyssa told me she'd just love macaroni and cheese. And it's usually so loud there that no one's going to complain if she gets a little vocal. But if you're too tired—"

"No, the Hip Hop sounds great," he assured her. It had been a busy week and he was beat. All he really wanted to do was to order a pizza for supper, play with Alyssa, and fall asleep later on the couch in front of the TV. But Summer's week had been as hectic as his—adjusting to living with a baby when she'd never been around one couldn't have been easy for her—and he couldn't really blame her for wanting a night out.

"Let me change into something a little more comfortable, and we can go."

He hurried up to their room, only to return less than five minutes later in jeans and a black-and-white sweater. Sweeping up Alyssa, who giggled in delight, he said, "Okay, ladies, let's get this show on the road. I'm starving!"

It was date night, and not surprisingly, the Hip Hop was doing a booming business. Every parking space in the café's lot was taken, and people were lined up three deep just inside the front door, waiting for a table.

Summer took one look at the crowd and groaned. "Maybe this wasn't such a good idea, after all."

"It's Friday night," Gavin reminded her. "Any other place is going to be just as crowded, unless you want fast food, and I'm not really in the mood for that."

Summer wasn't, either, but she wasn't sure how Alyssa would tolerate the wait. When she got hungry, she didn't hesitate to let the whole world know it. "We'll see how it goes. I brought some crackers in case she gets fussy, but that may not satisfy her."

Alyssa, however, hadn't been with anyone but one of them or Lettie for an entire week, so she was thrilled to be around other people, especially when she spied several children in the crowd. Grinning at a six-year-old who played peekaboo with her, she was perfectly content to wait with the grown-ups.

Chuckling at Alyssa's shy reaction to the little girl who played with her, Summer hardly noticed the gossip swirling about the café until the woman standing directly in front of her said to her companion, "I still can't believe Jordan Baxter's going to let Garrett Kincaid buy the Kincaid place. He's been bragging for over a year now that there was no way in hell he was letting the Kincaids have his inheritance, then all of a sudden, he just drops the whole suit. It makes no sense."

"Of course it does," her friend retorted. "The man's in love with Meg Reilly, and that little boy of hers is Garrett's grandson. If Jordan wants to adopt the boy when they get married, he'd better make peace."

"You mean, you think Garrett would try to stop the adoption?"

"Of course not!" she retorted. "The old man's not like that. He wants Meg to be happy. Why else do you think he's throwing them a wedding at the ranch and inviting the whole town? Can you imagine? It's going to cost him a fortune!"

"You're going, aren't you?" her friend asked eagerly. "It's going to be the biggest wedding this town's ever seen.

Everybody's going to be there. Damn, I've got to get a dress. Everyone's seen my old one."

That started a discussion about what to wear, but Summer hardly heard them. Ever since her uncle Garrett had discovered that his only son, Larry, had fathered seven illegitimate sons over the course of his lifetime before he died, Garrett had been trying to buy the Kincaid ranch as a legacy for his grandsons. He'd felt as if he'd failed Larry and had wanted to buy the ranch for his grandsons as a way to make up for Larry's indifference as a father. Until today, however, Jordan Baxter had thwarted him at every turn.

Glancing up at Gavin, she said quietly, "Did you hear that?"

He nodded. "That explains why half the town's here tonight. The gossips are eating up the latest news with a spoon."

It was always that way whenever a story broke, and after having been the brunt of so much talk himself, Gavin usually hated it. But in this particular instance, he was glad to hear that the old feud between the Baxters and Kincaids appeared to have ended—at least for now. If anyone deserved a break, it was Garrett Kincaid.

When no one else in town but Summer had believed in Gavin's innocence, she'd gone to her uncle and asked for his help. To this day, Gavin was still amazed that the old man had come to his rescue. The evidence against him had been damning, and everyone else in town had been ready to string him up from the nearest tree. Garrett, however, hadn't rushed to judgment. Instead he'd actually met with Gavin in his jail cell, believed his story, and hired Elizabeth Gardener to represent him. And for that, Gavin would always be grateful. They'd never know now if Elizabeth would have been able to clear his name, but that was really beside the point. Garrett hadn't known him from Adam and he'd still gone out on a limb for him. Gavin owed him.

The two women standing in front of them got a table, then it was their turn. Following Janie to the table at the back of the café, Gavin couldn't help but be aware of the interested looks he and Summer and the baby drew. Anytime the three of them went anywhere together, the reaction was always the same. To the interested eyes of the townspeople, they seemed to be the all-American family that had it all.

So much for appearances, he thought cynically as Summer held the high chair while he settled the baby into it. They were living a lie, pretending to be something that they weren't, and it was so damn easy. That was what threw him the most. He'd expected their arrangement to be awkward. He wasn't used to sharing his life—or his home—with anyone, and he'd thought he'd miss his solitude. But when he walked through his front door after a long, hard day at the clinic, he felt as if he was truly, finally coming home.

It wasn't supposed to be this way. He wasn't supposed to have any feelings for Summer except gratitude. But damn it, how was he supposed to resist her? he wondered as he watched her lean down to press a kiss to Alyssa's baby-soft cheek. She was so wonderful with the baby. She might not have had a child herself, but she was a natural mother, gentle and loving and incredibly patient. And she was everything that a man could ask for in a wife. Giving, hardworking, loyal, passionate.

Dear God, she was passionate! With just a touch, a kiss, a sigh, she could make the blood pound in his veins. And when she gave herself to him without inhibitions, he was helpless to resist her. His heart slammed against his ribs, his body turned hard as a rock—

Suddenly realizing where his thoughts had wandered—and right in the middle of the Hip Hop, damn it!—he stiffened, cursing under his breath as he jerked open the menu Janie had set in front of him. He was losing his mind, he thought furiously. He had to be. Why else would he be practically salivating over the woman right there in front of half the town?

At his low growl of disgust, Summer glanced up from her menu and blinked in surprise at the sight of the scowl wrinkling his brow. "What's wrong? Don't you see anything you like?"

That was the problem, he thought with a groan. He saw something he liked, all right, but he couldn't tell her that. Not when she'd done so much for him already. Twice, she'd come to his rescue—first, when she'd convinced her uncle to hire Elizabeth to represent him, then again, when she'd married him to improve his standing in the eyes of the community and the jury when he went to trial. If he told her how he felt about her now, that would only put pressure on her to stay with him after the year they'd agreed to was up, and that wouldn't be fair. They had an agreement, and the least he could do was honor it.

So he kept his feelings to himself and said stiffly, "It's nothing. I guess I'm just not that hungry."

"The flu's been going around," she said with a frown of concern. "Have you got a fever?"

She started to reach across the table to feel his forehead, only to have his fingers close around her wrist lightning-fast. "I'm fine," he said tersely and almost swore again when her eyes widened in surprise. Damn it, this wasn't the way he'd intended for things to go!

Feeling like a heel, he let out his breath in a huff. "Look, I'm sorry. I don't mean to be testy. I guess I'm more tired than I realized. It's been a long week."

"Then why don't we just do this another time?" she suggested. "We can go back to the house and order a pizza."

And once again, they would be alone, he thought, and immediately shook his head. "No, we're already here. We might as well stay. What do you think we should order for Alyssa?"

After that, Gavin tried to keep the conversation—and his thoughts—strictly impersonal. But she shared the same passion for medicine that he did, and they were soon discussing the clinic and the patients he'd treated that afternoon. Summer knew them all, of course, and spoke of them all fondly, as if they were family, and once again, he found himself bowled over by the lady. The medical field was filled with caring people, but he didn't know anyone who gave so unselfishly of her time and money and heart as Summer. And she didn't seem to have a clue how special she was.

He wanted to tell her—the words were right there on his tongue—but he bit them back before they could escape. And in growing desperation, he changed the subject to something he still wasn't sure he believed in—the ancient healing she had learned at the knee of Grandmother Gray Eagle.

But here, too, she fascinated him. Knowing full well that he was a skeptic, she wasn't the least offended. "Everyone's entitled to their opinion, but I witnessed firsthand many of the healings performed by Grandmother. She learned them from her grandmother, and she from her grandmother before her. And they knew what they were doing, Gavin."

She told him how the tribal healers of their ancestors ground up the bark of wild cherry trees to make cough syrup and how they extracted an aspirinlike acid from willow trees to treat the aches and pains of their tribesmen. And that was just a few of the examples she gave him. As their food arrived and they fed Alyssa, then ate themselves, she told him one story after another about their tribal history and the men and women who helped the tribe through epidemics and disasters, childbirth and death.

Captivated, Gavin could have sat there all night and listened to her. All around them, people were still talking about the surprising truce between Jordan Baxter and Garrett Kincaid, but all he heard was the soft, musical tone of Summer's voice. Then Alyssa decided she'd had enough fun for one night, and he and Summer were both jerked back to their surroundings.

"Uh-oh," Summer chuckled when the baby rubbed her eyes and began to whine. "Looks like somebody's ready to go to bed."

"No wonder," Gavin exclaimed, glancing at his watch. "It's nearly nine o'clock!"

He didn't have to ask where the time went, they both knew. They'd been so wrapped up in their conversation—and each other—that a team of storm troopers could have marched through the café and they never would have noticed. Suddenly feeling awkward and not quite able to look each other in the eye, they made preparations to leave.

"I'll get the baby."

"I'll pay the bill."

Five minutes later, flushed and loaded down with coats, Alyssa, and all the paraphernalia that went with a baby, they hurried out to the car and drove home without saying a word. And all the while, their hearts pounded in unison in the dark silence that surrounded them.

Confused, Summer wanted to ask what was wrong, but Gavin's stony expression didn't encourage conversation. And that was probably for the best, she told herself as they reached the house and she carried a now sleeping Alyssa upstairs to bed. When she talked about the clinic and Grandmother Gray Eagle and taking care of the people she loved so much, she gave away far too much of herself.

She couldn't keep doing that, she told herself as she carefully undressed Alyssa and eased her into her pajamas. She'd already given him far too much—her innocence, her heart. She wouldn't give her soul, too. She had to find a way to put some distance between them.

But how was she supposed to do that when she was sleeping with the man? Time and again, she swore she wasn't going to give in to the need he stirred in her by just breathing. But then in the dark of the night, when her defenses were down and he was as close as her dreams, she found herself in his arms.

Not this time, she promised herself as she left Alyssa asleep in her bed and went to her and Gavin's room to change. She'd wear her old maid flannel gown and socks and be sound asleep on her side of the bed by the time Gavin came upstairs. Tonight, her body would *not* betray her while she was sleeping!

She had it all worked out—or so she thought. But she hadn't counted on a need that was stronger than every survival instinct she possessed. Even though she fell asleep almost immediately, she somehow unconsciously knew the second he slipped into bed with her. Dreaming, she murmured something unintelligible in her sleep and shifted restlessly under the covers. Somewhere in the back of her mind, alarm bells clanged, but she never heard them. Aching for his touch, his kiss, even in her sleep, she felt the inexorable pull of his presence at her side. Dreamily, she half rolled toward him and in the next instant was gently wrapped in his arms.

Taking in the scent of him, she sighed in contentment.

He always smelled so wonderful. Clean and fresh and spicy. Unable to resist, she nuzzled close and pressed a lingering kiss to the side of his neck. It was the low sound of his groan that brought her fully awake.

Startled, her eyes flew open and she found herself snuggled close against the hard angles and planes of his body. If she'd been more alert, she would have immediately apologized and jumped from the bed with the excuse that she wasn't sleepy after all and was going to read for a while. But her blood was already hot, her body humming. And without quite knowing who moved first, they were suddenly kissing as if there were no tomorrow.

"Gavin—"

"I know, honey," he murmured when he swept his hands under her gown and caressed her naked back and hips. "Let's get rid of this gown. You don't need it anymore. I'll keep you warm."

He did that, all right. With just the slow glide of his hands, he made her burn.

But it was his tenderness that completely undid her. With a touch that was as soft as a feather, he stroked her breasts, her thighs, the curve of her belly, as if she was the most precious thing in the world to him. Over and over again, he caressed her, murmuring his need for her, until he was all that she heard in the darkness, all that she felt, and every thought began and ended with the ache he stirred in her very bones.

Seduced by the dark velvet tones of his voice in the night, she couldn't think, couldn't remember why she shouldn't do this. She loved him more than she'd ever thought it was possible to love anyone, and suddenly, the words just bubbled up inside her like a fountain. Kissing him softly, hungrily, she whispered, "I love you."

She barely spoke above a whisper, but in the heated quiet

of the bedroom, there was no question that he heard her.
Gavin stiffened, and Summer found herself holding her
breath, waiting for him to say that he loved her, too. But
in the sudden, tense stillness that enveloped them, the only
sound was the frantic beating of her own heart. Gavin
didn't say a word.

Eleven

She'd never been so mortified in her life.

Hot color surging into her cheeks, Summer wanted to take the words back, but it was too late. They hung there between them, throbbing like a neon light in the dark, impossible to ignore.

Pain lancing her heart, she called herself seven kinds of a fool. Idiot! Of course he didn't love her. That wasn't part of their deal. They had a business arrangement. Business, she told herself fiercely, swallowing a sob. Just business. How many times did she have to tell herself that before she got it through her thick head that what they had wasn't going to turn into some kind of fairy-tale romance? It was just sex.

She winced at that, but there was no denying the obvious. He didn't love her. He'd never claimed to. But he didn't have to love her to want her. He was a man, and he had certain needs. If she continued to persist in hoping that his feelings would grow into something deeper than that, she was only going to end up getting hurt more.

"Summer—"

His voice was rough in the darkness, and apologetic. And that only increased her embarrassment. Wishing she could just crawl into a hole somewhere and die, she said quickly, "It's okay, Gavin. I was just caught up in the heat of the moment. Forget I said anything."

To his credit, he didn't want to let the subject die there. "We need to talk—"

"That's not necessary," she replied stiffly, pulling out of his arms. He'd said too much already without saying a word. "It's late and I'm tired. You must be, too, so let's just say good-night and go to sleep." And not giving him a chance to argue, she rolled over onto her side of the bed and turned her back on him.

Her heart thundering, she could almost feel his frustration as he lay beside her, but he didn't, thankfully, force the issue. She didn't think she would have been able to bear it if he had. Instead, he turned his back on her, just as she'd done him, and pretended she didn't exist.

Later, Summer couldn't have said how long they lay just that way, stiff as a couple of boards, without moving so much as a muscle. It seemed like an eternity. More than once, she wanted to melt, to turn and try to make peace. But what, after all, was there left to be said? He couldn't help it that he didn't love her. He married her because she was a Kincaid and could help him clear his name. He enjoyed her company and made no secret of the fact that he desired her, but that was all there was to it, all there was ever going to be to it. All the talking in the world wasn't going to change that.

Her heart bruised and aching, she knew she should get out of the marriage now, before the hurt completely destroyed her. But she loved him so much, she couldn't imagine going back to the dull existence she'd had before they'd decided to marry to improve his image. And deep down inside, she couldn't help but think that he would grow to love her as much as she loved him. All she had to do was stay close and give him a little time.

As far as hope went, it wasn't much, but it was all she had. Beside her, she felt Gavin relax. Long minutes later, he softly started to snore. He didn't reach for her and she didn't dare turn to face him, but if this was all she could have of him, she told herself, it would be enough.

Exhausted, she fought sleep and stared wide-eyed at the darkness, afraid that if she dropped her guard, even for sleep, she'd wind up in his arms. She was, however, fighting a battle she couldn't win. Exhaustion stealing up on her in the dark, she sighed and felt the tension that gripped her ease. Moments later she, too, was asleep, and never knew when her body sought the warmth and comfort of his.

In the weeks that followed their night out at the Hip Hop, Summer tried to convince herself she had her life—and her emotions—under control again. And on the surface, it appeared that she did. Her days were comprised of work and Alyssa, and she made sure there was no time for anything personal with Gavin. There was no more talk of love, no more lovemaking, and if she gave herself away in the dead of night, when she sought his closeness in her sleep, she didn't speak of it and neither did he.

It was the kind of existence she'd imagined would develop between them when she'd first suggested that they get married, and she should have been pleased. But there was a hollowness inside her, an emptiness that ate at her, and as the days passed, she found it more and more difficult to keep a smile on her face and pretend that everything was perfect.

If Gavin noticed, he didn't say anything. But her aunts and cousins knew her better than most, and it was harder to hide things from them. When her aunt Celeste ran into her at the grocery store, she took one look at her and immediately hugged her. "What's wrong?"

It had been a hard day, one that had started out wrong when she woke to find herself lying in Gavin's arms. She'd quickly pulled free before she woke him, but denying herself his closeness did little good. She'd still spent the rest of the day aching for his touch.

That, however, was something she had no intention of discussing with her aunt, so she forced a smile and used work as an excuse for her melancholy. "It's nothing. I'm just worried about one of my patients. So, how're the girls? And Aunt Yvette and Uncle Edward? I've been meaning to stop by and see all of you, but I've just been so busy that I can't ever seem to find the time."

She saw by the look in her aunt's sharp eyes that she hadn't fooled her in the least, but Celeste took the hint and didn't push…well, not that much, anyway. "We're all fine," she replied. "I'm sorry about your patient. It must be someone you're really close to. When I first saw you, you looked like you'd lost your best friend. You haven't, have you?"

That was exactly how she felt. "No, of course not," she fibbed. "I'm fine. Really."

But she wasn't, and she didn't know if she ever would be again. As she talked with her aunt and caught up on all the family news, all she could think of was the mess she'd made of her and Gavin's arrangement. If she'd just protected her heart, everything would have been fine. But she hadn't, damn it, and with every passing day, she fell more in love with Gavin. And it was killing her. Living with him, sleeping with him, loving him and Alyssa—they'd both become so special to her in such a short time. How was she ever going to be able to walk away from them at the end of a year? Leaving them would destroy her.

The question nagged at her for days, eating at her until it was all she could do not to cry whenever she thought of Alyssa growing up without a mother and Gavin spending the rest of his life alone. It didn't have to be that way. They could forget the terms of their agreement and let things just continue as they were.

And then what? a caustic voice in her head retorted. *You end up spending years, possibly the rest of your life, with a man who doesn't love you? Is that your idea of happily ever after?*

She tried to tell herself that it wouldn't be that way, that he would grow to love her with time. But how much time did he need? Weeks? Months? There were no guarantees in life. She could give him that, and more, and he might still never come close to loving her the way she loved him. Would that be enough for her?

Even as she asked the question, she knew the answer was no. But it wasn't until the invitation to Jordan Baxter and Meg Reilly's wedding arrived at the house one afternoon while Gavin was working at the clinic that she accepted the fact that she had no choice but to end her marriage. Her intentions had been good, but that old line "the road to hell is paved with good intentions" was true, and right now, she felt as if she was, if not in hell, then certainly in purgatory. And all because she'd married Gavin for the wrong reasons. Marriage was supposed to be about love and commitment—the kind Jordan and Meg had—not deals or business or saving someone's reputation. She'd thought she was helping Gavin, but in the end, she'd only made a mess of things, and she couldn't go on as they were. It just hurt too much.

The decision made, there was nothing left to do but tell him. All the rest of the afternoon, she rehearsed in her mind how she was going to do it, but nothing seemed to work. How did you tell a man you'd changed your mind and didn't want to be married to him, after all? What excuse could she give? She certainly couldn't tell him the truth— because she loved him and she needed a husband who felt the same way about her. She'd already told him she loved him once. She wouldn't do it again.

At a loss as to where to begin or how to even introduce the subject, she was still stewing about it that evening when he gave her an opening as they were doing the dishes after dinner. "I see we got an invitation to Meg Reilly and Jordan Baxter's wedding," he said as he wiped the counter while she loaded the dishwasher. "There was no mention of no children being allowed, but I don't really think it would be a good idea to take Alyssa, do you? Maybe we can get Lettie to baby-sit."

Her heart pounding just at the idea of attending a wedding with him, she said huskily, "Actually, I don't think I'm going to go at all."

Surprised, he arched a brow at her. "Why not? I know your family isn't crazy about Jordan after all the trouble he caused your uncle, but now that he's no longer blocking the sale of the ranch, don't you think you should let bygones be bygones? Garrett certainly has since he's springing for the wedding."

"Oh, that's not why I'm not going," she replied. "I really hope Meg and Jordan are very happy. I'm just not in the mood for a wedding. Not that it matters. I probably won't be here, anyway. There's an opening at Mercy in Salt Lake City, and I've been told that it's mine if I want it. I could finish my residency with Clarence Bishop."

If she'd wanted to surprise him, she couldn't have done better if she'd knocked him over the head with a hammer. He froze, totally forgetting what he was doing as he stared at her searchingly. "What are you saying?"

Pale, her pulse pounding, she would have given anything to say she was just joking, but she couldn't. As much as it hurt to end things, she knew she had to do it now. Because if she gave herself too much time to think, she'd never be able to do it, and then they'd all get hurt.

Turning to face him squarely, her hands clutched in front of her in a white-knuckle grip, she said quietly, "There's no longer any reason to continue our arrangement, Gavin. Your name's been cleared and you have Alyssa. Rachel's not going to challenge you for custody—she knows you're a good father, and she has her own baby to take care of now. So there's no longer any reason for me to stick around."

"But our agreement was that I'd work in your clinic for a year," he reminded her.

"That doesn't have to change just because I won't be here. You know the routine now and the patients are comfortable with you. And it's not as if I'm going to drop off the face of the earth and leave you in the lurch with Alyssa," she added with a bright smile that didn't come easily. "I won't leave until I'm sure the baby-sitting situation is taken care of. If Lettie's agreeable, she can continue to keep her in the mornings, so we just have to find someone to watch her three afternoons a week. I could talk to Rachel, if you like. She's busy with the new baby, of course, but she is her aunt, and she's crazy about her. I'm sure she'd be willing to help until other arrangements can be made."

She had everything worked out to the smallest detail, but even as she rattled off her plan to him, she prayed he wouldn't accept it. Ask me to stay. You don't even have to tell me you love me. Just tell me not to go. Give me some hope, give me a reason to stay. That's all I need. Just one reason.

But her silent prayer fell on deaf ears, and she knew by his very silence that he wasn't going to say a single word to change her mind. He just frowned at her, then, when she didn't think she could stand it another second, he said stiffly, "You don't need to call Rachel. I'll do it. If she can't keep her, then I'll talk to Lettie. When are you planning to leave?"

She really hadn't thought that far ahead, but now she had no choice. "By the end of next week, if we have someone lined up to watch Alyssa," she said huskily.

"I'll call Rachel right now." His expression closed, he turned and walked out.

Summer, fighting tears, watched him head for his study and tried to take comfort in the fact that she'd done the right thing. He didn't love her—that much, at least, was obvious. If he'd cared the least bit about her he would have said something, *anything,* to change her mind. He hadn't. She should have been pleased her instincts were right. Instead she'd never been more miserable in her life.

She was leaving.

Gavin sank into the chair behind his desk in his study and tried to remember Rachel's phone number, but his mind was blank. He couldn't think, couldn't do anything but sit there and stare into space. Summer was leaving—and he felt as if she'd just pulled the rug out from under his feet.

What's the big deal? a voice in his head demanded. *You knew she would leave eventually. Your arrangement was only for a year, for God's sake! Okay, so she's ending things a little early. What do you care as long as you've got what you want—your daughter and your name cleared? Isn't that why you got married in the first place? You've accomplished what you set out to do. Let it go. Let her go.*

Common sense told him that this was for the best. But he didn't give a flying leap about common sense right now, damn it! He didn't want her to leave, didn't want to lose her. Couldn't she see that he and Alyssa needed her? That they *loved* her? That they—

Suddenly realizing where his thoughts had wandered, he froze, the truth slapping him hard in the face and stealing the air right out of his lungs. *He loved her!* Dear God, how had that happened? When? He'd sworn after his fiasco of an affair with Patricia Winthrop, then his rebound involvement with Christina, that he was never going to let himself love another woman again. But he had never been involved with anyone like Summer before. She was generous and giving and so gentle with Alyssa. And then there were those nights they'd spent in each other's arms making love. She'd turned him inside out with her sweet passion and stolen his heart and he'd never even realized it until now.

When she was leaving him.

No! he raged, suddenly furious. He couldn't let her go, not now that he'd finally found her. He'd talk to her, tell her how he felt, explain how much he loved her, needed her, and they'd work things out. They had to. She loved him, too.

Are you sure about that? that damning voice in his head drawled, irritating him to no end. *She only told you that she loved you once, and that was after you'd just made love. How do you know that she wasn't just caught up in the emotions of the moment? People mistake sex for love all the time. Maybe Summer did, too. Think about it. After her head cleared and she had time to think about it, she never said the L word again. I don't know about you, but it sounds like the lady came to her senses and realized she didn't love you, after all.*

No! he thought furiously. She did love him, damn it! He couldn't have been mistaken about something like that, not when it came to Summer. Regardless of the circumstances, she would have never said she loved him unless she meant it.

That didn't mean, however, that she wanted to love him. She'd married him for only one reason—to help him—and now that she'd done that, she was obviously ready to get on with the rest of her life. And he couldn't say he blamed her. Clarence Bishop was one of the most renowned immunologists in the country. Working with him would be the chance of a lifetime for Summer, and she was right to jump at the opportunity. This would be a real feather in her cap as far as her career went.

He knew that and could honestly say he was happy for her. But every instinct he had urged him to ask her to stay. Just for a little while. Just until they had time to explore their feelings for each other to see if they had any chance at a future. They could turn back the clock and start over, this time as husband and wife, not business partners with their own agendas working toward the same goal. And it would work, damn it! He knew it would. All she had to do was stay.

But he couldn't ask her. Not after she'd already done so much for him. Time and time again, she'd done nothing but give to him, and to now ask her to give up the career opportunity of a lifetime for him would be incredibly selfish. She deserved this chance, and he loved her enough to let her have it. Even if it meant letting her go.

But God, he didn't know how he was going to do it. They'd only been living together for a short time, but she'd carved a niche for herself in his life—and Alyssa's!—and he didn't know how he was going to live without her. Everywhere he turned in the house, there were reminders of her—her clothes hung next to his in the closet, her perfume was on his dresser, her car was next to his in the garage. She'd take her things with her, of course, when she left, but he knew it wouldn't help. Her essence would linger, along with the memories they'd created together, and every time he turned around, he knew he'd find himself looking for her.

And then there was his bed. What the hell was he supposed to do about that? He'd never shared it with another woman, never wanted to. In the past, when he'd needed a woman, he'd always gone to her place or to a hotel because he didn't want anyone intruding on his space. But he'd never had a wife before, and to create the kind of image he needed to improve his reputation, he'd had no choice but to share his bed with her. And somehow, it had become theirs. He didn't think he'd ever sleep in it again without thinking of her, aching for her, reaching for her.

Because he loved her.

Why had it taken him so long to realize what she meant to him? he thought, shaken. From the first time he kissed her, she'd stirred emotions in him that no woman ever had, and it had scared the hell out of him. He'd fought it and ignored it and tried to convince himself it was just sex, and all the while, he'd been falling more and more in love with her.

He should have told her. Time and time again, opportunities had presented themselves, and he'd let them pass him by for one reason or another. He had a lousy track record when it came to women, and every time he let down his guard, he got burned. Not this time, he'd promised himself.

Idiot! he chided himself. If he'd just told her how he felt when she'd first told him she loved him, everything would be different now. They'd have worked things out and been well on their way to a future together. He would have still wanted her to go to Salt Lake City, but he would have found a way for him and Alyssa to go with her. Instead, she was going alone and there was nothing he could say to stop her. Because if he told her how he felt now, it would sound like a weak excuse to keep her there. And he had nobody to blame but himself.

Resigned, his heart heavy in his chest, he was left with no choice but to accept the inevitable. It was over. After everything she'd done for him, the least he could do for her was end things as quickly as possible so she could get on with her life.

Finally remembering Rachel's number, he reached for the phone and punched it in. The second she came on the line, he said huskily, "Rachel, this is Gavin. I need to talk to you about Alyssa. I need a baby-sitter."

In one week she'd be gone.

Her heart breaking, Summer tried not to think about it as she bathed Alyssa, then sat to rock her to sleep in the old wooden rocking chair in the baby's bedroom. But she couldn't help herself. She had one week, seven short days to pack in a lifetime of memories of what might have been. She only had to hold Alyssa close to know that wasn't going to be nearly enough.

Fighting tears as she inhaled the fresh, clean baby scent of her, Summer sang to Alyssa softly, treasuring this precious time with her. She was so little. Her face lit up like a Christmas tree whenever Summer or Gavin walked into a room, and that just melted Summer's heart. Lord, she was going to miss her! And the sad thing was, Alyssa was so young that she'd soon forget her. By this time next month, she probably wouldn't even remember much about this time they'd had together.

She couldn't hold back the tears then. They welled in her eyes and spilled over her lashes, and she just wanted to bury her face in the baby's downy-soft hair and bawl.

But she heard a sound in the doorway at that moment, and she looked up to find Gavin standing there. Horrified he would see her tears, she quickly turned her head away before he could see she was crying. "She's almost asleep."

"I just wanted to let you know that I talked to Rachel," he said quietly. "She said she'd be happy to keep Alyssa for as long as I needed her to. So you can go ahead with your plans. Alyssa and I will be fine."

Her throat tight with tears, she nodded mutely, unable to manage a word. It was over. There was nothing left to say.

For the next five days they kept to their regular work schedule and no mention was made of the fact that Summer was leaving in a matter of days. They took turns caring for Alyssa, cooked dinner together at night, slept in the same bed, and shared patients at the clinic during the day. And all either one of them could think of was that they were running out of time.

His feelings locked away behind a stoic expression, Gavin tried to take comfort from the sure knowledge that he was doing the right thing. It didn't help. He'd never been more miserable in his life.

Still, he thought he hid it well. It wasn't until he had to make a house call on Janet Crow that he realized he wasn't fooling anyone, least of all the patients that he'd known all his life but had never really gotten to know and like until he'd married Summer. The older lady took one look at him and scowled. "What the hell's the matter with you? You look awful."

He hadn't cracked a smile in days but his lips twitched at that. "Gee, thanks, Janet. And here I thought I was such a big, strapping, good-looking guy. Guess I was wrong."

"You were not, and you know it," she chuckled, slapping him lightly on the arm as he took her blood pressure.

"Why, Janet," he teased, "don't tell me you're actually starting to like me. I thought you hated my guts."

Sobering, she stared at him with black eyes that were still as sharp as a hawk's in spite of the fact that she was seventy-five. "I never hated you," she said gruffly. "Hate kills the spirit and damages the soul. But I admit I had little sympathy for your problems. Just as you had little sympathy for the plight of our people."

Gavin had to give her credit, she didn't hold back when it came to speaking her mind. Not concerned with playing nicey-nice, she fired straight from the hip and nailed him right between the eyes. And there was little he could say in his own defense.

He met her gaze head-on and took responsibility for his selfishness. "I was wrong," he said huskily. "I know that now. I'm not the man I was then."

Still studying him, she said quietly, "Summer has been good for you. She's brought you back to your people."

He didn't deny it. "She's a good woman."

"Then why are you letting her go to Salt Lake City? She belongs here, with you and Alyssa."

Gavin wasn't surprised that she felt that way. Ever since the news had broken that Summer was leaving to work with a famous doctor in Utah, every patient who came into the clinic had voiced the same opinion. "We discussed it and decided this was a career move she couldn't pass up," he said, giving her the same standard response he'd given everyone else. "And it's not forever. She'll be back once her residency is completed." They would quietly divorce before then, but that was something he had no intention of telling anyone.

Janet, however, wasn't easily discouraged. As a tribal elder, she took full advantage of the fact that age gave her the right to speak her mind. "Horse poop! You're not happy about this. Why do you pretend you are?"

"It's Summer's decision," he insisted. "She has to do what's right for her."

"I see. So I guess that means that you haven't told her you love her."

Caught off guard, he blinked in surprise, giving himself away, before he quickly stiffened. "I'm not going to discuss my private life with you, Janet." And not giving her time to say another word, he stuck his stethoscope in his ears and listened to her heart and lungs.

Another woman might have taken the hint and changed the subject when he gave her a chance to talk again, but Janet was made of sterner stuff than that. Biding her time, she patiently waited for him to finish his exam. Then, the second he removed the stethoscope from his ears, she retorted, "I haven't asked you for any of the details of your marriage. I don't have to. I know who you are, Gavin Nighthawk. I know the kind of man you are. You hide your feelings to protect yourself and think you're being strong. That's how it is done in the world you live in."

"And what's wrong with that?"

"Nothing," she said simply. "But there are different ways of being strong, and sometimes a woman needs a man to do more than the right thing without a word of complaint. Sometimes she needs the man in her life to be strong enough to speak up and tell her what *he* needs and how *he* feels, especially when it comes to her. Because she can't always tell what's going on in his head. Sometimes, she just needs to hear the words."

What she said might have made sense—if Summer hadn't been so anxious to end their marriage and put three states between them. Those were hardly the actions of a woman in love. "She was the one who wanted to leave," he said stiffly. "What was I supposed to do? Stand in her way?"

"If necessary."

Irritated by her persistence, he growled, "C'mon, Janet, get real! We're talking about her career here! She's spent years studying to get to this point—"

"Yes, she has," she cut in smoothly, not the least disturbed that she'd ruffled his feathers. "And her career means a lot to her. But do you really think that's what she dreams about at night? Think about it," she suggested softly. "She's a sensitive, caring woman, Gavin. Ask anyone on this reservation. They'll tell you that no one has a softer heart than Summer. Yes, her career is important to her, but not more important than love. Not more important than her love for *you*."

Glaring at her, he told himself to not listen, to not hope, but it was too late. "Did she tell you she loved me?" he asked sharply. "Did you actually hear her say the words?"

"No," she admitted honestly, "but I didn't have to. I've seen it in her eyes every time she talked about you. I've heard it in her voice every time she mentioned your name. I'm not so old that I can't remember what it's like to be in love. Summer loves you. Why else do you think she tried to help you?"

Shocked, Gavin almost dropped his stethoscope. "You know about that?"

Janet laughed, truly amused. "I may be old, but I'm not stupid. I've known Summer all her life. She'd give her last dime to help somebody, but I've never known her to take chances with her heart. She wouldn't fall in love and rush into marriage after dating someone for just a couple of weeks…unless she was trying to help them. And I don't even think she would do that unless she felt a connection with that person that she'd never felt with anyone else."

Her eyes dark with kindness, she reached for his hand and squeezed it reassuringly. "I wouldn't mislead you on this, Gavin. Your destiny is entwined with Summer's and always has been. But sometimes, destiny isn't enough. For the two of you to have a future together, *you* have to make a move. You have to let her know how you feel or you could lose her forever. And that would be a shame. You two were made for each other."

She made it sound so simple. All he had to do was tell Summer how he felt—and lay his heart on the line. There'd been a time in the not too distant past when he would have flatly refused to take such a chance. No woman was worth risking that kind of rejection.

But that was before Summer had come into his life and changed everything. Before she'd taught him to love. Could he really let her go without saying a word just because he was afraid she might not love him back?

No.

Just that easily, the decision was made. Quickly repacking his medical bag, he impulsively hugged Janet. "You're a wise woman, Janet Crow. Thanks for the advice. I've got to go."

She grinned broadly as he hurried toward the door. "I knew you wouldn't let any grass grow under your feet once you came to your senses. Hey," she called after him when he strode toward the door. "What about my heart?"

"You're strong as a horse," he retorted with a chuckle. "Keep taking your pills and you'll outlive us all." Leaving her laughing, he rushed outside, his only thought to find his wife. They had to talk.

Twelve

It was one of those days when nothing seemed to go right. Alyssa woke up fussy, the kitchen sink stopped up, the phone never seemed to stop ringing. Summer had already quit her job at the hospital and had hoped to start packing, but one thing after another got in her way. She should, she supposed, have taken the baby to Lettie's, but she had so little time left with her that she hadn't been able to bring herself to do that. So the morning slipped away from her, and before she knew it, it was lunchtime. It had taken the entire morning to pack one box. And she was leaving in two days.

Frustrated, she pulled all of her things out of Gavin's closet and told herself not to panic—she could do this. She just had to remain calm and organized. But Alyssa didn't want the chicken tenders she made for her for lunch, the plumber arrived just as she finally convinced her to try some ravioli instead, and all the baby wanted to do then was get out of her high chair and crawl under the sink with the man and play. When she wasn't allowed to do that, she didn't hesitate to voice her displeasure.

The afternoon only went downhill from there.

By three o'clock, Summer was on the verge of pulling her hair out and having a screaming fit of her own when the phone rang again. At the end of her rope, she snatched it up and just dared the person on the other end of the line to be another telemarketer. "Hello?"

At her rough growl, the caller hesitated. "Summer? Is that you? This is Rachel. Is something wrong?"

Embarrassed, she wanted to sink right through the floor. "Oh, God, Rachel, I'm sorry! I didn't mean to bite your head off. It's just been one of those days."

Far from offended, she laughed softly. "I understand. Sometimes you just wish you could go back to bed and start the day over again."

That was exactly how she felt. "Actually, I don't even think I'd get up if I had it to do over again. A whole day in bed sounds wonderful."

"It happens to all of us at one time or another," Rachel assured her. "And you're still new at this mommy stuff. Maybe I can help. I called to see if I could take care of Alyssa this afternoon. I know you must have things to do, getting ready for your trip and everything, and I thought it would give Alyssa a chance to adapt to the baby before I start baby-sitting her next week.

"If that's okay with you," she added quickly. "Gavin told me you're not going to be able to come home very often, so I wouldn't blame you if you wanted to spend as much time as possible with her before you leave. In fact, now that I think of it, this probably isn't such a good idea, after all. I don't want to intrude."

So Gavin hadn't told her that they were getting a divorce. Why? she wondered. What explanation was he going to give when she didn't come home to visit? That she'd found somebody else? That she'd decided she didn't want to be a wife and mother, after all? That she didn't care?

Hurt, she tried to tell herself it didn't matter what he told people—the end result was that they were getting divorced. Nothing else mattered. But her emotions were in such a twist about leaving that he could have told Rachel and half the county that she was the most wonderful wife in the world and she still would have cried. She'd been holding back tears for days, pretending that she was happy with her decision to get on with her life, and it was killing her.

Suddenly desperately in need of some time to herself, she said huskily, "You're not intruding, Rachel. If you're really serious about taking Alyssa for a while, I could use an hour or so to run an errand. I'll be back as quick as I can."

"Take all the time you need," she insisted, pleased. "I've missed her. Just drop by whenever you're ready."

"I'll be there in ten minutes," Summer promised, and prayed she could last that long before she fell apart.

The drive back to town seemed to take forever. His hands clutching the steering wheel and his foot flattening the accelerator of his Chevy, Gavin never spared the speedometer so much as a single glance as he flew across the reservation like a man possessed. God, he'd wasted so much time! Janet was right. He should have told Summer long before now just how much he loved her. She had a right to know how he felt about her before she left for Salt Lake City. Then if she still chose to leave, he could hopefully take comfort in knowing that he'd done everything he could to give their marriage a chance.

He would tell her as soon as he got home, he decided. It wouldn't be the romantic declaration that most women dreamed of, but something like that took time to plan, and time was something he didn't have a lot of right now. Later, he would give her music and flowers and candlelight. For now, all he could give her was his love, straight from the heart. He prayed it would be enough.

He hit the town limits of Whitehorn and was forced to slow down or risk getting a ticket. He muttered a curse when a traffic light changed in front of him and would have shot through it if a sheriff's deputy hadn't pulled up next to him at that moment. Left with no choice but to stop, he sat for what seemed like ten minutes before the damn light changed and he was able to go through the intersection. And all he could think of was that he had to get to Summer.

He drove the rest of the way home like a model citizen, not even coming close to speeding, but the second he pulled into his driveway, he was out of his car and striding for the front door. "Summer, I'm home!" he called as he unlocked the door and hurried inside. "Where are you? We need to talk."

For an answer, all he got was silence.

On her afternoons off, she was usually in the kitchen with Alyssa, starting supper, but even as he headed for the back of the house, he knew he wouldn't find her there. Unless Alyssa was sleeping, she could almost always be counted on to be banging on a bowl or talking to herself or Summer as she played. The house, however, was as quiet as a tomb.

Still, he hurried into the kitchen to check the refrigerator, where he and Summer left messages for each other. Not surprisingly, there was a note there, just as he'd expected. Figuring she'd had to make a run to the store for something for dinner, he pulled the note from the magnet that held it in place and quickly skimmed it.

Gavin
Alyssa is at Rachel's. Please pick her up when you get home from the clinic. I had to leave—

The neatly printed words hit him right in the chest and nearly knocked him off his feet. *Leave?* he thought, panicking. She'd left him already? Like this, without even giving him a chance to say goodbye? No! Damn it, she couldn't do this to him! She couldn't do this to *them!* He had to talk to her, had to tell her he loved her. Now, before it was too late!

Crumpling the note in his fist, he whirled, his only thought to find her and tell her how he felt about her before she left town. Because if he didn't do it now, he might not ever get a second chance.

Rushing out to his car without even bothering to lock the front door, he threw the transmission into reverse and went flying backward out of the driveway like a maniac. Rachel, he thought frantically. Summer had taken Alyssa to her house. If he hurried, he might still catch her there.

Later, he never remembered the drive across town to Rachel's. He did know that it was only through the grace of God that he didn't hit anyone. He went through yellow lights, one red, and at least three stop signs without even touching his brakes, and more than a few drivers told him what they thought of him with obscene hand gestures. He couldn't have cared less. Nothing mattered but Summer, and finding her.

With a squeal of tires, he braked to a stop in front of Rachel's house ten minutes later and was out of the car and running for the front door without bothering to turn off the motor. There were two cars in the driveway, neither of which was Summer's, but Gavin refused to be discouraged. She wouldn't have just left Alyssa there without an explanation. She would have told Rachel what was going on, why she was moving out early, if she was actually leaving town today or just moving out of the house.

His heart pounding, he reached the front door and lifted his fist to pound it down if he had to, only to remember Alyssa. She wouldn't understand what was going on if he came barging inside like a madman, and the last thing he wanted to do was to scare her.

Dragging in a steady breath that cost him dearly, he punched the doorbell and told himself he was going to remain calm. But the second Rachel opened the door to him, his control snapped. "Where is she?" he growled. "And don't pretend you don't know. She must have told you. Damn it, Rachel, I'm not letting her leave me like this! Not until I get a chance to tell her I love her."

Surprised, Rachel fell back a step to allow him entry and had to bite her lip to hold back the smile that suddenly pulled at the corners of her mouth. She didn't think she'd ever seen the oh-so-stoic Gavin Nighthawk rattled. It was quite enlightening. He hadn't even blinked when he'd been charged with murder, but here he was, pacing her entrance hall like a restless tiger just at the thought that Summer might have left him. There was hope for the man yet.

Encouraged, she leaned a shoulder against the doorjamb and arched a brow at him. "Are you telling me that you convinced that woman to marry you without telling her you loved her? Shame on you, Gavin Nighthawk! No wonder she was so upset when she dropped off Alyssa."

Wincing as if she'd struck him, his frustration immediately turned to concern. "Was she crying? What did she say? You shouldn't have let her leave if she was that upset. If something happens to her—" Unable to finish the thought, he swore, "Damn it, Rachel, this is driving me crazy! I've got to find her. I know she told you where she was going."

She didn't deny it. "She needed some time to herself," she said quietly. "She didn't tell me not to tell you, but I really don't think she expected you to come after her."

"I'll follow her all the way to Utah if I have to," he said simply. "I love her, Rachel. All I want is a chance to tell her that."

For a man of few words when it came to his feelings,

he couldn't have spoken more eloquently. Touched, Rachel said, "She said she was going to the Crying Falls. But that was over an hour ago. I'm not sure she's still there."

"I'll find her," he promised in a voice thick with emotion. "Thanks, Rachel. I owe you one—again." Giving her a quick kiss on the cheek, he turned and rushed out the door.

Located deep in a remote canyon on the far north side of the reservation, the Crying Falls had been a sacred retreat for the Cheyenne long before Columbus came to America. It was here, according to legend, that a white buffalo had led a lost Indian maiden in a blinding snowstorm. Fed by hot springs that didn't freeze, even during the coldest of winters, the falls had called out to her during the worst part of the storm, crying her name and guiding her to the safe haven of its warmth. If not for that, she would have surely died.

It was said that the Great Spirit used the falls to speak to the maiden, and ever since then, the Cheyenne had sought solace there. It was there that the sick came to drink the warm, mineral waters of its bubbling springs and the troubled came to ask the Great Spirit for help and guidance. And it was there that Summer always came whenever her heart was heavy and she needed help to find her way again.

Usually, she had only to hear the murmur of the water and her spirit magically lightened. But not today. Her heart hurting, she sat slumped on a boulder next to the falls and found little comfort in the whispered gurgle of the water as it slipped and slid over moss-covered rocks that were older than time itself. Tears stung her eyes, and with a shuddering sob, she buried her face in her hands and gave in to the pain tearing at her.

Lost in her misery, she never noticed when Gavin pulled

up in his Chevy and parked next to her Jimmy, but he saw her immediately. And his heart broke at the sight of her. He'd never seen a more dejected figure in his life. Every instinct he had urged him to rush forward and sweep her into his arms, but he couldn't. Not until he knew why she was crying. Was it because she couldn't stand the thought of leaving him and Alyssa? Did she love them that much? Or did she regret the day she'd ever gotten involved with him by foolishly rushing to his rescue?

Torn, unsure what to do, what to believe, he approached her carefully, not wanting to scare her or, worse yet, hurt her again, but he had to talk to her. He wasn't leaving there until he did.

"Summer?"

He expected the sound of the falls to drown him out, but the second he called her name, she twisted around on the rock and gasped at the sight of him. Mortification washing over her, she scrambled to her feet and hastily wiped away the tears that trailed down her cheeks. "What are you doing here? I came here to be alone."

She stood poised like a deer, ready to run. "Wait!" he cried when she would have taken off into the woods just to get away from him. "Damn it, Summer, I'm sorry if I'm intruding, but Rachel told me you were here. I had to come. We need to talk."

Not meeting his eyes, she moved as if to brush past him. "There's nothing left to say, Gavin. Let it go before you ruin what's left of our friendship."

Lightning quick, he stepped in front of her, blocking her path. "Before *I* ruin it?" he growled. "You're the one who's leaving!"

"Because I've fulfilled my end of our bargain," she retorted, stung.

"Our agreement was for one year," he reminded her. "*One year,* Summer. Not one month."

"Your part of the agreement was for a year."

"Oh, no," he argued. "We both agreed we'd be married for one year, and during that time, you'd help me get back my daughter and my reputation, and I'd help you by working at the clinic."

He was right, and they both knew it, and to stand there and argue about it was ridiculous. "All right," she sighed, suddenly bone weary. "I'm cutting out early, I admit it. But if you had a problem with that, why didn't you say something last week when we discussed this? When I told you I wanted to change my residency so I could work with Dr. Bishop, you agreed it was too good an opportunity to pass up."

"So I changed my mind," he retorted. "We have an agreement, and I expect you to honor it. If you don't, I'll be forced to sue you for breach of promise."

Stunned that he would even threaten to do such a thing, Summer couldn't believe she'd heard him correctly. "You can't be serious."

"Try leaving," he dared her, "and you'll see just how serious I am."

Her eyes searching his, there was no doubting his sincerity. He would do it, she thought incredulously. After everything she'd done to try to help him, he would actually sue her if she didn't stand by her word!

"Why are you doing this?" she demanded, hurt. "Can't you see that I'm just trying to protect Alyssa? She's already lost one mother. How do you think she's going to feel if I stay and a year from now we divorce? After she's had all that time to grow closer to me? She's just a little girl, Gavin. She's never going to understand. Don't do that to her. She's the innocent one in all this. End it now before she gets too attached and gets hurt.''

For a moment she thought she'd actually gotten through to him. He hesitated and doubt flickered in the dark depths of his eyes. But just when she expected him to agree that she was doing the right thing, he set his jaw stubbornly. "No."

"Damn it, you can't do this! Alyssa—"

"Will be fine," he assured her. "I would never do anything to hurt her. And neither would you. If I thought you were really leaving to protect her, I'd help you pack your bags myself. But you're not."

Confused, she frowned. "What are you talking about? I just told you—"

"You told me everything but the truth," he cut in smoothly. "Why don't you try that for once and see what happens? Tell me why you're really leaving."

Caught in the trap of his eyes, Summer felt her heart start to pound. He knew, she thought, shaken. He knew she was leaving because she loved him, and he was determined to make her admit it. Why? she wanted to cry. Why was it so important to him to hear the words? He'd already heard them once. Why did he need to hear them again when his only response the first time had been nothing but silence?

Hurt, not sure she could ever say those words again to any man without knowing positively that he loved her, too, she set her jaw stubbornly. "I already did," she said flatly. "There's nothing left to say."

Resentment glittering in her eyes, she glared at him eye-to-eye, and it was all Gavin could do not to smile. Damn, she was something! And she loved him. She could hold the words close to her heart for the rest of her life, but he knew exactly how she felt about him. She'd given herself away countless times with her touch, her kiss, with the incredible way she made love with him. She was right—she didn't need to say another word. But he did.

"Alyssa is going to be fine," he assured her huskily. "Do you know why? Because she already loves you, and that could never be a mistake."

He only meant to reassure her, but he did the exact opposite. Stricken, she looked at him with tears welling in her eyes. "No! Don't say that!"

He reached for her then because he couldn't help himself. Because he had to touch her when he told her how much he loved her. "Easy," he murmured when she gasped as he took her hands and pulled her toward him. "I'm not laying a guilt trip on you, honey. I'm glad she loves you. You're so good with her—"

"But I'm leaving!"

"Because you love me. No, don't deny it," he said quickly when she immediately started to object. "You're not the type of woman who would ever say that lightly. You do love me. And that's why you're really leaving. Because you think you're the only one who's in love. But you're not."

Suspicious, she grew still in his hold, her eyes searching his. "What are you saying, Gavin? I'm not in the mood for guessing games. If you have something to say, just say it."

He should have known she'd reduce their entire future to just three little words. She didn't want diamonds or candlelight or flowery speeches—she just needed the words. "I love you," he said simply, and felt his heart expand with the words that had been waiting so long to be said. "I'm sorry it took me so long to see what was right in front of my nose, but I was afraid to let anyone get too close. I didn't want to get hurt again."

Summer just stared up at him and tried to convince herself she'd misunderstood him. He couldn't have just said he loved her. Her imagination must have been playing tricks on her, teasing her because she needed so badly to know that he cared.

But his gaze was direct, his heart in his eyes. Desperately wanting to believe him, she couldn't hold back the sob that rose in her throat. "Please don't say that just because you know it's what I want to hear. I don't think I could bear it."

"I *love* you," he said earnestly. "I would never say that unless I meant it. I love you more than I thought it was possible to love any woman, and I don't want to lose you."

Pulling her into his arms, he kissed her as if she was the most precious thing in the world to him, as if he never wanted to let her go, and finally, Summer believed him. *He loved her!* Joy bubbling up inside her, she threw her arms around his neck and kissed him back with all her heart.

When he finally let her up for air, he still didn't let her go. "If you still want to go to Salt Lake City, then Alyssa and I will go with you. This isn't a marriage of convenience, Summer. Not anymore. It's for real."

Unable to stop smiling, she nodded. "Forever."

"Damn straight," he agreed. "I want you to be my wife and Alyssa's mother and the three of us to be the family we were meant to be."

That was what she wanted, too, more than anything in the world. Kissing him softly, she said huskily, "Me, too. But we don't have to go to Utah, you know. You were right—Clarence Bishop is a wonderful doctor, but I never really wanted to change my residency. I just couldn't stay here any longer, thinking you didn't love me. It hurt too much."

"And now?"

A beautiful smile spreading across her face, she melted in his arms. "Now I have everything I want. I'm not going anywhere."

Epilogue

"By the power invested in me, I now pronounce you husband and wife. Jordan, you may kiss your bride."

Seated next to Gavin in the crowd of well-wishers that had flocked to the Kincaid ranch for Jordan and Meg's wedding, Summer watched the bride and groom kiss and grinned when her husband squeezed her hand. Since she and Gavin had admitted their love for each other two weeks ago, life had been so wonderful that sometimes she had to pinch herself just to make sure she wasn't dreaming. If Jordan and Meg were half as much in love as she and Gavin, which Summer was sure they were, they would be the second happiest couple in Whitehorn.

The second the newly married couple ended the kiss, the crowd broke into a rousing cheer and the party began. Immediately swarmed by well-wishers, Jordan and Meg found themselves hugged and kissed by family and friends and people they hardly knew. Laughing, they threw themselves into the festivities.

Unable to stop smiling, Summer looked around for her uncle Garrett and wasn't surprised to find him observing the proceedings with twinkling eyes. He'd done as he'd promised and arranged the wedding of their dreams for Meg and Jordan, but there was so much more to celebrate than just a wedding. All seven of Garrett's grandsons, along with the women in their lives, were there, united once again on Kincaid land just as he'd always longed for. From the love and pride in his eyes, it was obvious he relished playing the role of grandfather.

Nudging her husband, Summer said, "Look at Uncle Garrett. He's in hog heaven."

Watching his grandsons as they mingled among the guests and got to know each other, Garrett was, in fact, having the time of his life. Family had always meant so much to him, which is why, from the moment he'd learned about his son Larry's illegitimate children, it had been so important to him to find the boys after Larry's death and to not only introduce them to their legacy, but to share it with them. The ranch was for them, and he was thrilled that they were all there where they belonged.

The only thing that would have made the day perfect was Elizabeth's being there, but she'd gotten tied up unexpectedly with a case in Boise and it didn't look as though she would make it back in time for even the reception. Hiding his disappointment well, Garrett assured himself it was just a temporary separation, but still, he missed her. He stepped outside, enjoying the afternoon sun that warmed the November air.

"You're a powerful man, Garrett Kincaid, and you don't even know it. I see all your dreams coming true."

Turning to face Winona Cobbs, the town psychic, Garrett just barely bit back a smile. Dressed in a bright pink flowing gauze dress and matching turban, Winona had on enough beads to choke a horse, and she gloried in it.

"I don't know that I'd say I was powerful," he said dryly, "more like lucky. As for my dreams, they've already come true."

He looked inside toward his grandsons, who had all gathered together for a group picture. Winona didn't spare them a glance. "You have dreams you haven't even allowed yourself to dream yet. Those, too, will come true. Because you found a way to break the curse.''

His gaze on Cade, who was tickling his two-year-old half brother, Gabriel, Meg's son, it was a moment before her words registered. When they did, his eyes snapped to hers. ''What are you talking about, Winona?'' he asked with a frown.

''The curse your grandmother, Ruth Whitefeather, placed on the ranch when your father was cheated out of his share of the Kincaid land by his half brother Zeke.''

Garrett knew she was referring to the story about his Native American grandmother and how she, in a rage over the fact that her son had been denied his birthright, had called on the power of her Cheyenne heritage to curse the ranch. Because of her, anyone who sought wealth on the Kincaid ranch had found nothing but death, destruction, and unhappiness for decades to come.

''That old woman had powerful magic,'' Winona concluded, ''and that was her legacy to you. By reuniting the family and bringing Bart's great-grandsons back to the land of their ancestors, you have righted a terrible wrong and finally broken the curse.'' Pleased, she closed her eyes and lifted her face to the late afternoon sunshine that turned the air golden. ''Can't you feel it? There is an anticipation in the air that wasn't here in the past.''

Garrett almost told her he didn't feel anything but the wind. But just as he started to explain that he wasn't the sensitive type, there was a sudden flutter of wings from the bell tower of the chapel he'd had constructed for Jordan and Meg's wedding. A split second later a single white dove burst free to soar overhead like an eagle gliding on thermals.

A cynical man would have said that the dove was part of the wedding celebration, provided by the wedding planner to be released at just the right moment and it had broken free before it was supposed to. But he, along with Meg, had planned this wedding right down to the smallest after-dinner mint on the buffet table, and he knew for a fact that there were no doves of any kind included in the festivities.

"See," Winona said in satisfaction. "There is your sign. And there," she added, nodding toward a woman who made her way toward them from the parked cars, "is one of your dreams that will come true."

"Elizabeth!" His blue eyes lighting up at the sight of her and a delighted smile spreading across his strong, tanned features, Garrett stepped toward her, his hands outstretched for hers in welcome. "I'd just about given up on you!"

"I was able to get a postponement until next week," she said with a grin as she slipped her hands into his. Pretty as a picture in a deep blue silk suit that matched the blue of her eyes, she looked like a girl as the wind tousled her short blondish-gray hair. "Have I missed everything?"

"Not at all," he assured her. "The reception just started. In fact, Winona was just telling me—"

Turning to include the other woman in the conversation, he smiled crookedly when he saw she was nowhere in sight. "She was here just a second ago," he told Elizabeth with a shrug. "We had quite an interesting conversation. Remind me to tell you about it later. Right now, let me just look at you. It seems forever since I've seen you."

It had, in fact, been only a few days, and even then, they'd never been out of touch. They talked on the phone every day, regardless of where the other was.

Cocking her head at him, uncaring that they were drawing interested eyes, she flirted with him shamelessly as they entered the ranch house. "Missed me, did you? Maybe I should go away more often."

"Only if you'll promise me you'll always come back," he retorted, and meant every word.

It still amazed him the unexpected joy she had brought to his life. He and his wife Laura had been happily married for almost fifty years, and when she'd died, he'd resigned himself to the fact that he would spend what was left of his life alone. Then he'd hired the famous Elizabeth Gardener to represent first Emma Stover, then Gavin Nighthawk, and for the first time in God knew how long, Garrett smiled and laughed and actually found himself looking forward to each new day.

On this day when everything was so perfect, he wanted, needed, to tell her what she meant to him. But before he could find the words, the bride stepped up onto the staircase of the ranch house and called everyone's attention as Jordan rang the old-fashioned dinner bell attached to the wall next to the front door.

Smiling down at the guests, Meg announced, "Ladies and gentlemen, I know it's not proper procedure to throw my bouquet until I'm about to leave, but there's someone here who needs its magic right now more than I do." And with no more warning than that, she threw it right at Garrett.

Laughing, he had no choice but to catch it. And suddenly, he didn't need words to tell Elizabeth what she meant to him. His blue eyes twinkled with a mixture of love and mischief, and he handed the bouquet to her with a courtly bow that brought the glint of tears to her eyes.

All around them, people gasped, most of them only just then realizing that she was there as his date. The whispers started then, the quiet speculation, and it didn't take an Einstein to figure out that everyone wanted to know about their relationship. His eyes meeting Elizabeth's, Garrett almost laughed out loud when she slipped her arm through his, uniting them in front of the whole town.

Enough said.

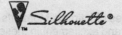

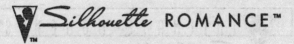

Silhouette ROMANCE™

What's a single dad to do when he needs a wife by next Thursday?

Who's a confirmed bachelor to call when he finds a baby on his doorstep?

How does a plain Jane in love with her gorgeous boss get him to notice her?

From classic love stories to romantic comedies to emotional heart tuggers, **Silhouette Romance** offers six irresistible novels every month by some of your favorite authors!

Such as...beloved bestsellers **Diana Palmer, Stella Bagwell, Sandra Steffen, Susan Meiner** and **Marie Ferrarella,** to name just a few—and some sure to become favorites!

Silhouette Romance—always emotional, always enjoyable, always about love!

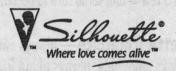